Mystic and the Black Diamond

The Adventures of Finn Thornwood, Volume 1

Wallace Berry

Published by Wallace Berry, 2024.

MYSTIC AND THE BLACK DIAMOND

First edition. June 17, 2024.

Copyright © 2024 Wallace Berry.

ISBN: 979-8990123649

Written by Wallace Berry.

Table of Contents

Chapter 1

Finn followed Mystic along the familiar forest trail, weaving between the towering pines as shafts of sunlight filtered through the canopy above. The early morning air was crisp and filled with the earthy scents of the forest. Mystic trotted happily ahead, tail wagging, her golden coat gleaming in the dappled light.

As they reached a small clearing blanketed in ferns and moss, Mystic suddenly stopped, nose quivering. She caught an intriguing scent and began sniffing intently at a patch of ground nestled against the roots of an old oak. Before Finn could react, Mystic started digging furiously, paws tearing into the soft loam.

"Whoa girl, what did you find?" Finn knelt beside her, watching in astonishment as she continued tunneling. With a final flurry of dirt, Mystic unearthed something and sat back proudly tongue lolling. Finn's eyes widened in disbelief.

Sitting in the freshly turned soil was a large black truffle, nearly the size of a baseball. Finn recognized it immediately from the books he'd read - a rare and valuable Périgord truffle. Gingerly, he picked it up, marveling at the pungent aroma and peculiar warty texture of the subterranean fungus. A culinary black diamond, truffles like this sold for over $300 a pound in gourmet markets.

Finn whooped excitedly, jumping to his feet. "Mystic, you clever girl! Do you think there could be more around here?" Mystic barked happily, tail wagging, ready to search. Finn quickly stashed the truffle in his backpack. This was an incredible, potentially life-changing find.

"Alright girl, lead the way! Let's go hunting!" With renewed vigor, Finn and Mystic continued down the trail, the tantalizing scent of riches filling the morning air. The forest held hidden treasures, and today, they had found one. Their truffle hunting journey was just beginning.

FINN GAZED IN WONDER at Mystic as she happily chomped down on the truffle she had just unearthed. He had known his loyal companion had a talented nose, but uncovering such a rare delicacy by scent alone was astonishing.

Crouching down, Finn gently stroked Mystic's velvety ears. "You really are incredible, girl. I can't believe you sniffed out a truffle!"

Mystic's tail thumped happily in response as she licked Finn's hand.

Finn's mind raced as he examined the peculiar fungus. Truffles only grew in certain forest ecosystems and were notoriously difficult to find. Yet Mystic had zeroed in on one buried inches underground, hidden among the tangle of tree roots.

He recalled reading something about truffles being extremely valuable, with certain varieties fetching steep prices. Intrigued, Finn pulled out his smartphone to research them further. His eyes widened as he read about European white truffles selling for thousands of dollars per pound.

Finn looked around the shaded forest, taking in the towering pines and fertile soil. If rare truffles could grow here, then perhaps their forest was valuable truffle territory waiting to be tapped.

The budding scientist in Finn was fascinated, but then another thought struck him. Finding and selling truffles could be a way to grow his college fund. With his high school graduation just a few years away, earning money to supplement his college savings was becoming crucial. Truffle hunting could be the solution.

Filled with excitement, Finn sprang to his feet. "Mystic, how would you like to become a truffle hunter?" Mystic yipped and jumped in circles around him.

"I'll take that as a yes!" Finn laughed.

He gazed out at the expanse of the forest before them. It seemed full of potential now, hiding underground treasures just waiting to be found.

"Alright girl, it's settled. Our new mission is Operation Black Diamond. We're going to scour every inch of this forest until we uncover enough truffles for college. What do you say, are you ready?"

Mystic barked eagerly in response. With his trusted companion by his side, Finn felt a thrill of anticipation. Their future felt ripe with possibility.

The winding trails and shadowy thickets of the forest no longer seemed daunting or perilous. Instead, they called to Finn like a siren song, concealing riches beneath their layers of pine needles and loam. He couldn't wait to venture forth and unravel their secrets, with Mystic leading the way.

Their lives were about to become an adventure, with new mysteries and treasures awaiting around every bend. As Finn scratched Mystic behind her ears, he whispered, "Let Operation Black Diamond begin."

FINN SAT ON THE WEATHERED back porch of his family's modest home on the outskirts of Loblolly Springs, absentmindedly running his fingers through Mystic's soft golden fur. The late afternoon sun filtered through the canopy of towering pines that surrounded their property, bathing everything in a warm, honey-colored glow.

Mystic rested her head contentedly on Finn's lap as he replayed the incredible events of the day in his mind. It had started like any other Saturday - Finn and Mystic venturing into the depths of the forest in search of adventure. But today's expedition had taken an extraordinary turn when Mystic's keen nose detected something special buried beneath the leaf litter near a mossy creek bed. Finn watched in awe as she carefully unearthed a peculiar, gnarled fungus the size of a small apple, its brownish-gray skin marbled with white veins. Mystic had proudly presented her find to Finn, tail wagging excitedly.

Though Finn didn't know exactly what it was, he could tell it was rare and valuable. After returning home, he had shown it to his father Ethan, whose eyes widened in delighted surprise. "Finn, this is a truffle!" he had exclaimed. "And not just any truffle, but a rare Périgord truffle, one of the most prized culinary delicacies in the world."

Ethan explained that renowned local chef Jacques Renoir was an authority on truffles, and could confirm the identity and value of their extraordinary find. He promised to call his friend Jacques and arrange a meeting.

Now, sitting with Mystic as the evening chorus of crickets and frogs began, Finn couldn't believe their luck. Hunting for truffles could be his ticket to achieving his dream of attending the elite wildlife biology program at the state university. But more importantly, selling truffles could ease the financial burden on his family.

The screen door creaked open, jolting Finn from his thoughts. His father stepped out onto the porch, a broad smile on his usually serious face.

"Jacques can meet with us first thing tomorrow morning at his restaurant," Ethan said. "He was thrilled when I told him what Mystic found. If it's a real Périgord truffle, he'll pay top dollar for it."

Mystic lifted her head at the sound of her name, tail thumping happily against the weathered wooden boards.

Finn grinned. "Hear that girl? You're going to make us rich!" He hugged the delighted dog as excitement and optimism bloomed within him. Their future felt brighter than the fireflies winking to life in the encroaching twilight. Tomorrow couldn't come soon enough.

THE PUNGENT, EARTHY aroma filled Chef Jacques' kitchen as he carefully examined the tuber Mystic had dug up. "Remarkable, simply remarkable!" he exclaimed, holding the lumpy black specimen up to the light.

Finn bounced on the balls of his feet, unable to contain his excitement. "So it's real? A real Périgord truffle?"

"But of course!" Chef Jacques replied in his thick French accent. He grinned at Finn's eager face. "Your dog 'as quite ze nose for truffles. Zis is a fine example of Tuber melanosporum, ze Périgord truffle."

Mystic wagged her tail proudly as Finn scratched her behind the ears. He had heard whispers around town of Chef Jacques' renown as an expert in rare ingredients, though Finn never imagined he'd be standing in the famous chef's kitchen with a priceless truffle his own dog had sniffed out.

Chef Jacques set the truffle down gently on a cutting board and beckoned Finn to have a closer look. "You see ze dark exterior and ze pale marbling inside? And ze earthy perfume?" Finn leaned in and inhaled the exotic aroma. "C'est magnifique! You 'ave found a treasure, mon ami."

The chef's praise filled Finn's heart with pride. He had always felt a special connection to the forest, but he never dreamed his rambles with Mystic would lead to a discovery like this.

Chef Jacques began regaling Finn with tales of the rare truffle hunters who sourced these precious delicacies across Europe. "In ze forests of France and Italy, ze trufflers search for truffles at night, when ze scent travels best in ze cool, moist air. Zey use pigs or dogs, just like your Mystic, to sniff out ze ripe truffles."

The chef explained how the truffle hunters kept their best spots secret, sometimes even blindfolding their dogs on the drive over to hide the location. Competition over prime truffle real estate was fierce.

Some hunters had even had their trusted truffle dogs stolen right before the height of truffle season!

Finn listened, enraptured by the drama and secrecy surrounding the exotic tubers. He had trouble imagining anything nefarious going on in the tranquil forests around Loblolly Springs, though this new insight into the world of truffle hunting intrigued him.

"And ze treasure you 'ave found!" Chef Jacques continued. "Ze Périgord truffle is considered la crème de la crème, ze finest of all truffles, wiz its complex aroma and delicate flavor. Top restaurants around ze world will pay 'andsomely for truffles of zis quality."

Finn's eyes grew wide. He had heard truffles were valuable but had no idea just how coveted the Périgord variety was. His mind raced as he imagined what he could do with money like that. College tuition for himself, some home repairs his dad had put off, a long overdue anniversary trip for his parents - the possibilities made his head spin.

This unexpected discovery seemed like a stroke of tremendous luck. Finn glanced down at Mystic, her tail still wagging happily. He smiled and patted her golden head, silently thanking his clever companion for this chance discovery.

Maybe Mystic's nose for truffles could help Finn achieve his dreams after all. But how did one actually become a truffle hunter? Chef Jacques' tales hinted at a world of mystery and competition surrounding the prized tubers. As Finn and the talented Mystic headed home, dozens of questions bubbled in his mind, eager to learn the secrets of the trade from Loblolly Springs' newest truffle hunters.

JACQUES LEANED BACK in his creaking rocking chair, puffing thoughtfully on his pipe as he regarded Finn with twinkling eyes.

"Those truffles you brought me - mighty fine specimens, I'll say. Mystic sure has a keen nose for finding them."

He paused, letting a wisp of smoke curl upwards. "You know, folks pay a pretty penny for truffles like those in the fancy big city restaurants. Why, a single Perigord truffle can fetch over $1000 easy. The rarer the truffle, the higher the price."

Finn's eyes grew wide. "A thousand dollars? For one truffle?" He could hardly believe the numbers Jacques was suggesting.

The old man chuckled. "I know, it's hard to fathom. But truffles only grow in certain conditions, can't be farmed like regular crops. That makes them a delicacy. Top chefs will pay just about anything to get their hands on even an ounce or two."

Leaning forward intently, Jacques met Finn's gaze. "With Mystic's talent, you could harvest quite a bounty out there in the forest. Why, if you become the truffle hunter of Loblolly Springs, you're looking at some real money."

Finn's mind began to race. Money for college had always been a concern hovering over his family like a raincloud. His parents worked tirelessly to provide for him and his siblings. But truffle hunting could be an answer. An exciting, adventurous answer.

If a single truffle fetched so much, just think what he could earn from consistent foraging with Mystic! Why, he could pay his entire college tuition in no time. The prospect left him breathless, his heart hammering with exhilaration.

This was more than just a childhood fantasy of exploring the great outdoors. With Mystic by his side, he could achieve his dreams of pursuing higher education and easing the financial strain on his family.

Jacques seemed to read his thoughts. "It won't be easy, Finn. You'll have to put in the time learning the forest's secrets. And truffle hunting has its risks - it's just you, the wilderness, and your wits. But I believe you and Mystic have what it takes. That dog's a natural forager, and you have a drive like no other."

Filled with purpose, Finn stood tall. "We can do it. I'm going to be the truffle hunter of Loblolly Springs!" Saying it out loud ignited a fire within. Mystic would help sniff out his way to college. The sprawling forest now teemed with potential and purpose. Their adventures had taken on new meaning.

FINN RUMMAGED THROUGH the cluttered garage, gathering the tools his dad said he would need for foraging in the woods. Rakes, trowels, kneeling pads, pouches to collect any truffles he might find - it was all coming together. But Finn was anxious to get going.

"Dad, I think I've got everything," he called out.

His father, Ethan, came around the corner, wiping engine grease from his hands with a rag. As a wildlife biologist, he knew these woods better than anyone.

"Not so fast there, kiddo," Ethan said. "I know you're eager to get out there, but we need to go over a few safety tips first."

Finn sighed, but listened as his dad shared words of wisdom from his years of field work. Always bring more water and snacks than you think you'll need. Carry a compass and map, and know how to use them. Keep an eye on the sky in case a storm blows in. Watch out for critters that might be startled by your presence - best give them a wide berth.

"Most importantly, pay attention to your surroundings at all times. It's easy to get turned around or lost out there if you're not careful." Ethan put a hand on Finn's shoulder. "I know you've got good instincts, but don't push them too far till you've got some experience under your belt."

Mystic, Finn's yellow lab, gave an excited bark, as if to say she would help keep an eye on things.

Finn took a deep breath, letting his dad's advice wash over him. He knew Ethan only wanted him to be prepared. And he had to admit, some of those tips were really useful.

"Thanks Dad," he said. "I'll be careful. And I've got Mystic to watch my back."

Mystic's tail thumped approvingly.

"Alright you two, looks like you're all set." Ethan handed Finn one last item - a walkie talkie. "If you need anything, just holler. And be home before dark."

"We will," said Finn, clipping on the walkie talkie. He gave his dad a quick hug, then headed out to the woods, Mystic bounding eagerly at his side. It was time to start the grand adventure of becoming Loblolly Springs' master truffle hunter.

ONE LAST TIME, FINN double-checked his backpack, ensuring he had all the essentials for another day of truffle hunting deep in the forest of Loblolly Springs. Trowel, gloves, first aid kit, water, snacks - it was all there, neatly packed and ready for adventure. Mystic stood attentively by his side, her tail wagging with anticipation. She knew these preparations well, a ritual that signaled the start of their favorite pastime.

Slipping on the backpack, Finn felt a swell of determination in his heart. It had been three days since Mystic had unearthed that first Périgord truffle, a rare and valuable delicacy, in a shaded glen near the whispering pines. The taste was still fresh in his mind - earthy, complex, and entirely new. Now, they were heading back to that very spot, spurred on by the possibility of more hidden treasures beneath the soft forest floor.

The early morning air was crisp and fragrant as they set out across the back field towards the edge of the woods. Finn breathed it all in, gazing at the treetops silhouetted against the brightening sky. The forest seemed to beckon them forward, branches swaying as if to say, "Come, let us share our secrets."

With Mystic bounding ahead, Finn stepped across the threshold into the shaded world beneath the pines. There was that familiar sense of the outside world receding as the forest welcomed them into its embrace. Finn's senses came alive - the muted light filtering through the canopy, the crunch of needles underfoot releasing their woody scent, the playful breeze that set the leaves whispering of adventures to come.

For over an hour they hiked deeper into the heart of the forest, following half-remembered trails. Finn knew this landscape well, yet it revealed itself anew with each journey. Every mossy log, hidden clearing, and burbling stream was a treasure to be explored.

Finally, they arrived at the ring of towering pines guarding the glen where their first truffle discovery lay. Mystic was quivering with anticipation now, her nose leading the way. "This is it girl," Finn said, patting her excitedly. "Let's see if we can find more!"

With trowel in hand, Finn selected his first spot. The soil was damp and soft as he gently loosened it, careful not to damage any truffles that might lie beneath. Scooping away the earth, he searched intently for any sign of the peculiar mushrooms. Mystic watched, nose twitching as she sniffed curiously at the freshly turned soil.

At first, there was nothing. Then, as Finn sifted through another trowel of dirt, he saw it - the unmistakable pecan-sized shape of a Périgord truffle! "We did it!" he cried, quickly retrieving and cleaning the treasure. Mystic barked joyfully, dancing around him. Finn smiled, savoring the thrill of discovery. This was just the beginning.

FINN GAZED OUT HIS bedroom window at the towering pines silhouetted against the setting sun. The forest of Loblolly Springs stretched as far as he could see, full of mysteries and secrets yet to be uncovered.

"Just think Mystic," he said, as the yellow lab resting by his feet perked up her ears. "There could be a small fortune buried out there under those trees. People pay hundreds of dollars for real truffles."

Mystic tilted her head quizzically.

"We find enough truffles, I can pay for college on my own. No student loans, no money worries." Finn sighed. "No burden on Mom and Dad."

The old floorboards creaked as Mystic got up and rested her chin on Finn's lap, looking up at him with trusting eyes. She gave a soft woof.

Finn scratched behind her ears. "You and me Mystic, we can do it. We'll be the truffle hunting team of Loblolly Springs!"

Her tail thumped excitedly against the wooden floor.

"It'll take patience and hard work," said Finn. "But we've explored every inch of those woods together. If anyone can find them, it's you and me."

Mystic bounced up and licked Finn's face, eliciting a laugh.

"I'm counting on that legendary nose of yours to lead the way," he said.

Mystic's eyes shone with devotion. She would be at his side, no matter what mysteries the forest held.

Finn gave her a hug, feeling hopeful. The road ahead would be challenging, but the bond between them was unbreakable.

He took a deep breath, gazing out once more at the sea of pines that swayed gently in the evening breeze. Somewhere beneath those trees lay the promise of adventure.

FINN WALKED SLOWLY through the dense underbrush, Mystic by his side, as he approached the oak grove. The trees here were ancient, broad trunked giants that seemed to radiate a quiet wisdom. Their branches stretched outwards and upwards, leafy limbs intertwined with one another to form a cathedral-like ceiling. Dappled sunlight filtered down through the canopy, bathing the forest floor in shifting patterns of light and shadow.

He recalled Chef Jacques' words about prime truffle territory as he surveyed the grove. "Old oaks are where you'll strike gold," the chef had said, his French accent rolling over the 'r' in 'gold.' Finn wasn't sure this was quite the El Dorado the chef had described, but there was something magical about this place. It felt ripe with potential, like a land that had yet to reveal its hidden treasures.

Mystic ranged ahead of Finn, nose to the ground as she explored every hollow and hole. Finn smiled as he watched his faithful companion. Her enthusiasm was contagious. He paused to take a deep breath, inhaling the rich, loamy scents of the forest. There was that earthy aroma Chef Jacques had told him to keep an eye out for. Could this be it? Could this be their moment of discovery?

Finn's heart quickened with excitement and apprehension. This spot seemed familiar, like a place he had visited in a dream, yet it also felt unknown and thrilling. He was an explorer standing on the precipice of the undiscovered. This grove represented untapped potential and the first step toward achieving his dreams.

With eager anticipation, Finn began to search, peering under bushes and poking at soft patches of soil with a stick. He tried to calm his racing mind, remembering the chef's advice: "Walk slowly, breathe deeply, and focus all your attention on the ground below you."

He slowed his pace, taking it all in. The way the sunlight danced on a fallen log. A sparrow flitting from branch to branch. The rich scent of earth and leaf litter. For now, the grove held its secrets, but Finn remained patient and hopeful. This was only their first foray into this hidden gem of Loblolly Springs. If today wasn't the day for discovery, they would return again soon. The forest would reveal itself when the time was right.

WITH ONE HAND RESTING on Mystic's back as she sniffed intently at the base of the massive oak, Finn crouched low. Its gnarled roots twisted out of the earth like ancient tentacles, and its branches stretched overhead, filtering the late afternoon sunlight into dappled patches on the forest floor.

Finn inhaled deeply, catching the subtle scent Mystic had alerted to. It was faint but unmistakable - the earthy, nutty aroma of truffles. Excitement quickened his pulse as Mystic whined eagerly, pawing at the leaf litter around the oak's base.

"Good girl," Finn whispered, not wanting to disturb the tranquil hush of the forest. He grabbed a stick and gently raked away the detritus around the oak's roots, watching intently for any glimpse of the hidden treasure.

Seconds later, there it was - a Pecan truffle, round and brown, nestled against one of the gnarled roots. Finn's breath caught in his throat as he carefully plucked it from the earth and held it up. It was smaller than a golf ball, caked in dirt, but to Finn it may as well have been a flawless diamond.

Mystic sniffed the truffle curiously. Finn smiled and slipped it into his pocket before resuming his search. If there was one truffle, there were likely more. He scanned the ground, looking for more subtle mounds or disturbances in the leaf litter.

Over the past few weeks, he and Mystic had honed their skills in tracking these elusive fungi. He vividly remembered their first discovery - the joy and disbelief he felt when Mystic unearthed that initial truffle. It had seemed like a miracle. Now, he understood it was simply a matter of patience, perseverance, and learning to understand nature's hidden signals.

Finn paused, tuning his senses to the forest around him. A woodpecker's staccato tap echoed from somewhere deep in the woods.

Squirrels chittered as they chased each other along the boughs overhead. From nearby, the gurgle of the creek murmured over stones smoothed by centuries of flowing water. Finn closed his eyes and breathed it all in - the scents, sounds, and feelings of this ancient place.

When he opened them, details seemed to leap out - a slight depression at the base of a hickory tree, a cluster of mayapple shoots emerging from the undergrowth, signs of rodent burrowing around the roots of a pine. Subtle clues that may reveal more hidden treasure.

With Mystic by his side, Finn moved slowly, methodically from tree to tree, scanning and sniffing. The search took time, but he was learning patience. With a truffle already in his pocket, he felt no rush. Their first success had taken weeks of learning and discovery. Now he knew - the forest would reveal its secrets in its own time.

Under the patient tutelage of the woods, Finn was discovering much about his role within it. With focus, open senses, and respect, nature would unveil her wonders. And with care and restraint, those wonders could be sustained.

The sun drifted lower, gilding the trees in a warm, late afternoon glow. Finn foraged in contented silence, Mystic a panting, eager presence by his side. And though he found no more truffles that day, when Finn left the shaded oak grove, he carried so much more. Patience. Awareness. Understanding. His connection to this place flowed in his veins as sure as sap in the towering pines. And he knew - their journey was just beginning.

FINN'S EYES TRACKED the slight rustle of ferns along the forest floor. At first he thought it might be the wind, the way the broad fronds swayed ever so gently. But his instincts told him something else was afoot.

That's when he saw it - the flash of white behind the undergrowth. Too big to be a rabbit, too nimble to be a possum. A fox.

The creature crept forward, its movements fluid and graceful, yet with a sense of purpose. As it emerged fully into view, its intelligent eyes regarded Finn with curiosity tinged by wariness.

With his breath caught in his throat. The fox was mesmerizing, its coat a vivid red-orange with black legs and white underbelly. But more than its beauty, what struck Finn was the feeling that this was no chance encounter. The fox had sought them out deliberately.

For weeks now, Finn and Mystic had been exploring the ancient forest of Loblolly Springs. And for weeks, Finn had felt they were on the cusp of something big. Some revelation lurked among the whispering pines and hidden hollows - he was sure of it.

Staring at the fox, Finn wondered if this creature was meant to divert their path. With its cunning and stealth, it could easily lead them astray. He'd heard tales of foxes tricking hunters and hikers in the woods. Finn looked down at Mystic, sensing her calm alertness. They couldn't afford to lose focus now. Not when they seemed so close.

The fox took a step forward, fixing Finn again in its unblinking gaze. Finn stood frozen, torn between fear and wonder. With a flick of its bushy tail, the fox turned and padded back into the ferns. Finn let out his breath. Had the fox sensed his doubts? Finn shook his head. No, he couldn't start second-guessing himself or the journey now. He gave Mystic's neck a reassuring pat.

"Let's keep going, girl," he said softly. "We can't let anything distract us from our destiny."

Mystic nuzzled his hand, ready to follow wherever he led. With the image of the fox still fresh in his mind, Finn continued onward. He hoped they were still on the right path, the one that would lead to their dream. If the fox was a test, he was determined not to fail it.

FINN KNELT DOWN AND ruffled Mystic's fur, her golden coat gleaming in the dappled sunlight.

"Ready girl?" he asked, excitement evident in his voice. Mystic's tail thumped enthusiastically against the forest floor in response.

Together, they surveyed the landscape, taking in the rolling hills blanketed in pines, oaks and hickories. A light breeze rustled through the trees, carrying the earthy scent of the forest. Somewhere in these woods, hidden beneath the fallen leaves and rich soil, lay their future - the elusive truffles.

He unclipped Mystic's leash, knowing she would keep close. They had spent countless hours traversing these trails, Finn on foot and Mystic leading the way, her nose guiding them unerringly through the maze of trees. Their bond had been forged through these explorations, a wordless connection built on trust.

Mystic circled Finn, her brown eyes bright with excitement, before turning and plunging into the underbrush. Finn laughed and hurried after her, dodging low-hanging branches and vaulting over moss-covered logs. The morning dew dampened his shoes but he hardly noticed, focused only on keeping Mystic in sight.

They moved swiftly through the forest, the land sloping gently beneath their feet. The cool shade beneath the trees was a welcome respite from the late summer heat. Birdsong and the scurrying of small animals accompanied their passage.

Eventually, the trees thinned and they emerged into a sun-dappled clearing. A small creek burbled along the far edge, disappearing into a dark thicket downstream. Mystic paused, nose to the air, carefully sampling each scent on the breeze. Her ears pricked forward intently.

"What is it girl?" Finn whispered, crouching down beside the retriever. Mystic turned and met his gaze, her eyes bright with an unspoken message - they were close.

Finn's breath quickened, his hands trembling faintly as they brushed through the leaf litter. Somewhere beneath the rich blanket of decaying matter lay their future, the truffles that would fund his college dreams and lift the financial burden from his family.

All it would take was faith, patience, and persistence. Traits Mystic already possessed in abundance. Finn just had to trust her, as he had so many times before.

With a deep breath, he rose and followed as Mystic ventured into the shadows beneath the trees. An air of purpose surrounded them both as they slipped into the forest's embrace. The hunt had begun.

Chapter 2

Finn and Mystic had been on a successful truffle hunt the day before, finding several specimens of a type they couldn't identify. Curious about their discovery, Finn decided to seek out the expertise of Chef Jacques, a local culinary master known for his knowledge of wild ingredients.

The next day after school, Finn caught a ride with his father to Chef Jacques' restaurant, "Le Chêne Doré". As they pulled up to the quaint bistro, Finn couldn't help but feel a mix of excitement and nervousness. He clutched the small bag containing the mysterious truffles, hoping Chef Jacques could shed some light on their identity and value.

Mystic, ever the loyal companion, trotted alongside Finn as they entered the restaurant. The delightful aroma of simmering sauces and freshly baked bread greeted them, making Finn's stomach growl despite his anticipation.

Chef Jacques emerged from the kitchen, his white chef's coat pristine and his smile warm. "Ah, Finn! And Mystic, of course. Welcome, my young truffle hunters," he greeted them, his French accent adding a touch of charm to his words.

Finn grinned, immediately put at ease by the chef's friendly demeanor. "Hi Chef Jacques. We found some truffles yesterday, but we're not sure what kind they are. I was hoping you could take a look?"

"But of course! Let's see what treasures you've brought," Chef Jacques said, leading them to a quiet corner of the restaurant.

Opening the bag, Finn presented the truffles to the chef. They were small, roughly the size of a walnut, with a mottled brown exterior and a faint, earthy aroma.

Chef Jacques took one of the truffles, examining it closely. He turned it over in his hands, sniffing it delicately. His eyes widened in recognition.

"My boy, you've found something quite special," he said, a note of excitement in his voice. "These are Bianchetto truffles, a variety of white truffle. They're not as well-known as the Périgord or the Alba, but they're still highly prized by chefs."

Finn's eyes lit up. "Really? That's amazing! What are they worth?"

Chef Jacques chuckled. "Well, while not as valuable as some other varieties, Bianchetto truffles can still fetch a good price. I'd say around $200 to $300 per pound, depending on the quality and the market."

Finn couldn't believe his ears. The truffles he and Mystic had found could be worth that much? It was more than he had ever imagined.

CHEF JACQUES HELD THE Bianchetto truffle up to the light, admiring its marbled surface. "You know, Finn, the world of truffles is a secretive one. Hunters guard their best spots jealously, and buyers can be just as competitive."

Finn leaned in, his curiosity piqued. "Really? I had no idea."

"Oh yes," Jacques continued, his eyes twinkling with mischief. "I once knew a truffle hunter in Provence who would only search for truffles at night, so no one could follow him to his secret spots. He'd come to my restaurant at dawn, his basket filled with the most exquisite truffles you've ever seen."

Finn's imagination ran wild, picturing himself and Mystic scouring the forest under the cover of darkness, uncovering hidden treasures. "That's incredible. I never knew truffle hunting could be so... mysterious."

Jacques chuckled. "It's a world full of characters, that's for sure. But it's also a world that rewards dedication and skill. And from what I can see," he said, gesturing to the truffles, "you and Mystic have both in spades."

Finn felt a surge of pride at the chef's words. He glanced down at Mystic, who sat patiently at his feet, her tail wagging slightly. "We make a good team," he said, scratching her behind the ears.

"Indeed you do," Jacques agreed. He carefully placed the truffle back in the bag and handed it to Finn. "These are some of the finest Bianchetto truffles I've seen in a while. If you keep finding specimens like these, you'll have no trouble making a name for yourself in the truffle world."

Finn's heart raced at the prospect. He had started truffle hunting as a way to save for college, but now he could see it becoming something more - a passion, an adventure, a future.

"Thank you, Chef Jacques," he said, his voice filled with gratitude. "For everything. Your advice, your stories... it means a lot."

Jacques smiled, placing a hand on Finn's shoulder. "It's my pleasure, Finn. I see great potential in you. Keep following your instincts, and let Mystic guide you. The forest has many secrets to share with those who are willing to listen."

As Finn listened to Chef Jacques' tales of the secretive truffle world, a realization dawned upon him. While the stories of midnight hunts and jealously guarded spots were undeniably thrilling, Finn knew in his heart that his path lay elsewhere.

"Chef Jacques," Finn began, his voice steady with resolve, "I appreciate everything you've shared with me. The stories, the knowledge... it's all incredible. But I have to be honest with you. I don't see myself becoming a full-time truffle hunter."

The chef's eyebrows raised slightly, but his expression remained warm and understanding. "Oh? And why is that, Finn?"

Finn glanced down at Mystic, finding comfort in her unwavering presence. "It's just... I have other dreams. College, for one. And while I love the adventure of truffle hunting, I don't think I want to make it my life's work."

Jacques nodded, his eyes filled with a wisdom that seemed to stretch beyond his years. "I understand, Finn. The truffle world is not for everyone. It takes a certain kind of dedication, a certain kind of obsession, even."

Finn felt a wave of relief at the chef's understanding. "Exactly. But that doesn't mean I don't want to keep hunting. In fact, I was hoping..." He paused, gathering his courage. "I was hoping that I could sell my truffles to you. That way, I can still be a part of this world, but on my own terms."

Chef Jacques leaned back in his chair, considering Finn's proposition. The kitchen bustled around them, the clatter of pots and the sizzle of pans creating a symphony of culinary creation. Finally, he spoke.

"You know, Finn, I think that's a wonderful idea. I'd be more than happy to buy your truffles. With specimens like these," he said, gesturing to the bag of Bianchetto truffles, "I know my customers will be thrilled."

Finn's heart soared. "Really? That's fantastic! Thank you, Chef Jacques. This means so much to me."

The chef waved off his gratitude with a good-natured chuckle. "No need to thank me, Finn. It's a mutually beneficial arrangement. You get to fund your dreams, and I get to serve some of the finest truffles in Loblolly Springs. It's a win-win."

With those words echoing in his mind, Finn left the restaurant, Mystic trotting happily at his side. He felt a new sense of purpose, a determination to uncover all the secrets the forest of Loblolly Springs had to offer. The world of truffles had opened up before him, and he was ready to explore it, one precious fungus at a time.

AS THE SUN DIPPED BELOW the horizon, Finn sat on the porch steps, his mind whirling with the events of the day. Mystic lay at his feet, her head resting on her paws, a picture of contentment.

Finn, however, was far from content. His heart raced with a mixture of excitement and trepidation. The prospect of financial independence, of being able to pay for college without burdening his parents, was tantalizing. But with that promise came pressure, a weight that settled heavily on his young shoulders.

He thought back to his conversation with Chef Jacques, the way the chef had spoken of the truffle world with such reverence and passion. Finn wanted that for himself, that sense of purpose and dedication. But he also knew that the path ahead would not be easy.

School would soon let out for the summer, giving Finn and Mystic ample time to hone their truffle-hunting skills. But Finn knew that time alone would not be enough. They would need to learn, to adapt, to persevere in the face of challenges.

He thought of the forest, of its vast expanse and hidden secrets. It was a world unto itself, a realm of mystery and wonder. And yet, it was also a world of danger, of unseen perils lurking in the shadows.

Finn's hand absently stroked Mystic's fur, finding comfort in the warmth of her presence. She was his partner in this, his loyal companion on the journey ahead. Together, they would face whatever the forest had in store.

As the last light of day faded, Finn stood, his resolve hardening like steel. He would succeed, not just for himself, but for his family, for his future. The path ahead was uncertain, but one thing was clear: Finn Thornwood was ready to become the truffle hunter of Loblolly Springs.

WHILE THE THORNWOOD family gathered around the dining room table, the aroma of homemade spaghetti and freshly baked bread filled the air. Finn, his mind still buzzing with the day's events, eagerly shared his plans with his father.

"Dad, I've been thinking," Finn began, twirling a forkful of spaghetti. "I want to start searching the woods for truffles more seriously. But I know I need to be prepared."

Ethan Thornwood, his wildlife biologist father, nodded thoughtfully. "That's a smart approach, Finn. The forest can be unpredictable, and it's crucial to know your way around."

Finn's eyes lit up. "That's where I was hoping you could help. Do you think we could map out the woods together? Mark key landmarks, compass directions, distances... the whole works?"

Ethan smiled, pride shining in his eyes. "Absolutely. It's important to have a solid understanding of your surroundings, especially when you're spending a lot of time out there."

Clara Thornwood, Finn's mother, chimed in. "It's a wonderful idea, Finn. But remember, safety always comes first. The forest is beautiful, but it can also be dangerous."

Finn nodded solemnly, understanding the weight of his mother's words.

The conversation flowed as easily as the meal, with the family discussing the intricacies of Loblolly Springs and its surrounding woods. The forest, they knew, was vast, spanning over 200,000 acres. It was a mosaic of rolling hills, steep ridges, and dense canopies that seemed to touch the sky.

Ethan spoke of the diverse flora and fauna that called the forest home. Towering Loblolly Pines stood sentinel over a rich undergrowth of ferns and wildflowers. Deer roamed the woods, their paths crisscrossing with those of raccoons, foxes, and the occasional black bear.

The weather, they agreed, was as varied as the landscape. Spring brought a burst of color and life, summer a blanket of humidity, fall a spectacular show of changing leaves, and winter a serene stillness broken only by the soft crunch of snow underfoot.

As the meal wound down and the plates were cleared, Finn's excitement only grew. With his father's guidance and the promise of adventure ahead, he felt ready to take on the challenge of the forest and all its secrets.

THE FIRST LIGHT OF dawn began to paint the sky when Finn was gently roused from his slumber by his father's hand on his shoulder. Ethan Thornwood, his face illuminated by the soft glow of the bedside lamp, spoke in a low, excited tone.

"Finn, it's time to get up. We're starting our first trip into the woods today, and I'm going to teach you how to set up a campsite for an overnight stay. Once you've mastered this, we'll move on to the next lesson."

Finn, his sleepiness quickly replaced by a surge of excitement, nodded eagerly. He quickly dressed and joined his family in the kitchen, where the aroma of freshly brewed coffee and sizzling bacon filled the air. As they ate, the conversation buzzed with anticipation for the day ahead.

After breakfast, Finn made his way to the pantry, grabbing a scoop of dog food and carefully measuring out enough to last Mystic for the day. He packed it into a small, waterproof bag, ensuring his faithful companion would be well-fed on their adventure.

Ethan, meanwhile, had retrieved one of his own backpacks from the garage. He laid it out on the living room floor, motioning for Finn to join him.

"Alright, Finn, let's go over what you'll need for your overnight stay," Ethan began, his voice taking on the tone of a seasoned instructor.

One by one, he pulled out items from the backpack, explaining their purpose and importance. A compact sleeping bag, designed for the cool nights in the forest. A small axe for cutting firewood and tent stakes, a lightweight, waterproof tent that could be set up in minutes. A flashlight with extra batteries, a compass, a map of the area with permanent marker, 40 foot of heavy string, and a whistle for emergencies.

Ethan also included a small first-aid kit, a fire starter, and a water filtration system. He explained how to use each item, patiently answering Finn's questions and ensuring he understood their significance.

As Finn carefully repacked the backpack, his mind raced with the possibilities of the day ahead. With his father's guidance and the necessary equipment, he felt ready to take on the challenges of the forest and learn the skills that would serve him well in his future truffle-hunting adventures.

FINN, HIS BACKPACK now filled with the essential gear for their overnight stay, turned to his father with a question that had been nagging at his mind.

"Dad, the forest is huge. Where do we start?" he asked, his eyes filled with a mix of excitement and uncertainty.

Ethan smiled, understanding his son's apprehension. He placed a reassuring hand on Finn's shoulder and led him to the large, wooden table in the living room. Spread out on the table was a detailed topographical map of the Loblolly Springs forest.

"That's a great question, Finn," Ethan began, his finger tracing the contours of the map. "The key to navigating any wilderness is to break it down into manageable sections. We'll start with the areas closest to our home and work our way outwards."

Ethan pointed to a section of the map that was shaded in a light green. "This area here, just a couple of miles from our backyard, is where we'll begin. It's a relatively flat section of the forest, with a mix of hardwoods and pines. It's the perfect place to practice setting up camp and getting a feel for the terrain."

Finn nodded, his eyes following his father's finger as it moved across the map. Ethan continued, "Once you're comfortable with this area, we'll move on to this section here." He indicated a slightly darker green area, further from their home. "This part of the forest is a bit more challenging, with some steeper hills and denser undergrowth. But by then, you'll have the skills and confidence to handle it."

Ethan then pointed to a series of blue lines that snaked through the map. "These are the streams and rivers that run through the forest. They'll be important landmarks for you to navigate by, and they're also prime spots for finding truffles."

Finn leaned in closer, studying the map with renewed interest. The forest, which had seemed so vast and daunting just moments ago, now appeared as a series of interconnected puzzles, each one waiting to be solved.

"Remember, Finn," Ethan said, his voice taking on a more serious tone, "the forest is a beautiful place, but it can also be dangerous if you're not prepared. Always carry your map and compass, and never hesitate to use your whistle if you get into trouble. Your safety is always the top priority."

Finn nodded solemnly, understanding the weight of his father's words. With the map now etched in his mind and the gear packed securely in his backpack, he felt a surge of readiness for the adventure ahead. The forest of Loblolly Springs, with all its mysteries and potential, awaited him, and he was eager to uncover its secrets, one step at a time.

ETHAN AND FINN STEPPED into the embrace of the Loblolly Springs forest, the towering pines welcoming them with a gentle rustle of their needles. The early morning sun filtered through the canopy, casting a dappled light on the forest floor. The air was crisp and filled with the earthy scent of pine and damp soil.

For the first half hour of their trek, the going was easy. The understory was sparse, allowing for unobstructed views and comfortable walking. The tall, straight trunks of the loblolly pines stood like sentinels, guiding their path deeper into the woodland.

As they walked, Ethan took the opportunity to teach Finn the finer points of forest navigation. He handed Finn a compass, showing him how to hold it level and align the needle with the orienting arrow.

"Always trust your compass, Finn," Ethan said, his voice carrying a mixture of wisdom and patience. "It's your most reliable guide in the woods. Keep your heading steady, and you'll always find your way."

Finn nodded, his eyes focused on the compass as he adjusted his direction. He felt a surge of pride as he successfully navigated a straight line through the trees.

But Ethan had more to teach. He pointed to a distinctive tree in the distance, its crown rising above the others. "Now, Finn, sometimes you might not have a compass handy. In those situations, you can use the landscape itself to guide you."

He gestured towards the tree. "Pick a landmark, like that tall pine over there. Fix your eyes on it, and walk straight towards it. When you reach it, find another landmark in the same direction and repeat the process. This way, you can maintain a relatively straight course, even without a compass."

Finn listened intently, absorbing his father's wisdom. He picked his own landmark, a gnarled oak with a unique branch pattern, and set off towards it. As he walked, he felt a growing sense of connection with the forest around him. Each tree, each landmark, became a waypoint in his mental map of the woods.

Ethan watched his son with a mix of pride and nostalgia, remembering his own early adventures in these woods. He knew that these lessons, these moments shared between father and son, would stay with Finn forever. They were more than just navigational skills; they were life lessons, teaching Finn the value of observation, patience, and self-reliance.

As they continued their journey deeper into the forest, the pines stood tall around them, silent witnesses to the passing of knowledge from one generation to the next. The forest of Loblolly Springs, in all its timeless wisdom, seemed to embrace this moment, knowing that in Finn, it had found a new guardian, a young man ready to uncover its secrets and cherish its wonders.

THE LANDSCAPE BEGAN to change as Ethan and Finn ventured deeper into the Loblolly Springs forest. The easy, level terrain gradually gave way to a wet bottomland, where shallow pools of standing water dotted the forest floor. The ground became softer, and their footsteps started to sink into the damp earth with each step.

As they navigated this new terrain, Ethan's keen eyes spotted a set of tracks in the soft mud. He called Finn over, pointing to the unmistakable imprints left by wild hogs. Mystic, curious as ever, trotted over to investigate, her nose twitching as she sniffed the tracks.

Ethan gently pulled Mystic away, his voice firm but calm. "Finn, it's important to remember that wild pigs can be very dangerous. If you ever come across them in the forest, it's best to give them a wide berth. Don't try to approach them, and definitely don't let Mystic chase after them."

Finn nodded solemnly, understanding the gravity of his father's words. He looked at Mystic, who was still straining to investigate the scent, and called her back to his side.

Ethan continued, "Wild hogs are incredibly strong and can be very aggressive, especially if they feel threatened. Their tusks can cause serious injuries, even to a dog as big as Mystic. It's always better to be safe than sorry out here."

Finn absorbed this new piece of forest wisdom, his respect for the untamed wilderness growing with each passing moment. He realized that the forest, for all its beauty and wonder, also held its share of dangers. It was a place that demanded respect and caution, a place where knowledge and awareness could mean the difference between a thrilling adventure and a perilous encounter.

As they pressed on, leaving the wild hog tracks behind, Finn kept a closer eye on Mystic, ensuring that she stayed close by his side. The forest around them seemed to take on a new character, its shadows deeper, its sounds more mysterious. But with his father's guidance and Mystic's loyal presence, Finn felt ready to face whatever challenges lay ahead, eager to uncover the secrets and treasures hidden within the depths of Loblolly Springs.

AS ETHAN AND FINN CONTINUED their journey through the Loblolly Springs forest, the landscape began to transform once more. The wet, muddy bottomland gradually gave way to rising terrain, and in the distance, tall cottonwoods stood like sentinels, their white bark gleaming in the sunlight that filtered through the canopy.

The soft, yielding mud of the bottomland was replaced by a vibrant red clay, a stark contrast to the earthy tones they had encountered earlier. Rocks and small patches of gravel began to appear sporadically, adding texture and variety to the forest floor. Mystic, ever curious, paused to sniff at these new elements, her tail wagging with each discovery.

As they walked further, the understory of the forest grew denser. Briars and vines began to dominate the landscape, their tendrils reaching out to grasp at passing hikers. These hardy plants thrived in the spaces between the tall trees, taking advantage of the sunlight that managed to penetrate the dense canopy.

Ethan pointed out the different species of vines and briars to Finn, explaining how they played a vital role in the forest ecosystem. Some, like the blackberry vines, provided food for wildlife, while others, like the poison ivy, were best avoided altogether.

Finn marveled at the diversity of the forest, how each step revealed a new facet of this complex world. The rising terrain, the red clay, the rocks, and the vines all contributed to the rich tapestry of Loblolly Springs, each element playing its part in the grand symphony of nature.

As they navigated this new terrain, Finn and Ethan had to be more mindful of their steps. The briars and vines, when not in the deep shade of the tall trees, could easily snag clothing and skin, demanding a heightened level of awareness and caution.

Mystic, too, had to adapt to this change in the landscape. Her usual bounding gait was tempered by the need to navigate the tangles of vegetation, her keen senses helping her to avoid the most troublesome patches.

A NEW SOUND BEGAN TO permeate the air as Ethan and Finn ventured further into the heart of the Loblolly Springs forest. It was the gentle, persistent murmur of flowing water, a whisper that grew louder with each step they took. Though still hidden from view by the dense foliage, the presence of the Loblolly Major, the large creek that carved its way through the forest, was unmistakable.

Ethan, his eyes scanning the surrounding landscape, suggested that it was time to start looking for a suitable campsite. Finn, eager to learn, listened attentively as his father began to share his wisdom on the art of selecting the perfect spot to set up camp.

"First," Ethan began, "we need to find a flat, dry area that's elevated above the stream. We don't want to wake up in the middle of the night to find our sleeping bags soaked because of a sudden rise in the water level."

Finn nodded, his eyes already searching for potential sites that fit this description. Ethan continued, "We also need to make sure that there aren't any dead trees or large dead branches nearby that could fall on us during the night."

As they walked, Ethan pointed out a few spots that looked promising, but he always found a reason to move on. "This one's too exposed to the wind," he would say, or "That one's a little too close to that dense brush over there. We don't want any surprise visits from the local wildlife."

Finn, absorbing every word, started to understand the nuances of selecting a campsite. It wasn't just about finding a clear patch of ground; it was about reading the landscape, understanding the potential hazards and benefits of each location.

Ethan paused at a small clearing, his experienced eye surveying the area. "Now this," he said, a smile spreading across his face, "this might just be perfect."

ETHAN STOOD AT THE edge of an open area as he surveyed the potential campsite, his eyes were drawn to a particular tree standing near by, away from the towering giants of the forest. It was an Eastern Redbud, a deciduous tree native to the region. Ethan recognized its distinctive heart-shaped leaves and the remnants of the pink to purple flowers that would have covered its twigs in early spring.

"Finn, come take a look at this," Ethan called out, beckoning his son over. Finn, who had been investigating a nearby patch of wildflowers, hurried over to his father's side.

"You see that tree over there?" Ethan pointed to the Redbud. "That's an Eastern Redbud. It's a perfect addition to our campsite."

Finn looked at the tree, curious. "What makes it so perfect, Dad?"

Ethan smiled, always eager to share his knowledge. "Well, for one, it's not too tall. It can give us some shelter from the sun, rain, or morning dew without being so high that it might attract lightning away from the taller trees."

Finn nodded, understanding the logic. "And it's away from the other trees, so we don't have to worry about anything falling on us, right?"

"Exactly," Ethan confirmed, proud of his son's quick grasp of the situation. "Plus, it's just a beautiful tree. It'll be nice to have it watching over us as we sleep."

Finn grinned, already picturing their tent set up beneath the Redbud's branches. Mystic, who had been exploring the perimeter of the clearing, trotted over to join them, her tail wagging with excitement.

"What do you think, Mystic?" Finn asked, ruffling the dog's golden fur. "Is this a good spot for us?"

Mystic barked once, as if in approval, and Finn laughed. "I guess that settles it then."

Ethan chuckled, setting down his backpack and stretching his arms. "Alright, let's get started on setting up camp. We've got a lot to do before nightfall."

Chapter 3

E than and Finn worked diligently to set up their campsite beneath the welcoming branches of the Eastern Redbud tree. The clearing they had chosen was a perfect spot, with soft, level ground and a canopy of leaves that filtered the sunlight into a dappled pattern on the forest floor.

Ethan, with his years of experience, guided Finn through the process of pitching the tent. Together, they unfurled the lightweight fabric, threading the poles through the loops and raising the structure until it stood tall and sturdy. Finn, eager to learn, watched intently as his father demonstrated how to secure the tent with stakes, ensuring it would withstand any unexpected gusts of wind.

Next, they turned their attention to the fire pit. Ethan showed Finn how to clear a small area of ground, removing any dry leaves or twigs that could catch fire. With a small shovel, they dug a shallow pit, encircling it with a ring of stones to contain the flames. Finn gathered a pile of dry wood from a nearby fallen tree, carefully selecting pieces that would burn long and hot, perfect for cooking and keeping them warm through the night.

As the day grew warmer, Ethan suggested they head to the nearby Loblolly Major creek to collect water. Mystic, ever-eager for an adventure, bounded ahead of them, her nose to the ground as she explored the new scents of the forest. The sound of the creek grew louder as they approached, a soothing melody of rushing water over rocks.

At the creek's edge, Ethan pulled a small water filtration system from his backpack. He explained to Finn the importance of purifying any water they collected from natural sources. Finn watched, fascinated, as his father demonstrated how to use the filter, pumping the creek water through the system and into their waiting water bottles. The water emerged crystal clear, free of any impurities that could make them ill.

By noon, their campsite was fully set up, a cozy haven in the heart of the Loblolly Springs forest. The tent stood proudly beneath the Eastern Redbud, its bright green leaves casting a cool shade over the entrance. The fire pit waited, ready to be lit when evening fell, and their water bottles were filled with fresh, clean water from the creek.

THE CAMPFIRE CRACKLED and popped as Ethan and Finn huddled around the small pot of simmering instant soup. The aroma of the savory broth mingled with the earthy scent of the forest, creating a comforting atmosphere in their little campsite. Mystic lay nearby, her tail thumping contentedly as she watched her human companions prepare their meal.

Finn stirred the soup thoughtfully, his mind still buzzing with the excitement of their truffle hunting adventure. He glanced up at his father, who was carefully adding a pinch of dried herbs to the pot. "Dad," Finn began, his voice curious, "where do you think the best place is to find truffles?"

Ethan smiled, his eyes crinkling at the corners. He had been expecting this question, knowing his son's keen interest in their foraging endeavors. "Well, Finn," he said, settling down on a nearby log, "truffles are a bit of a mystery, even to the most experienced hunters. They grow underground, in symbiosis with the roots of certain trees, like oaks and hickories." This term comes from the Greek word *symbioun*, which means "to live together," and it defines a relationship such as that between a truffle and a tree root.

Finn nodded, remembering the information Chef Jacques had shared with him. "So, we should look near those kinds of trees?" he asked, his eyes scanning the surrounding forest.

"That's a good start," Ethan agreed, "but it's not just about the trees. Truffles also prefer specific soil conditions - well-draining, slightly alkaline, and rich in organic matter. They need just the right balance of moisture and nutrients to thrive."

Finn's brow furrowed as he tried to process the information. "How do we find spots like that in the forest?" he wondered aloud, stirring the soup absently.

Ethan chuckled, reaching over to ruffle his son's hair affectionately. "That's where experience and a keen eye come in handy," he explained. "Over time, you'll learn to read the signs - the type of trees, the undergrowth, the texture of the soil. It's a skill that develops with practice and patience."

Finn sighed, realizing that truffle hunting was more complex than he had initially thought. "I guess I still have a lot to learn," he admitted, looking down at the bubbling soup.

Ethan placed a reassuring hand on Finn's shoulder. "Don't worry, son," he said, his voice warm with encouragement. "You've already shown a natural talent for this. With Mystic by your side and a willingness to learn, I have no doubt you'll become an excellent truffle hunter."

Finn smiled, his enthusiasm rekindled by his father's words. He ladled the steaming soup into two bowls, handing one to Ethan. As they sat together, enjoying their simple meal in the heart of the Loblolly Springs forest, Finn felt a renewed sense of determination. He was ready to embrace the challenge of truffle hunting, to learn the secrets of the forest, and to pursue his dreams, one step at a time.

ETHAN AND FINN SAVORED the last spoonfuls of their instant soup. The warm meal had rejuvenated their spirits, and they were now ready to embark on their truffle hunting adventure. Mystic, their faithful canine companion, sat patiently nearby, her tail wagging in anticipation of the impending exploration.

Ethan set his empty bowl aside and turned to Finn, his eyes sparkling with the excitement of sharing his knowledge. "Alright, son," he began, his voice clear and purposeful, "here's the plan. We'll start by walking out from the camp in a straight line, keeping track of our path so we can easily find our way back. We don't want to get lost in these woods, especially on our first outing."

Finn nodded, his attention focused on his father's words. He understood the importance of staying oriented in the vast wilderness, and he was grateful for Ethan's guidance.

"As we walk," Ethan continued, "we'll be on the lookout for specific types of trees and soil conditions that are ideal for truffle growth. We want to focus on old-growth pecan and oak trees. These trees have a symbiotic relationship with the truffles, providing them with the nutrients they need to thrive."

Finn's brow furrowed as he processed the information. "What about the soil?" he asked, curious to learn more about the factors that influenced truffle growth.

Ethan smiled, pleased by his son's inquisitive nature. "Good question, Finn," he praised. "Truffles prefer well-draining soil with a slightly alkaline pH. The soil type and vegetation can give us clues about the pH levels."

Finn's eyes widened with realization. "But how will we know what the pH is?" he wondered aloud, unsure of how to determine the acidity or alkalinity of the forest floor.

Ethan reached into his backpack and pulled out a small booklet, its pages worn and weathered from years of use. "This field guide," he explained, holding it up for Finn to see, "will help us identify the plants and trees that thrive in alkaline soils. For example, if we spot a patch of wild ginger or trillium, it's a good indication that the soil is more alkaline."

Finn took the booklet from his father, flipping through the pages with newfound appreciation. He marveled at the intricate illustrations and detailed descriptions of the various plant species, eager to put his newfound knowledge to the test.

As they prepared to set out on their truffle hunting expedition, Ethan placed a reassuring hand on Finn's shoulder. "Remember, son," he said, his voice filled with encouragement, "truffle hunting is as much an art as it is a science. It takes patience, observation, and a willingness to learn from the forest itself. With time and practice, you'll develop an intuitive understanding of where to look." Finn nodded, his determination growing with each passing moment.

Ethan's words resonated with Finn as they prepared to embark on their truffle hunting expedition. The young boy's eyes sparkled with determination, eager to learn the secrets of the forest and train Mystic to become an expert truffle hunter.

"Mystic will be our secret weapon," Ethan said with a grin, patting the Labrador's golden head. "Her keen sense of smell and natural instincts will guide us to the hidden treasures beneath the soil."

Finn nodded, his heart swelling with pride as he looked at his loyal companion. He knew that Mystic's unwavering spirit and sharp senses would be invaluable in their quest for the elusive truffles.

As they set out from their campsite, Ethan led the way, his steps sure and confident as he navigated the dense undergrowth. Finn followed closely behind, his eyes scanning the forest floor for any signs of the prized fungi.

Mystic trotted alongside them, her nose to the ground, sniffing intently at every root and hollow. Her tail wagged with excitement, as if she could sense the adventure that lay ahead.

"Watch how she moves, Finn," Ethan instructed, his voice low and steady. "Notice how she pauses and investigates certain spots more thoroughly than others. Those are the places where we should focus our search."

Finn observed Mystic's behavior, marveling at the way she seemed to instinctively know where to look. He made mental notes of the areas she lingered, committing them to memory for future reference.

As they ventured deeper into the forest, Ethan pointed out the various trees and plants that indicated the presence of truffles. He showed Finn how to identify the telltale signs of the fungus, from the subtle changes in soil texture to the faint, earthy aroma that hung in the air.

Finn absorbed every detail, his mind whirring with the newfound knowledge. He felt a deep connection to the forest, as if the secrets of the truffles were slowly revealing themselves to him.

Mystic, too, seemed to be learning with each passing moment. Her movements became more focused, her nose more attuned to the scents that wafted through the undergrowth. Finn couldn't help but smile as he watched his faithful companion work, her dedication and enthusiasm mirroring his own.

THE TERRAIN BEGAN TO change as Ethan, Finn, and Mystic ventured further into the heart of Loblolly Springs forest. They had been walking due west from their campsite for roughly half a mile, and the landscape started to slope upward gradually. The dense undergrowth gave way to a more open canopy, dominated by towering oak trees that stood like sentinels along the ridge.

At the base of the slope, a string of native pecan trees lined the lower portion of the rise, their branches reaching out to embrace the sunlight that filtered through the leaves. The soil here was noticeably different, with well-drained earth at the top of the slope and wetter, more moisture-rich soil where the pecan trees thrived.

Finn's eyes widened with excitement as he recognized the potential for truffles in this area. He reached into his pocket and pulled out the map his father had given him, carefully studying the grid system that divided the forest into manageable sections.

With a steady hand, Finn placed a mark on the map at the coordinates O45, indicating their current location. He knew that this would be a crucial reference point for future truffle hunts, allowing them to retrace their steps and explore the surrounding areas with greater precision.

Ethan nodded approvingly as he watched his son's meticulous approach. He knew that Finn's attention to detail and willingness to learn would serve him well in the art of truffle hunting.

Mystic, too, seemed to sense the importance of their location. Her nose twitched with anticipation as she caught the faint, earthy scent of truffles on the breeze. She looked up at Finn, her eyes bright with eagerness, ready to begin the search.

Finn took a deep breath, inhaling the rich, loamy aroma of the forest. He could feel the excitement building within him, the thrill of the hunt coursing through his veins. With Mystic by his side and his father's guidance, he knew that he was ready to embark on this new adventure.

As they prepared to start their truffle hunt, Finn couldn't help but feel a sense of purpose and determination. He knew that every step he took, every truffle he found, would bring him closer to his dream of attending college and securing a bright future for himself and his family.

With a nod to Ethan and a gentle pat on Mystic's head, Finn set off into the forest, ready to uncover the hidden treasures that lay beneath the soil. The hunt had begun, and the young truffle hunter was determined to make his mark on the world, one precious fungus at a time.

AS FINN AND MYSTIC begin to search the forest, a sense of anticipation hung in the air. The young truffle hunter's heart raced with excitement, his mind focused on the task at hand. He knew that this moment marked the beginning of a new chapter in his life, a journey that would test his skills and determination.

Mystic, ever the loyal companion, trotted alongside Finn, her golden coat shimmering in the filtered light. Her keen nose twitched as she caught the scent of the forest floor, a tapestry of earthy aromas that hinted at the treasures hidden beneath the soil.

Finn paused for a moment, taking in his surroundings with a discerning eye. The towering oak trees and native pecan trees that dominated the landscape created a canopy of green, their leaves rustling gently in the warm breeze. The undergrowth was sparse here, allowing for easier movement and a clearer view of the ground.

With a deep breath, Finn knelt down and ran his fingers through the rich, loamy soil. He could feel the moisture and the slight alkalinity that Chef Jacques had described as ideal conditions for truffles. The knowledge that he had gained from his mentor and his father swirled in his mind, guiding his actions as he began to search.

Mystic, too, was in her element. Her tail wagged with enthusiasm as she put her nose to the ground, her instincts guiding her towards the most promising spots. She moved with purpose, her body language conveying a sense of focus and determination that mirrored Finn's own.

Together, the boy and his dog worked in tandem, their movements synchronized by an unspoken understanding. Finn followed Mystic's lead, trusting in her keen senses to guide them towards their quarry. He watched as she paused at the base of a particularly old oak tree, her nose working furiously as she caught the scent of something hidden beneath the soil.

With a gentle command, Finn encouraged Mystic to investigate further. He watched as she began to dig, her paws working with precision and care. The anticipation built as the soil gave way, revealing a small, round object nestled in the earth.

Finn's heart skipped a beat as he reached down and gently lifted the truffle from its resting place. It was a Bianchetto, a delicate white truffle that gleamed in the sunlight. He marveled at its beauty and the promise it held, a tangible symbol of the adventure that lay ahead. As he carefully placed the truffle in his satchel, Finn couldn't help but feel a sense of pride and accomplishment.

THE GURGLING MELODY of Loblolly Major Creek beckoned them to follow its serpentine path, as Finn and Mystic ventured deeper into the forest. The sun's rays danced through the canopy, casting a broken light on the leaf-strewn ground. Finn's keen eyes, ever observant, scanned the forest floor as they walked, taking in the intricate details of the natural world around them.

Suddenly, a glint caught Finn's attention, a flash of something metallic peeking out from beneath the carpet of leaves. Curiosity piqued, he knelt down to investigate, gently brushing away the debris with his hands. As he cleared the area, a series of old artifacts emerged, their presence oddly incongruous in the untouched wilderness.

Finn's heart raced with excitement as he carefully examined each item. There were rustic metal implements, their surfaces weathered and tarnished by time. They appeared to be tools used for digging, their handles worn smooth from use. A cracked leather pouch lay nearby, its contents long since lost to the elements. But it was the faded map that truly captured Finn's imagination.

The map was a mystery, its edges frayed and its surface marred by the passage of time. Strange symbols and partially eroded text dotted its surface, hinting at secrets waiting to be uncovered. Finn's mind raced with possibilities, his adventurous spirit ignited by the discovery.

Eager to share his find, Finn called out to Ethan, who was a short distance away. "Dad, come look at this!" he exclaimed, his voice filled with excitement. Ethan, intrigued by his son's enthusiasm, made his way over to where Finn knelt.

As Ethan examined the artifacts, his brow furrowed with curiosity. He carefully picked up one of the metal implements, turning it over in his hands. "These are old, Finn," he said, his voice tinged with wonder. "They could be from the early days of Loblolly Springs, when the first settlers arrived."

Finn's eyes widened at the thought. "Really? That's incredible!" He held up the map, its mysteries calling to him. "And what about this map? What do you think it means?"

Ethan studied the map closely, his fingers tracing the faded lines and symbols. "I'm not sure, son. But it's clear that someone left these here for a reason. Perhaps they were searching for something, just like we're searching for truffles."

HIS MIND DRIFTED TO the whispered tales that had long circulated among the residents of Loblolly Springs, as Ethan examined the weathered map and ancient tools. The stories spoke of a legendary truffle-rich area, a hidden enclave within the vast forest that the locals had dubbed the "Mycelium Haven."

According to the folklore, the early settlers of the region had stumbled upon this extraordinary place, a pocket of land where the soil and conditions were perfect for the growth of rare and valuable truffles. The tales described an abundance of these subterranean delicacies, a bounty that could transform the lives of those fortunate enough to find it.

However, as time passed and generations came and went, the exact location of the Mycelium Haven became lost to history. The once-vivid details faded into obscurity, and the legend took on a more mythical quality. Many dismissed it as nothing more than a charming story, a bit of local color designed to entertain tourists and captivate the imaginations of children.

But now, as Ethan held the tangible remnants of the past in his hands, he couldn't help but wonder if there might be more to the legend than mere folklore. The map, with its cryptic symbols and faded lines, seemed to hint at a purposeful journey, a quest undertaken by someone long ago.

Ethan's mind raced with possibilities. Could these artifacts be connected to the Mycelium Haven? Were they clues left behind by a determined truffle hunter from a bygone era? The thought sent a shiver of excitement down his spine.

Finn, observing his father's pensive expression, couldn't contain his curiosity. "Dad, what is it? Do you think this map could lead us to something special?"

Ethan looked at his son, a glimmer of adventure in his eyes. "I'm not sure, Finn. But there are stories, old tales about a place in this forest where truffles grow in abundance. A place called the Mycelium Haven."

Finn's eyes widened, his imagination ignited by the prospect of a hidden treasure within the forest he knew so well. "Do you think that's what this map is pointing to? Could it be real?"

ETHAN AND FINN MADE their way back towards their camp as the sun dipped low in the sky, painting the forest in a warm, golden glow. The day's adventures had left them both invigorated and hungry, eager to settle in for the evening and reflect on the discoveries they had made.

Once they reached the campsite, Finn set about starting a fire, his hands working deftly to arrange the kindling and strike a match. As the flames began to crackle and dance, he placed a pan of water over the heat, preparing to make their instant soup for the evening meal.

Mystic, ever the loyal companion, wagged her tail in anticipation as Finn opened a bag of dry food and poured it into her bowl. The dog's enthusiasm brought a smile to Finn's face, and he gave her a gentle pat before returning to his own dinner preparations.

With the soup simmering and the coffee brewing, Ethan and Finn settled down by the fire, the warmth of the flames chasing away the encroaching chill of the evening. They sipped their coffee, savoring the rich aroma that mingled with the woodsy scent of the forest.

As they sat, Ethan's gaze wandered to the edge of the camp, where a clump of small, delicate plants caught his eye. He recognized them instantly as chickweed, a common edible weed that could be found throughout the woods of Arkansas.

"Hey, Finn," Ethan called out, gesturing towards the plants. "See those over there? That's chickweed."

Finn looked up from his soup, curiosity piqued. "Chickweed? Is it edible?"

Ethan nodded, a smile playing at the corners of his mouth. "It sure is. Chickweed has these small, oval-shaped leaves and tiny white star-shaped flowers. You can usually find it in cool, damp areas like this."

He went on to explain how the plant could be used in salads, sandwiches, or even cooked as a leafy green. Finn listened intently, absorbing the knowledge his father imparted.

"You know," Ethan continued, "there are other edible weeds out here too. Like dandelions. The leaves can be used in salads, and the roots can even be used to make tea."

Finn's eyes widened with interest. "I had no idea there was so much out here that we could eat."

Ethan chuckled, patting his son on the shoulder. "The forest is full of surprises, Finn. It's all about knowing where to look and what to look for."

FINN'S EYES LIT UP with curiosity as he considered the possibility of adding the chickweed to their evening meal. "Can we cook it with our soup?" he asked, eager to put his newfound knowledge to the test.

Ethan smiled at his son's enthusiasm, pleased to see him taking an interest in the natural world around them. "We sure can," he replied, nodding his head in affirmation. "Chickweed is a versatile plant, and it would make a great addition to our soup."

However, as Ethan began to rise from his seat by the fire, ready to gather some of the delicate greens, a thought occurred to him. He paused, turning back to Finn with a serious expression on his face.

"But before we do that, Finn, there's something important I want you to remember," Ethan said, his tone taking on a note of gravity. "Never eat something from the wild unless you know for sure what it is. Some plants out here can make you very ill if you're not careful."

Finn nodded solemnly, understanding the weight of his father's words. He knew that the forest, for all its beauty and bounty, could also hold hidden dangers for those who were unprepared or unaware.

Ethan placed a hand on Finn's shoulder, his eyes locking with his son's. "I know you're excited to learn about all the edible plants out here, and that's great. But always make sure you double-check with me or consult a reliable field guide before you try anything new, okay?"

Finn nodded again, his expression serious. "I will, Dad. I promise."

Ethan smiled, giving Finn's shoulder a gentle squeeze before rising to his feet. "Good. Now, let's see about adding some of that chickweed to our soup, shall we?"

Together, father and son made their way to the edge of the camp, carefully selecting a handful of the tender, green leaves. As they returned to the fire, Mystic watched with interest, her tail wagging in anticipation of the delicious smells that would soon be wafting from the pot.

And as the chickweed simmered in the broth, releasing its subtle, fresh flavor, Finn felt a sense of pride and accomplishment. He was learning, growing, and discovering the secrets of the forest, one step at a time, with his father and his faithful dog by his side.

THE FIRE DWINDLED, its flickering light casting shadows on the surrounding trees. Finn and Ethan began to prepare for the night ahead. Ethan carefully banked the coals, ensuring that the embers would continue to provide a gentle warmth throughout the night without posing a risk to their campsite.

Finn, his energy spent from the day's adventures and discoveries, helped his father lay out their sleeping bags beneath the protective branches of the Eastern Redbud tree. Mystic, ever the loyal companion, settled herself nearby, her watchful eyes scanning the perimeter of the camp.

With their beds prepared, Finn and Ethan took a moment to appreciate the beauty of the night sky above them. Far from the light pollution of the city, the stars shone with a breathtaking intensity. The Milky Way stretched across the heavens like a luminous river, its ethereal glow casting a soft light over the forest below.

Ethan, his voice low and soothing, began to discuss their plans for the following day. He spoke of the areas they would explore, the techniques they would practice, and the wonders they might discover. Finn listened intently, his mind racing with possibilities and excitement for the adventures that lay ahead.

However, as Ethan continued to outline their itinerary, he noticed a change in Finn's demeanor. The boy's eyelids had grown heavy, his head nodding gently as he struggled to stay awake. The warmth of the fire, the comfort of his sleeping bag, and the soothing sound of his father's voice had all conspired to lull him into a peaceful slumber.

Ethan smiled softly, his heart swelling with love and pride for his son. He knew that the day had been long and full, and that Finn's young body needed rest to prepare for the challenges and discoveries that tomorrow would bring.

As the last of the coals burned down to a soft, pulsing glow, Ethan carefully adjusted Finn's sleeping bag, ensuring that he was warm and comfortable. He then settled into his own bed, his eyes drifting shut as the sounds of the forest – the gentle rustling of leaves, the distant hooting of an owl – filled the night air.

And so, beneath the canopy of the Loblolly Springs forest, the Thornwood family slept, their dreams filled with the promise of truffles, adventure, and the unbreakable bonds of love and companionship that had brought them to this moment, and would guide them through all the moments yet to come.

Chapter 4

The first rays of sunlight had just pierced through the forest canopy as Ethan and Finn emerged from their tent, ready to break camp and begin their journey back home. The morning air was crisp and invigorating, filled with the gentle sounds of birdsong and the rustling of leaves in the breeze.

With practiced efficiency, father and son worked together to dismantle their campsite, packing away their gear and ensuring that no trace of their presence remained. Mystic, eager for the day's adventures, bounded around them, her tail wagging with excitement.

Once everything was stowed away, Ethan shouldered his backpack and nodded to Finn, signaling that it was time to depart. With Mystic leading the way, her nose to the ground and her ears perked for any signs of danger or intrigue, they set off into the heart of the Loblolly Springs forest.

As they walked, Ethan took the opportunity to share his knowledge of the forest with Finn, pointing out various edible plants and explaining the soil conditions that were most favorable for truffle growth. He showed Finn how to identify landmarks – a gnarled tree, a distinctive rock formation, a patch of wildflowers – that could serve as guideposts, helping them to find their way if they ever became lost or disoriented.

Finn listened intently, absorbing every word and committing the information to memory. He knew that these lessons would be invaluable in his future truffle-hunting endeavors, and he was determined to learn as much as he could from his father's vast store of knowledge.

As they continued their trek, they came across a small, natural spring flowing at the bottom of a hill. The water was crystal clear and inviting, and Ethan instructed Finn to fill his water bottle from the source. He explained that it was always best to save their water filters when possible, as this would help to extend their lifespan and ensure that they had access to clean drinking water for future adventures.

Finn nodded, understanding the importance of resource management in the wilderness. He knelt down beside the spring, carefully filling his bottle and marveling at the purity and sweetness of the water.

Just as he was about to stand up, something caught his eye – a glint of metal, half-buried in the soft earth beside the spring. Intrigued, Finn reached out and brushed away the dirt, revealing a small, intricately carved bronze medallion. The design was unlike anything he had ever seen before, a complex pattern of interwoven lines and symbols that seemed to shimmer and dance in the sunlight.

Finn's eyes widened as he held the medallion in his hand, marveling at its intricate design and the way it seemed to pulse with an ancient energy. He turned to show it to his father, but before he could speak, a sharp yelp pierced the tranquil morning air.

Finn and Ethan spun around to see Mystic emerging from a clump of low, shrub-like bushes, her fur snagged with thorny branches. Finn rushed to her side, carefully extricating her from the prickly foliage and checking her for any injuries.

"Easy there, girl," he soothed, running his hands over her golden coat. "Let's see what you've gotten yourself into."

As Finn approached the bushes, he noticed that the limbs were covered in long, wicked-looking thorns. The leaves were dark green and glossy, and the bark had a distinctive, warty appearance. He turned to his father, a questioning look on his face.

Ethan smiled, recognizing the plant instantly. "That's a Hercules' Club tree," he explained, moving closer to examine the spiny branches.

"It's also known as the toothache tree, because the bark and leaves contain compounds that can numb pain when chewed."

Finn's eyes widened in surprise. "Really? That's incredible!"

Ethan nodded, his expression thoughtful. "The Hercules' Club has a long history of use by indigenous peoples and early settlers. The thorns were sometimes used as needles for sewing or tattooing, and the wood was crafted into walking sticks and clubs for self-defense."

He reached out and carefully snapped off a small twig, holding it up for Finn to see. "The bark and leaves can also be used to make a tea that's said to have medicinal properties, helping to relieve everything from toothaches to rheumatism."

Finn took the twig from his father, turning it over in his hands and marveling at the ingenuity of those who had first discovered the plant's many uses. He glanced down at Mystic, who was now sniffing curiously at the base of the tree, her tail wagging with renewed enthusiasm.

"I guess even the prickliest things can have a purpose," Finn mused, tucking the twig into his pocket alongside the mysterious medallion. "It's all about knowing how to use them."

Ethan clapped a hand on his son's shoulder, pride shining in his eyes. "That's the key to surviving in the wilderness, Finn. Everything has a role to play, and it's up to us to learn how to work with the forest, not against it."

ETHAN AND FINN REACHED home by mid-morning, Clara, Ethan's mother, came out to greet them, carrying a tray laden with steaming cups of coffee and freshly baked breakfast rolls. She led them to the small table by the garden shed, where they sat down to enjoy their meal and regale her with tales of their overnight adventure.

Finn, still captivated by the possibility of solving the historical puzzle, eagerly showed his mother the artifacts they had found in the forest. Clara, whose logical mind was adept at parsing fact from fiction, examined the items with a keen eye. She suggested that they clean and analyze the artifacts to see if they could uncover any clues about their origin and purpose.

Under Clara's guidance, Finn carefully cleaned the old tools and leather pouch, revealing more details that had been obscured by dirt and grime. As he worked, he noticed that the digging tools bore an old company stamp, which they thought could be traced back to a group of settlers known for harvesting truffles in the region generations ago.

Meanwhile, Ethan and Clara focused their attention on the faded map. Though eroded and difficult to read, they noticed that it contained contour lines that seemed to match a section of the topographical map of the Loblolly Springs forest that Ethan had brought with him.

Excited by this discovery, Finn and his parents huddled around the two maps, comparing them side by side. They looked for landmarks and other identifying features that might help them pinpoint the exact location depicted on the old map.

As they worked, a sense of anticipation and wonder filled the air. The possibility that they might be on the verge of uncovering a long-lost truffle haven was both thrilling and daunting. Finn couldn't help but feel a surge of excitement at the thought of what they might find if they could decipher the map's secrets.

FINN TURNED TO HIS father, his eyes sparkling with newfound curiosity. "Dad, would it be alright if I borrowed your book on wild edibles?" he asked. "I'd like to try and find some on our farm land and show you what I've discovered."

Ethan's face lit up with pride at his son's initiative. He knew that Finn's interest in the natural world was growing, and he was more than happy to encourage it. "Of course, Finn," he said, nodding his approval. "That's a great idea. I think you'll be surprised at how much you can find right here on our own property."

He walked over to the bookshelf and pulled out a well-worn field guide, handing it to Finn. "This should help you identify what's safe to eat and what to avoid," he explained. "And don't forget, if you're ever unsure, just leave it be."

Finn took the book gratefully, already flipping through the pages and marveling at the detailed illustrations and descriptions. "Thanks, Dad," he said, his mind already racing with the possibilities of what he might find.

Ethan smiled, recognizing the look of determination on his son's face. "You know, I bet you could easily find ten or so different edibles within a few hours," he said, his tone encouraging. "Just take your time, be observant, and trust your instincts."

Finn nodded, his resolve strengthening with his father's words. He tucked the book under his arm and headed for the door, eager to begin his new quest. As he stepped outside, he paused and looked back at his father. "I won't let you down, Dad," he said, his voice filled with determination. "I'll show you what I find."

With that, he set off towards the fields and forests that surrounded their home, the field guide clutched tightly in his hand and a sense of purpose guiding his steps. The world around him seemed to hum with potential, and he couldn't wait to uncover its hidden treasures.

FINN SAT AT THE KITCHEN table, his father's well-worn field guide open before him. He pored over the pages, his eyes scanning the detailed illustrations and descriptions of various wild edibles. As he read, a mental list began to form in his mind, a checklist of the plants he would seek out first on his foraging adventure.

At the top of his list was the Loblolly Pine, a tree that was ubiquitous in the forests surrounding their home. But while the pine was certainly a viable option, Finn's heart was set on finding a white oak. He knew that the inner bark of the oak could be harvested and eaten, and he had already decided on the perfect method: he would cut a strip of bark, about a foot high and four inches wide, careful not to harm the tree too much.

Next on his list were cattails. He had read about the many edible parts of this aquatic plant, from the starchy roots to the young shoots and even the pollen. He knew that he would need to dig up the whole plant, roots and all, and then carefully process each part before washing and preparing them for consumption.

As he continued to read, Finn's list grew longer. He would keep an eye out for any nuts he could find - acorns, walnuts, hickory nuts, and pecans - knowing that they could provide a valuable source of protein and healthy fats. He also made a note to himself to watch for any ripe berries or fruits that he might come across, knowing that they could add a burst of flavor and nutrients to his wild-foraged meals.

Finn's excitement grew as he imagined himself out in the woods, foraging for these hidden treasures. He could almost feel the rough bark of the oak tree beneath his fingers, the cool mud of the cattail bed squishing between his toes. He knew that the process of finding and preparing these wild edibles would be a challenge, but it was a challenge he was more than ready to take on.

With a final glance at the field guide, Finn closed the book and stood up from the table. He had his list, and he had his determination. All that was left was to head out into the wilderness and put his newfound knowledge to the test. With a deep breath and a sense of purpose, he stepped out the door and into the waiting forest.

FINN AND MYSTIC SET out into the Loblolly Springs forest, the early morning sun cast a welcome warmth as they walked. The air was crisp and cool, and the scent of pine and earth filled their nostrils as they walked. Finn had his father's field guide tucked under his arm, his mental list of wild edibles at the forefront of his mind.

Finn scanned the forest floor for any signs of the plants he sought. Mystic, ever the loyal companion, trotted along beside him, her nose to the ground as she sniffed out any interesting scents.

Before long, they came across a stand of Loblolly Pines, their tall, straight trunks reaching up towards the sky. Finn knew that the inner bark of these trees was edible, but he had his heart set on finding a white oak instead. They pressed on, deeper into the forest.

Finn spotted a patch of cattails growing along the edge of a small stream. He remembered reading about the many edible parts of this plant, and he eagerly waded into the shallow water to harvest a few specimens. Mystic watched from the bank, her tail wagging as Finn carefully dug up the roots and cut the young shoots.

With the cattails safely tucked away in his backpack, Finn and Mystic continued their search. They came across a grove of hickory trees, last years crop scattered on the ground. Finn gathered a handful, cracking them open with a rock to reveal the sweet, buttery meat inside.

As Finn gazes into the distance, he notices the telling characteristics of an Arkansas white oak tree (Quercus alba) tall and sturdy against the backdrop of the forest. Its size is impressive, the tree reaching between 80 to 100 feet into the sky, with a sprawling canopy that seems to match its height in width. The bark catches Finn's eye next, the light ash-gray color distinct even from afar, deeply furrowed and textured, forming scaly ridges that distinguish it from the bark of other trees in the forest.

The rounded lobes of the tree's leaves flutter in the light breeze, the bright green tops contrasting with paler undersides, hinting at the spectacular shades of red or purple they will display come autumn.

Even from a distance, Finn can discern the rounded shape of acorns dotting the branches, shorter and more plump than those of other oaks, with their distinctive warty caps. Despite the tree's slow growth, its immense presence speaks to its age, and Finn knows that the strength and resilience of this white oak are a testament to the ancient, enduring beauty of the Arkansas forests he so loves to explore.

As the sun climbed higher in the sky, Finn and Mystic found themselves in a small clearing. There, in the center of the glade, stood a magnificent white oak tree, smaller than the first he had spotted in the distance. Finn's heart leapt with excitement as he approached the tree, his hand outstretched to touch its rough bark.

With great care, Finn used his knife to cut a strip of bark from the tree, just as he had read in the field guide. The bark was tough and fibrous, but Finn knew that it could be boiled and eaten in times of need.

As they made their way back towards home, Finn's backpack was heavy with the bounty of the forest. He had found many of the plants on his list, and he felt a sense of accomplishment and pride in his newfound skills. Mystic, too, seemed pleased with their adventure, her tail held high as she trotted along beside him.

AS THE SUN BEGAN TO set over Loblolly Springs, Ethan Thornwood pulled into the driveway of his family's home. The day's work as a wildlife biologist had been fulfilling but tiring, and he was looking forward to a quiet evening with his family.

Inside, Finn was practically bouncing with excitement, eager to show his father the wild edibles he had gathered from the forest that day. As soon as Ethan walked through the door, Finn rushed to greet him, his backpack in hand.

"Dad, you'll never guess what I found in the forest today!" Finn exclaimed, his eyes shining with pride.

Ethan smiled, setting down his own bag and giving his son his full attention. "What did you find, Finn?"

Finn unzipped his backpack and began to carefully lay out his treasures on the kitchen table. "I found cattails by the stream," he said, pointing to the roots and shoots. "And hickory nuts from the grove near the clearing."

Ethan nodded, impressed by his son's knowledge and skills. "Those are some excellent finds, Finn. Cattails and hickory nuts are both very nutritious."

But Finn had saved the best for last. With a flourish, he produced the strip of white oak bark he had harvested. "And look at this, Dad," he said, holding it out for his father to see. "I found a white oak tree and cut some of the inner bark, just like the field guide said."

Ethan took the bark, examining it closely. "This is perfect, Finn," he said, his voice filled with pride. "You've done an incredible job today. I'm so proud of you."

Finn beamed, his chest swelling with happiness at his father's praise. "Thanks, Dad," he said. "I can't wait to go out and find even more wild edibles. Maybe next time, we can go together?"

Ethan smiled, ruffling his son's hair affectionately. "I would love that, Finn. We can make a whole day of it, just you and me and Mystic out in the forest."

The Thornwood family settled in for the evening, Finn's mind was already racing with ideas for their next foraging adventure. With his father's guidance and Mystic by his side, he knew that there was so much more to discover in the wild and wonderful world of Loblolly Springs.

THE THORNWOOD FAMILY gathered around the dinner table that evening, the aroma of a hearty meal filled the air. Finn, his excitement barely contained, took a deep breath and looked at his parents. "Mom, Dad," he began, "I want to pack up and spend the day and night in the forest with Mystic. I'll come back the next afternoon."

Ethan and Clara exchanged a glance, their expressions a mix of concern and understanding. They knew their son's adventurous spirit and his growing love for the forest, but the thought of him spending the night alone in the wilderness gave them pause.

"Finn," Clara said gently, "we understand your desire to explore, but we need to make sure you're prepared and safe."

Ethan nodded, his brow furrowed in thought. "Your mother's right, Finn. The forest can be unpredictable, and we want to ensure you have everything you need."

The family discussed the matter at length, weighing the risks and benefits of Finn's proposed adventure. They talked about the supplies he would need, the importance of staying on marked trails, and the necessity of having a way to communicate in case of an emergency.

Finally, after much deliberation, Ethan and Clara agreed to let Finn embark on his overnight journey. "Alright, Finn," Ethan said, his tone serious but supportive, "you can go, but there are some conditions."

Finn leaned forward, eager to hear his father's instructions.

"First," Ethan continued, "you must pitch your camp in the same place we stayed last time. That way, we'll know exactly where to find you if there are any problems."

Finn nodded, committing the location to memory.

"And second," Ethan added, "you must take a portable radio with you. A citizen band transceiver, so you can contact us if you need help."

"I understand, Dad," Finn said, his voice filled with determination. "I promise I'll be careful and stay in touch."

That night, as the house grew quiet, Finn busied himself with packing his supplies. He carefully selected his gear, double-checking his list to ensure he had everything he needed. With his backpack ready and his heart full of anticipation, Finn climbed into bed, setting his alarm for before dawn. As he drifted off to sleep, his mind wandered to the adventures that awaited him and Mystic in the depths of Loblolly Springs forest.

AS DAWN BROKE OVER Loblolly Springs, Finn Thornwood emerged from his house, his loyal companion Mystic by his side. The early morning mist hung low over the forest, a veil of mystery that seemed to beckon them into its depths. With a deep breath, Finn shouldered his backpack, the weight of his essential gear a comforting presence against his back.

Among the carefully packed supplies, the mysterious map and artifacts found earlier nestled safely, their secrets waiting to be unraveled. Finn's mind wandered to the legend of the Mycelium Haven, a place said to be rich with rare truffles. The thought of uncovering this hidden treasure filled him with a sense of purpose and excitement.

Mystic, her golden coat gleaming in the soft morning light, trotted ahead, her nose twitching as she caught the scent of the forest. She seemed to sense the importance of their mission, her tail wagging with eager anticipation.

As they stepped into the dense undergrowth, Finn paused, his eyes scanning the ground. He noticed a set of unusual animal tracks, the imprints distinct and unfamiliar. A flicker of apprehension passed through him, a reminder of the potential dangers that lurked in the wilderness. But with Mystic by his side, he felt a surge of courage.

"Alright, Mystic," Finn said, his voice low and determined. "We've got a big day ahead of us. If we can find more truffles and uncover the secrets of the Mycelium Haven, it could change everything. Not just for us, but for our family and the whole town."

Mystic looked up at him, her brown eyes filled with understanding and loyalty. With a nod, Finn adjusted his backpack and set off into the forest, the dappled sunlight filtering through the canopy above. The journey had begun, and with each step, they ventured deeper into the heart of Loblolly Springs, the promise of discovery and adventure guiding their way.

SUDDENLY, MYSTIC PAUSED near the base of an ancient oak tree, her nose twitching with interest. She began to paw at the ground, her tail wagging with increasing excitement. Finn, curious about his companion's behavior, approached the spot where Mystic was digging.

As Mystic's paws worked to unearth something hidden beneath the roots, Finn's heart raced with anticipation. What secrets lay buried in this ancient forest? With a final tug, Mystic pulled out an old, rusted key, its surface covered in strange, intricate symbols.

Finn took the key from Mystic's mouth, turning it over in his hands. As he examined the peculiar markings, his eyes widened with recognition. The symbols on the key matched those on the map they had discovered earlier. A surge of excitement coursed through him as he realized the significance of this find.

"Good girl, Mystic," Finn whispered, his voice trembling with excitement. "I think you just found our first real clue."

He pulled out the map, his fingers tracing the lines and symbols that seemed to correspond with the key. As he studied the map, a sense of direction began to form in his mind. The key and the map were guiding them deeper into the heart of the forest, towards a destination that promised answers and perhaps even greater mysteries.

Just as Finn was about to share his revelation with Mystic, a distant noise echoed through the trees. It was a sound unlike anything he had heard before in the forest - a low, eerie moan that seemed to carry on the wind. Finn felt a shiver run down his spine, and Mystic's ears perked up, her body tensing with alert.

For a moment, they stood still, listening intently for any further signs of the strange noise. But the forest had fallen silent once more, leaving them with only the pounding of their own hearts and the weight of the key in Finn's hand.

AS FINN AND MYSTIC ventured further into the depths of the forest, they stumbled upon a narrow, overgrown path that seemed to have been forgotten by time itself. The path, barely visible amidst the dense underbrush, stretched out before them, leading towards the northeast. An eerie stillness hung in the air, broken only by the occasional rustling of leaves in the gentle breeze.

Finn hesitated for a moment, realizing that this hidden path deviated from the route that would take them to their first campsite. He glanced down at Mystic, who looked up at him with curious eyes, her tail wagging slowly. With a deep breath, Finn made the decision to follow the mysterious trail, his curiosity outweighing his apprehension.

As they pushed through the tangled vines and low-hanging branches, Finn felt a growing sense of unease. The path seemed to close in around them, the dense foliage creating a claustrophobic atmosphere. Mystic stayed close to Finn's side, her keen senses alert for any signs of danger.

After what felt like an eternity of struggling through the undergrowth, they came upon an old, weathered signpost. The wooden post was covered in cryptic markings, each pointing in a different direction. Finn stepped closer, his eyes narrowing as he tried to decipher the strange symbols.

As he studied the markings, a sudden realization dawned upon him. The symbols seemed to be a code, a hidden message left by someone long ago. With a surge of excitement, Finn worked to unravel the meaning behind the cryptic signs.

After several minutes of careful examination, Finn believed he had deciphered the code. One particular marking stood out, a series of lines and dots that seemed to point towards a specific direction. Finn's heart raced as he realized that this path, according to the signpost, led to the legendary Mycelium Haven.

GUIDED BY THE CRYPTIC signpost, the dense forest gradually gave way to a small clearing. In the center of the glade stood an old, abandoned cabin, its weathered wooden walls and sagging roof a testament to years of neglect. The structure seemed to emit an aura of mystery and foreboding, as if it held secrets long forgotten.

Finn approached the cabin cautiously, his heart pounding in his chest. Mystic stayed close by his side, her ears perked and her body tense, as if sensing the same unease that gripped her human companion. As they drew nearer, Finn noticed that the door of the cabin was slightly ajar, creaking softly in the gentle breeze.

With a deep breath, Finn pushed the door open, wincing as the hinges groaned in protest. The interior of the cabin was shrouded in darkness, the only light filtering in through the dusty windows and the open doorway. Finn stepped inside, his eyes slowly adjusting to the gloom.

As he surveyed the cabin's interior, Finn's gaze fell upon a collection of old truffle-hunting equipment scattered across the floor. Rusted trowels, weathered baskets, and worn-out boots lay haphazardly, as if abandoned in haste. Amidst the clutter, a small leather-bound journal caught Finn's attention.

With trembling hands, Finn picked up the journal and gently brushed away the layer of dust that had accumulated on its cover. As he flipped through the yellowed pages, his eyes widened in surprise. The journal contained detailed entries about the Mycelium Haven, describing its location and the abundance of rare truffles that could be found there.

Finn delved deeper into the journal, he discovered a passage that made his heart race with excitement. The author mentioned a hidden entrance to the Haven, a secret path known only to a select few. However, just as Finn turned to the next page, he found that the rest of the journal was torn out, the remaining pages jagged and incomplete.

A sense of unease crept over Finn as he surveyed the cabin once more. The scattered equipment and the abruptly ended journal entries hinted at a struggle, as if the cabin's previous occupant had met with an untimely fate. The air seemed to grow heavy with a sense of foreboding, and Finn couldn't shake the feeling that they were being watched.

FINN STOOD IN THE ABANDONED cabin, the torn journal clutched in his hands, a sense of unease settled over him. The incomplete entries and the scattered truffle-hunting equipment hinted at a mysterious and potentially dangerous past. Finn glanced at Mystic, who remained alert and watchful, her tail held low.

Deciding to investigate further, Finn stepped out of the cabin and into the clearing. The sun's rays filtered through the canopy, casting dappled shadows on the ground. Finn's eyes scanned the area, taking in the details of the cabin's surroundings.

To the left of the cabin, Finn noticed a small, overgrown garden. The once neatly tended rows were now a tangle of weeds and wildflowers, the remnants of a long-abandoned vegetable patch. Finn carefully navigated through the undergrowth, his boots crunching on the dry leaves and twigs.

As he approached the garden, Finn spotted a weathered wooden post, its surface worn smooth by the elements. Tied to the post was a faded piece of twine, its frayed ends fluttering in the breeze. Finn's curiosity piqued, and he gently untied the twine, revealing a small, rusted key dangling from its end.

Finn turned the key over in his palm, wondering what it could unlock. He glanced back at the cabin, his mind racing with possibilities. Could this key be connected to the secrets mentioned in the journal? Or was it simply a relic of the cabin's past, long forgotten by its previous occupants?

A few paces from the garden, Finn discovered the remains of a fire pit. The charred stones were arranged in a circle, the ashes long since scattered by the wind. Finn knelt beside the pit, his fingers tracing the blackened rocks. He couldn't help but wonder about the stories that had been shared around this fire, the laughter and the tears that had echoed through the clearing.

As Finn stood up, his gaze drifted to the path that led away from the cabin and deeper into the forest. He knew that their original plan had been to set up camp at their first location, but the discovery of the cabin and the journal had thrown a wrench in their plans.

Finn felt torn, unsure of whether to continue the search for the Mycelium Haven or to turn back and stick to their original route. The promise of rare truffles and the thrill of uncovering a long-lost secret tugged at his adventurous spirit, but the nagging worry about straying too far from their intended path gnawed at the back of his mind.

Mystic sensed Finn's hesitation and nuzzled his hand, her warm breath tickling his skin. Finn looked down at his loyal companion, drawing strength from her presence. Together, they stood at the edge of the clearing, the weight of the decision heavy on Finn's shoulders.

FINN TOOK A DEEP BREATH, the weight of the decision pressing on his shoulders. He glanced down at the rusted key in his palm, then at the torn journal, the pages fluttering in the gentle breeze. The allure of the Mycelium Haven and its rare truffles tugged at his adventurous spirit, but the nagging worry about straying too far from their intended path couldn't be ignored.

With a sigh, Finn made his choice. He would backtrack along the hidden path, retracing their steps until they reached the point where they had deviated from their original route. It was the safest option, ensuring that they wouldn't get lost in the depths of the forest.

But before they left, Finn knew he had to document their findings. He reached into his backpack and pulled out a notebook and a pencil. With careful precision, he sketched the layout of the abandoned cabin, noting the location of the garden and the fire pit. He jotted down the cryptic markings from the weathered signpost and the symbols on the old map, hoping that he could decipher their meaning later.

Finn also made a detailed entry about the torn journal, copying down the legible passages and making note of the missing pages. He couldn't shake the feeling that the journal held the key to unlocking the secrets of the Mycelium Haven, and he was determined to unravel the mystery.

As he worked, Mystic kept watch, her keen senses alert for any signs of danger. The forest seemed to hold its breath, the only sounds the rustling of leaves and the occasional chirp of a bird.

Finally, satisfied with his notes, Finn tucked the notebook back into his backpack. He gave the cabin one last glance, committing its location to memory. He knew that he would return someday, armed with more knowledge and better prepared to face whatever challenges lay ahead.

With a nod to Mystic, Finn set off along the hidden path, retracing their steps with cautious determination. The forest closed in around them, the dappled sunlight filtering through the canopy above. Finn's mind raced with thoughts of the Mycelium Haven and the secrets it held, but for now, he focused on the task at hand: finding their way back to the main trail and continuing on to their first camp location.

As they walked, Finn couldn't help but feel a sense of excitement mixed with trepidation. The forest of Loblolly Springs had already revealed so many surprises, and he knew that there were more discoveries waiting to be made. With Mystic by his side and the old map as his guide, Finn felt ready to face whatever challenges lay ahead, one step at a time.

Chapter 5

Finn and Mystic carefully retraced their steps along the hidden path, the dense forest of Loblolly Springs seemed to close in around them. The midday sun filtered through the canopy, casting dappled shadows on the forest floor. Finn's determination was palpable, but it was tempered with a sense of caution. He knew that one wrong turn could lead them deeper into the wilderness, far from their intended destination.

With each step, Finn consulted his compass, ensuring that they were heading in the right direction. The needle pointed steadily towards the southwest, guiding them back to the main trail. Mystic trotted alongside him, her nose to the ground, alert for any signs of danger or potential clues.

As they walked, Finn couldn't help but reflect on their adventure so far. The discovery of the abandoned cabin and the torn journal had only deepened the mystery surrounding the Mycelium Haven. He couldn't shake the feeling that they were on the cusp of something extraordinary, but he also knew that they needed to proceed with caution.

Suddenly, Mystic stopped in her tracks, her ears perked up. Finn followed her gaze and noticed a peculiar formation of mushrooms growing at the base of a tree. They were unlike any he had seen before, with delicate, lace-like caps and slender stems. Could they be a sign of the Mycelium Haven?

Finn crouched down to take a closer look, being careful not to disturb the fragile fungi. He pulled out his notebook and sketched a quick drawing, noting the location and any identifying features. It was a small clue, but it only served to heighten the sense of mystery surrounding their quest.

As they continued on, Finn couldn't shake the feeling that they were being watched. The hair on the back of his neck stood up, and he scanned the surrounding forest for any signs of movement. Mystic, too, seemed on edge, her tail held high and her body tense.

Was it just his imagination, or were there other hikers in the area? Or could it be something else entirely, some unseen presence that called the forest home? Finn shook his head, trying to clear his thoughts. They needed to stay focused on their goal, to reach the campsite before nightfall.

FINN AND MYSTIC PRESSED on, the dense forest seemed to breathe around them, the leaves rustling in a gentle breeze. The compass in Finn's hand was a steadfast guide, pointing them in the right direction. With each step, they drew closer to their original path, the familiarity of the terrain growing with every passing minute.

Finn's mind wandered as they walked, reflecting on the strange events that had unfolded since they first set out on this adventure. The discovery of the old map, the abandoned cabin, and the cryptic journal entries - each piece of the puzzle seemed to lead them deeper into the heart of Loblolly Springs and its secrets.

But for now, their focus was on reaching their first campsite. Finn knew that they needed to set up camp before nightfall, to have a safe place to rest and regroup before continuing their exploration. He mentally cataloged the tasks ahead: pitching the tent, gathering firewood, and securing their supplies.

As they trekked on, Finn couldn't shake the feeling that they were not alone in the forest. Every snap of a twig or rustle of leaves made him pause, his senses heightened. Mystic, too, seemed on alert, her ears pricked and her body tense. Was it just the natural sounds of the forest, or was there something else out there, watching them from the shadows?

Finn shook his head, trying to clear his mind of such thoughts. They had to stay focused on their goal, to reach the campsite safely. He consulted the compass once more, adjusting their course slightly to account for the winding path.

They finally emerged into the familiar clearing of their first campsite as the sun began its slow descent towards the horizon. Finn let out a sigh of relief, his shoulders sagging as the tension drained from his body. They had made it, despite the detours and unexpected discoveries.

Mystic bounded ahead, sniffing around the perimeter of the campsite as Finn set down his pack. He surveyed the area, taking note of the best spot to pitch the tent and the nearby stream that would provide fresh water. There was much to be done before nightfall, but for now, he allowed himself a moment to savor their small victory.

FINN TOOK A DEEP BREATH, taking in the earthy scent of the woods. He could feel a mix of excitement and nervousness coursing through his veins. This was their first night alone in the wilderness, a true test of his skills and resilience.

With a determined nod, Finn set about unpacking his gear. He carefully laid out the tent, sleeping bag, and other essentials, organizing them neatly on the ground. Mystic, ever the vigilant companion, sniffed around the perimeter of the campsite, her keen senses alert for any signs of danger.

Satisfied that the area was safe, Finn turned his attention to the tent. He spread out the tarp, creating a protective layer between the ground and the tent floor. Then, he began assembling the poles, fitting them together with practiced ease.

As he worked, Mystic watched intently, her tail wagging with curiosity. Every so often, she would nudge Finn with her nose, as if offering encouragement or simply seeking attention. Finn couldn't help but smile at his faithful friend, grateful for her presence in this moment.

With the poles in place, Finn carefully draped the tent fabric over the structure, securing it with clips and ties. He double-checked each connection, ensuring that the tent was stable and ready to withstand the night ahead.

As he stepped back to admire his handiwork, a sense of accomplishment washed over him. The tent stood tall and sturdy, a beacon of safety in the midst of the wilderness. Finn felt a growing confidence in his abilities, knowing that he had the skills and knowledge to thrive in this environment.

FINN TURNED HIS ATTENTION to the next essential task: building a fire pit. He surveyed the clearing, searching for the perfect spot to create a safe and efficient campfire. With a keen eye, he began to gather stones from the surrounding area, carefully selecting ones that were smooth and relatively flat.

Finn carried the stones back to the center of the clearing, arranging them in a circle with meticulous precision. He recalled the lessons his father had taught him about fire safety and the importance of creating a stable fire ring. As he placed each stone, Finn felt a sense of responsibility and pride in his growing outdoor skills.

With the fire ring complete, Finn set about collecting tinder, kindling, and firewood. He searched the forest floor for dry leaves, twigs, and small branches, gathering them in a neat pile near the fire pit. Next, he ventured a short distance from the campsite, seeking out larger branches and logs that would sustain the fire throughout the evening.

Finn returned to the fire pit with an armful of wood, carefully arranging the tinder and kindling in the center of the stone circle. With a steady hand, he struck a match and gently coaxed the flames to life. The fire slowly grew, consuming the dry materials and casting a warm glow across the clearing.

As the fire crackled and danced, Finn felt a sense of accomplishment wash over him. He had successfully built a campfire, just as his father had taught him. The flickering light and the gentle heat emanating from the flames filled him with a comforting sense of security and self-reliance.

With the fire burning steadily, Finn turned his attention to preparing dinner. He retrieved a small pot from his backpack and filled it with water from his canteen. Carefully, he placed the pot over the flames, balancing it on a sturdy log to allow the water to boil.

As the water bubbled and steamed, Finn reached for a packet of instant soup he had packed for the trip. He tore open the package and poured the contents into the pot, stirring it with a long-handled spoon. The aroma of the soup began to fill the air, mingling with the scent of the campfire and the earthy fragrance of the forest.

AS THE SOUP SIMMERED over the crackling fire, Finn's thoughts turned to his loyal companion, Mystic. The golden-coated Labrador had been by his side throughout their adventures in Loblolly Springs, and Finn knew that her well-being was just as important as his own.

With a smile, Finn reached into his backpack and pulled out a collapsible bowl and a bag of dry dog food. He poured a generous portion of the kibble into the bowl, the sound of the food hitting the plastic catching Mystic's attention. The dog's ears perked up, and her nose twitched as she caught the scent of her dinner.

Finn carried the bowl over to a spot near the tent, setting it down on a patch of soft grass. "Here you go, girl," he said, giving Mystic a gentle pat on the head. "Enjoy your dinner."

Mystic wagged her tail enthusiastically, her brown eyes shining with gratitude. She stepped forward and buried her nose in the bowl, eagerly digging into her meal. The sound of her crunching on the kibble filled the campsite, a comforting and familiar noise that reminded Finn of home.

As he watched Mystic eat, Finn felt a surge of affection for his four-legged friend. She had been a constant source of comfort and companionship throughout their journey, always ready with a wagging tail and a wet nose to lift his spirits. Feeding her was a small but significant act of love, a way to show her that he cared for her just as much as she cared for him.

Finn returned to the fire, stirring the simmering soup and inhaling the savory aroma. The routine of feeding Mystic and preparing his own dinner brought a sense of normalcy to their wilderness adventure. It was a reminder that, no matter how far they ventured into the unknown, they would always have each other to rely on.

FINN'S THOUGHTS TURNED to the comforts of home. He reached into his backpack and pulled out a carefully wrapped slice of his mother's homemade pie, a treasured treat she had insisted he take along on his adventure.

The aroma of the pie filled the campsite as Finn unwrapped it, the scent of cinnamon and baked apples mingling with the woodsmoke from the fire. He sat down on a log near the glowing embers, holding the slice reverently in his hands.

With the first bite, a wave of nostalgia washed over Finn. The familiar taste transported him back to the warmth of his family's kitchen, where his mother's love and care infused every dish she made. The pie was a reminder of the support and encouragement he had received from his parents, a tangible connection to home even in the heart of the forest.

As Finn savored each bite, he reflected on the day's events and the adventure that lay ahead. The challenges he and Mystic had faced, the clues they had uncovered, and the mysteries that still awaited them – all of it seemed more manageable with the comforting taste of home on his tongue.

The sky above the campsite darkened, and Finn knew it was time to check in with his parents. He retrieved the CB radio from his pack, carefully tuning it to the frequency they had agreed upon before he set out.

"Mom, Dad, this is Finn. Do you read me? Over," he spoke into the radio, his voice carrying a mix of excitement and reassurance.

The radio crackled to life, and his father's voice came through, clear and strong. "Finn, this is Dad. We read you loud and clear. How are you and Mystic doing out there? Over."

Finn grinned, the connection with his parents lifting his spirits even further. "We're doing great, Dad. We've set up camp for the night, and everything is going according to plan. Mystic is right here with me, and we're both looking forward to what tomorrow will bring. Over."

His mother's voice chimed in, her tone warm and encouraging. "We're so proud of you, Finn. Remember, if you need anything at all, we're just a radio call away. Stay safe and have fun out there. Over."

"Thanks, Mom. I will. I love you both. Over and out," Finn replied, feeling a surge of love and gratitude for his parents' unwavering support.

With the radio call complete, Finn turned his attention to settling in for the night. He ensured that the campfire was properly feed, the embers glowing softly in the darkness. Inside the tent, he unrolled his sleeping bag, creating a cozy spot for himself and Mystic.

As he lay down, Mystic curled up beside him, her warm presence a comforting reminder that he was never truly alone in the wilderness.

THE SOUNDS OF THE FOREST enveloped Finn like a soothing lullaby as he lay in his sleeping bag. The rustling of leaves in the gentle breeze and the distant calls of nocturnal creatures created a symphony that seemed to whisper secrets of the wilderness. The crackling of the dying embers in the campfire added a rhythmic backdrop to the natural melody.

In the stillness of the night, Finn's mind wandered to the events of the day. He reflected on the hidden path they had discovered, the cryptic clues that had led them deeper into the forest, and the mysterious abandoned cabin that had filled him with both intrigue and unease. Each discovery had brought them closer to unraveling the secrets of the Mycelium Haven, and Finn couldn't help but feel a sense of excitement and anticipation for what lay ahead.

Despite the challenges they had faced, Finn felt a deep connection to the natural world around him. The forest had become more than just a setting for their adventure; it had become a part of him, a place where he felt alive and purposeful. He marveled at the way the trees seemed to whisper ancient knowledge, and how the earth beneath his feet thrummed with a hidden energy that he could almost feel.

As he lay there, lost in his thoughts, Mystic curled up beside him, her warm body pressed against his side. The loyal dog's presence was a constant comfort, a reminder that he was never truly alone in the wilderness. Finn reached out and gently stroked Mystic's soft fur, feeling the steady rise and fall of her breathing.

The rhythmic sounds of the forest and the warmth of Mystic's companionship slowly lulled Finn into a peaceful slumber. As his eyes fluttered closed, he felt a sense of contentment wash over him. Whatever tomorrow would bring, he knew that he and Mystic would face it together, ready for the adventures that awaited them in the depths of Loblolly Springs.

AT THE FIRST LIGHT of dawn filtering through the canopy of the Loblolly Springs forest, Finn stirred from his slumber. He emerged from his sleeping bag, the cool morning air sending a slight shiver down his spine. Beside him, Mystic stretched her limbs, her tail wagging in anticipation of the new day.

Finn set about building up the campfire, carefully arranging the kindling and striking a match. As the flames licked at the wood, he placed a small pan over the heat and began cooking breakfast. The sizzle of two eggs and sausage patties filled the air, mingling with the aroma of the warming dry biscuit.

Mystic watched intently as Finn prepared their meal, her nose twitching at the enticing scents. Finn poured a serving of dry dog food into a separate pan for his loyal companion and broke one of the sausage patties into small pieces, scattering them over the kibble. Mystic's tail thumped against the ground in eager anticipation.

As the breakfast cooked, Finn retrieved the map and artifacts they had discovered the previous day. He spread them out on a flat rock near the fire, studying the intricate details and cryptic symbols. His mind raced with possibilities, trying to decipher the clues that could lead them to the legendary Mycelium Haven.

Finn and Mystic savored their breakfast in companionable silence, the sounds of the awakening forest surrounding them. As they ate, Finn shared his thoughts with Mystic, his voice filled with excitement. "You know, girl, they say the Mycelium Haven is a place of unimaginable wonders. Rare truffles, ancient secrets, and a connection to the very heart of the forest. Can you imagine what we might find there?"

Mystic tilted her head, her intelligent eyes fixed on Finn as if she understood every word. Finn smiled, feeling a surge of gratitude for his loyal friend.

As they finished their meal, Finn studied the map once more, tracing his finger along the route they would take. "We'll head due east today, towards the Loblolly Major. But first, we need to break camp and pack up our gear."

Finn stood up, stretching his limbs and surveying the campsite. That's when he noticed the unusual animal tracks near the edge of the clearing. They were unlike any he had seen before, larger and deeper than the typical woodland creatures. A flicker of unease passed through him, but he pushed it aside, focusing on the task at hand.

Together, Finn and Mystic set about breaking camp, their movements efficient and practiced. They packed their belongings, doused the fire, and erased any trace of their presence. With one last glance at the map, Finn shouldered his backpack, ready to embark on the next leg of their adventure.

THEIR STEPS FELL INTO a steady rhythm, carrying them eastward as Finn and Mystic ventured deeper into the Loblolly Springs forest. The morning sun lay broken on the forest floor, casting a golden glow through the canopy of leaves above. Mystic trotted ahead, her nose to the ground, her tail wagging with each new scent she encountered.

Finn's mind wandered to the mysterious artifacts they had discovered and the cryptic map that hinted at the location of the legendary Mycelium Haven. The promise of rare truffles and untold secrets fueled his determination, and he couldn't help but feel a sense of excitement building within him.

However, as they traversed the forest, Finn's keen eyes noticed something that gave him pause. Near the edge of their previous campsite, he spotted a set of unfamiliar tracks imprinted in the soft earth. They were larger and deeper than any animal tracks he had encountered before, and their shape was distinct, almost human-like.

Finn crouched down, examining the tracks more closely. The size and depth suggested that whatever had left them was significantly heavier than the typical woodland creatures. His mind raced with possibilities. Could they belong to another person, someone who was also searching for the Mycelium Haven? Or were they the tracks of an unknown animal, something that roamed these woods unseen?

A flicker of unease passed through Finn as he considered the implications. If someone else was out there, it meant that they were not alone in their quest. The thought of competition or potential danger added a layer of tension to their exploration.

Mystic, sensing Finn's change in demeanor, padded over to him, her warm brown eyes filled with curiosity. Finn reached out and stroked her soft fur, finding comfort in her presence. "What do you think, girl?" he murmured. "Should we be worried about these tracks?"

Mystic tilted her head, her ears perked up as if listening intently to Finn's words. She gave a soft whine, pressing her nose against Finn's hand in a gesture of reassurance.

Finn took a deep breath, trying to calm his racing thoughts. He knew that they couldn't let this discovery deter them from their mission. They had come too far to turn back now. With renewed determination, Finn stood up, adjusting his backpack on his shoulders.

"Come on, Mystic," he said, his voice steady. "We have a haven to find."

HALF AN HOUR HAD PASSED since Finn and Mystic had set out from their campsite, their steps carrying them eastward through the Loblolly Springs forest. The sun, which had been their constant companion, slowly faded behind a veil of gathering clouds. The once vibrant greens of the forest took on a muted tone, and the air grew heavy with an unseen presence.

As they trekked further, a fog began to roll in, creeping through the trees like a silent phantom. It enveloped the forest in an ethereal mist, obscuring the path ahead and transforming the familiar landscape into a realm of uncertainty. The tendrils of fog curled around the trunks of the towering pines, casting an eerie glow that seemed to emanate from within the forest itself.

Finn and Mystic found themselves navigating through the low visibility, their senses heightened by the sudden change in atmosphere. The mist clung to their skin, cool and damp, as if nature itself was reaching out to touch them. The sounds of the forest, once clear and distinct, now seemed muffled and distant, as if the fog had created a barrier between them and the outside world.

Finn squinted, trying to pierce through the dense curtain of mist, but he could barely see more than a hundred feet in any direction. The familiar landmarks and trails he had relied on were now obscured, making it difficult to orient himself. He reached into his pocket and retrieved his compass, the cool metal reassuring against his fingertips.

Remembering the lessons his father had taught him, Finn knew that in times like these, he had to trust his compass. He held it steady in his palm, the needle pointing resolutely towards the east. With each step, he checked the compass, ensuring that they were staying on course despite the challenges posed by the fog.

Mystic, too, seemed to sense the shift in their surroundings. Her nose twitched as she sniffed the air, her keen senses picking up on scents that Finn could not detect. She stayed close to Finn's side, her presence a comforting anchor in the midst of the disorienting mist.

As they pressed on, Finn made sure to mark their trail, leaving subtle signs that would guide them back if needed. He snapped small twigs at eye level, creating a breadcrumb trail of sorts. The fog seemed to swallow the markers as soon as he placed them, but he knew that they would be there, hidden in plain sight, should they need to retrace their steps.

THE FOG CONTINUED TO swirl around Finn and Mystic as they cautiously made their way eastward through the Loblolly Springs forest. The mist seemed to have a life of its own, pulsating and shifting with each step they took. It was as if the forest had been transformed into a living, breathing entity, with the fog serving as its ethereal breath.

As they ventured deeper into the heart of the forest, strange sounds began to echo through the misty veil. At first, they were faint and distant, barely discernible above the muffled stillness that had settled over the woods. But gradually, the sounds grew louder and more distinct, their origins impossible to pinpoint amidst the fog.

Whispers, eerie and unintelligible, drifted through the air like ghostly voices carried on the wind. They seemed to come from everywhere and nowhere at once, their words lost in the mist. Finn strained his ears, trying to make sense of the whispers, but they remained frustratingly out of reach, their meaning shrouded in mystery.

Alongside the whispers, the sound of footsteps began to emerge, their rhythm irregular and unsettling. They seemed to be coming from different directions, sometimes drawing closer, sometimes fading into the distance. Finn and Mystic exchanged glances, their eyes conveying a shared sense of unease. Were they truly alone in this fog-shrouded forest, or was someone—or something—stalking them from the shadows?

The distant cries of animals added to the eerie symphony that surrounded them. The calls were unfamiliar, unlike anything Finn had heard before in the forest. They were haunting and mournful, echoing through the mist like the lamentations of lost souls. Each cry sent a shiver down Finn's spine, and he found himself instinctively drawing closer to Mystic for comfort.

The fog seemed to distort the sounds, making it impossible to determine their true origin or distance. Finn and Mystic could only rely on their other senses as they navigated through the unsettling atmosphere. The fog had transformed the once familiar forest into a labyrinth of uncertainty, where every sound could be a potential threat lurking just out of sight.

Despite the growing sense of unease, Finn and Mystic pressed on, their determination to reach their destination unwavering. They knew that the fog and the eerie sounds were just another challenge they had to overcome in their quest for the Mycelium Haven. With each step, they drew upon their courage and the strength of their bond, ready to face whatever lay ahead in the mist-shrouded depths of the Loblolly Springs forest.

WITH MYSTIC LEADING the way, Finn navigated the dense underbrush, his eyes fixed on the topographical map. The day's sun trickled through the canopy, casting flickering shadows as they ventured deeper into the heart of Loblolly Springs Forest. Finn felt a surge of excitement with every step, anticipating the hidden treasures the forest might unveil today.

Suddenly, without warning, Finn's foot snagged on a vine concealed beneath the carpet of leaves. His heart lurched as he lost his balance, arms flailing in a vain attempt to steady himself. Time seemed to stretch, the moment unfolding in slow motion as he pitched forward. His hand, clutching the precious compass, jerked open.

"No!" Finn's cry was swallowed by the forest as the compass slipped from his grasp, somersaulting through the air. He crashed to the ground, the impact forcing the air from his lungs. Leaves and dirt scattered around him, and he scrambled to his knees, eyes desperately scanning the forest floor.

The compass was gone.

"Mystic, find it!" Finn urged, his voice tinged with desperation. The Labrador's keen sense of duty kicked in, and she began sniffing through the leaves, her nose working overtime. Finn, on his hands and knees, sifted through the detritus, heart pounding in his chest. Each second felt like an eternity.

As the minutes dragged on without a sign of the compass, panic seeped into Finn's mind. He could feel the tight knot forming in his stomach. This wasn't just any compass; it was a trusted tool, crucial for their navigation. The anxiety of being lost in the sprawling forest without it gnawed at his thoughts.

"How could I have been so careless?" He berated himself, frustration rising. The confidence that had buoyed him through many adventures now felt fragile, his fear of the vast, uncharted forest closing in. Without the compass, how would they orient themselves? What if they lost their way, wandered aimlessly through the rolling hills and dense pines until nightfall?

"Mystic, anything?" His voice shook, betraying the calm he tried to maintain. Mystic, determined and loyal, continued her search, but Finn could see the growing confusion in her eyes.

As minutes turned to what felt like hours, Finn's fear transformed into a palpable presence. He realized just how much he depended on that simple device. Every rustling leaf, every distant call of the forest now seemed to mock his plight. The fear of being stranded out here, vulnerable to the elements and wildlife, was overwhelming.

Finn took a deep breath, trying to calm his racing thoughts. "Stay focused. Panicking won't help." He reminded himself, drawing on the lessons his father, Ethan, a seasoned wildlife biologist, had taught him. He needed to think clearly, to strategize.

Finn glanced at Mystic, her brown eyes reflecting concern. "We'll find it," he said, more to reassure himself than Mystic. "We just have to keep trying." He continued to comb through the leaves, determined not to let fear take the reins.

In the quiet of the forest, surrounded by the whispering pines and hidden creeks, Finn understood the gravity of his predicament. But he also knew that giving up was not an option. With Mystic by his side, he would keep searching, relying on their bond and the forest's subtle guidance to carry them through.

FINN AND MYSTIC'S SEARCH for the lost compass proved futile. Despite their best efforts, the forest floor remained an inscrutable maze of leaves and undergrowth. With each passing minute, Finn's hope of recovering the crucial navigational tool dwindled. The realization that they could no longer pinpoint the exact location of his fall settled heavily in his mind.

As the fog thickened, shrouding the forest in an eerie, disorienting blanket, Finn knew a decision had to be made. Should they stay put, waiting for the mist to dissipate and hoping for a clearer view of their surroundings? Or should they retrace their steps, following the trail of broken twigs and disturbed foliage that Finn had left in their wake?

Uncertainty gnawed at Finn's thoughts. While the markings he had made seemed like a lifeline back to familiarity, doubt crept in. Were the signs clear enough to follow in this fog? Would they lead them back to safety, or would they end up wandering in circles, lost in the labyrinthine depths of Loblolly Springs?

In a last-ditch attempt to seek guidance, Finn reached for the CB radio. His fingers fumbled with the device, hope and trepidation intermingling as he awaited a response. Static crackled through the speaker, a disheartening silence that offered no comfort. Was the radio malfunctioning, or were they simply too deep in the forest, the dense foliage blocking the signal?

Questions raced through Finn's mind, each one met with the same unsettling absence of answers. In the end, it was the memory of their first campsite that tugged at his decision. That familiar clearing, with its reassuring landmarks and the lingering sense of safety, beckoned to him.

With a resolute nod to Mystic, Finn made his choice. They would turn back, retracing their path to the campsite that had sheltered them the night before. It was a gamble, trusting in the faint trail they had left behind, but it seemed the most promising course of action in the face of the unknown.

AS FINN AND MYSTIC ventured through the fog-shrouded forest, a glimmer of hope emerged when Finn spotted a familiar sight. Several minutes into their back tracking efforts, he noticed a broken tip on a low-hanging limb, a clear indication of their earlier passage. The discovery rekindled his determination, and he pressed onward with renewed hope.

Finn's mind raced back to his father's teachings, recalling the invaluable lessons Ethan had imparted during their camping trips. He remembered his father's words about moss growth in the forest, how it tended to flourish on the north side of trees. With this knowledge firmly in mind, Finn deduced that since they had traveled due east on their initial journey, the path back to safety would lead them due west.

Minutes ticked by as Finn and Mystic navigated the misty labyrinth of trees, their eyes scanning the surroundings for any sign of their previous trail markers. The broken limb had been a promising start, but as time stretched on without further indications of their route, doubt began to creep into Finn's thoughts once more.

In the absence of clear markers, Finn clung to the one constant he could rely on: the moss on the trees. He studied the green growth, noting its position and using it as a natural compass to guide their westward trajectory. Each step was measured, each glance at the moss a silent prayer for direction in the disorienting fog.

THE PASSAGE OF TIME seemed to blur. Finn realized at the start of their trip, that they had been walking for about an hour before the fog had disoriented them, but now, as they retraced their steps, he found himself unsure of how long they had been navigating back towards their first campsite.

The dense fog swirled around them, obscuring their vision and muffling the sounds of the forest. Each tree looked like the last, and the once-familiar landscape had become a labyrinth of uncertainty. Finn's heart raced as he tried to quell the rising panic within him, focusing instead on the steady presence of Mystic by his side.

In an attempt to gauge their progress, Finn glanced back over his shoulder, peering into the direction from which they had just come. As his eyes scanned the misty expanse, something odd caught his attention. Squinting through the haze, Finn's gaze settled upon a weathered signpost, its wooden surface beaten and worn by the elements.

Curiosity mingled with apprehension as Finn approached the sign, Mystic close at his heels. As he drew nearer, the faded letters carved into the wood became clearer, and a chill ran down Finn's spine as he read the ominous message: "Beware the Fog."

The warning sent a shiver through Finn's body, and he found himself questioning the path he had chosen. What dangers lurked within the fog? Was he leading himself and Mystic into peril? The doubts swirled in his mind, as thick and disorienting as the mist that enveloped them.

Finn's hand instinctively reached for Mystic, seeking comfort in her presence. As his fingers brushed against her soft fur, he drew strength from their bond. They had faced challenges together before, and they would overcome this one as well. The signpost's warning echoed in his mind, but Finn refused to let fear dictate their path. He exchanged a determined look with Mystic, a silent understanding passing between them.

Chapter 6

As Finn and Mystic pressed onward through the misty forest, their steps were measured and cautious. The fog had transformed the once-familiar landscape into a disorienting maze, but they remained undeterred. Finn's mind was focused on retracing their path back to their first campsite, using the moss on the trees as a natural compass to guide them westward.

Every half hour or so, Finn would pause and reach for the CB radio, hoping to establish contact with the outside world. The static crackled and hissed, the silence on the other end a stark reminder of their isolation. But Finn refused to let despair take hold, knowing that perseverance was their key to safety.

As time passed and the fog showed no signs of relenting, Finn made the decision to reach out once more. With a steady hand, he pressed the button on the radio and spoke, his voice cutting through the static. "Mom, it's Finn. Can you hear me?"

The response was immediate, his mother's voice filled with a mixture of relief and concern. "Finn! Are you alright? Where are you?"

Finn took a deep breath, his words measured and reassuring. "We're okay, Mom. Mystic and I got caught in a thick fog, and we're trying to make our way back to our first campsite. We're not lost, but the visibility is pretty low."

He could hear the worry in his mother's voice, but he continued, his tone calm and confident. "We're going to find a good spot to set up camp for the night. Hopefully, the fog will lift by morning, and we can continue our journey."

His mother's response was filled with understanding and support. "Alright, Finn. Be safe and take care of each other. Keep us updated when you can."

Finn smiled, the weight on his shoulders feeling a little lighter. "Will do, Mom. Talk to you soon."

With renewed determination, Finn and Mystic continued their slow trek westward, their eyes scanning the misty forest for a suitable place to set up camp. They knew that the night ahead would be challenging, but they had each other and the skills they had learned to rely on. Together, they would weather this storm and emerge stronger on the other side.

FINN AND MYSTIC CONTINUED their slow, westward trek through the misty forest, Finn's mind raced with the lessons his father had taught him about finding a safe campsite. He knew that the trees themselves could pose a danger, their heavy branches capable of falling without warning. Water, too, was a concern; a sudden rainstorm could flood a poorly chosen site, leaving them drenched and vulnerable.

His eyes scanned the surrounding forest, searching for the ideal spot. He knew that protection from the elements was key - a small, low-hanging canopy of thick branches could offer shelter from the wind, rain, hail, and even the harsh rays of the sun.

Finn's gaze fell upon a promising area. It was a small clearing, nestled between a cluster of sturdy, low-growing trees. The canopy above was dense, the interwoven branches forming a natural roof that would shield them from the worst of the weather.

He approached the site cautiously, his eyes taking in every detail. The ground beneath his feet was dry and level, free from the telltale signs of previous flooding. The surrounding trees were healthy and strong, their trunks thick and their roots deep.

He knelt down, running his hand over the soft, leaf-littered ground. It was the perfect spot, offering both protection and comfort. Mystic, too, seemed to approve, her tail wagging as she sniffed around the perimeter of the clearing.

Finn felt a surge of gratitude for his father's wisdom. Without Ethan's guidance, he might have chosen a less suitable site, one that could have put them both in danger. But armed with the knowledge he had gained, Finn felt confident in his decision.

He turned to Mystic, a smile on his face. "This is it, girl. This is where we'll make our camp for the night."

Mystic barked in agreement, her eyes bright with excitement. Together, they began to unpack their gear, ready to set up their temporary home in the heart of the misty forest.

FINN SURVEYED THE CHOSEN campsite, his mind already planning the necessary tasks to set up a safe and comfortable shelter for the night. He approached a nearby tree and carefully broke off a low-hanging limb, its sturdy form perfect for the job at hand. With the makeshift broom in hand, Finn meticulously raked the ground where he would pitch the tent, clearing away debris and ensuring a level surface.

Once satisfied with the tent area, Finn ventured into the surrounding forest, his eyes scanning for suitable firewood. He knew that dry, dead wood would be crucial for maintaining a fire throughout the night. Finn methodically collected branches and twigs, testing each piece for its dryness before adding it to his growing bundle. He made sure to gather enough to last until morning, knowing that a well-stocked fire would provide warmth, light, and a means to cook their meager meals.

With the firewood secured, Finn turned his attention to the fire pit. He chose a spot at a safe distance from the tent, ensuring that any stray embers would not pose a threat. Using a small shovel from his pack, Finn dug a shallow pit, his movements precise and purposeful. He then retrieved his hatchet and carefully selected several long branches from a nearby tree. With skilled strokes, he cut the branches to length, creating a sturdy framework for the fire. Finn arranged the branches in a tepee shape over the pit, providing shelter from any potential rain and a convenient structure to hang his cooking pot.

As Finn assessed their food supplies, a slight frown creased his brow. They had only two packages of instant soup remaining, barely enough for a meager dinner. Mystic's dry dog food would suffice for the evening, but Finn knew they would need to head back home in the morning, as their provisions were running low. He contemplated saving one package of soup for the journey back, but the growling of his stomach persuaded him otherwise.

With the fire pit prepared and the food situation assessed, Finn turned his attention to the tent. He carefully unpacked the tent and began the process of setting it up. Finn selected sturdy branches and used his hatchet to fashion long, reliable stakes. He drove the stakes deep into the ground, ensuring that the tent would remain secure even in the face of inclement weather. As he worked, Finn's mind wandered to the challenges that lay ahead, but he found comfort in the knowledge that he had the skills and determination to face whatever the forest might throw their way.

WITH THE TENT SET UP, Finn turned his attention to their dwindling food supplies. He retrieved the last two packages of instant soup from his backpack and carefully measured out a portion of the remaining dry dog food for Mystic. The thought of their limited provisions weighed heavily on his mind, but he pushed the concern aside, focusing on the task at hand.

Finn set about boiling water for the soup, the small campfire flickering bravely against the encroaching fog. As he stirred the pot, a distant sound caught his attention. It was faint at first, barely audible above the crackling of the fire, but it gradually grew louder, echoing through the mist-shrouded trees.

Mystic's ears perked up, and she turned her head towards the source of the noise, her body tensing with alert curiosity. Finn strained his ears, trying to identify the sound, but the fog seemed to distort and muffle it, making it impossible to discern its origin.

As they sat by the fire, sipping the hot soup and listening intently to the eerie noises that drifted through the fog, Finn couldn't shake the feeling of unease that had settled over him. The isolation and mystery of their surroundings weighed heavily on his mind, and he found himself wondering what secrets the fog-shrouded forest might hold.

FINN AND MYSTIC SETTLED down by the flickering campfire, seeking solace in its warmth and light. The eerie atmosphere that had followed them throughout the day still lingered, but the crackling flames provided a small measure of comfort.

He reached for his CB radio and made a short call to his parents, his voice steady and reassuring. "Mom, Dad, it's Finn. We're settled in for the night. Everything's fine, just wanted to check in." He could sense their worry even through the static-filled response, but he knew they trusted him and his abilities.

As he set the radio aside, Finn's thoughts drifted to their journey so far. The challenges they had faced, from the dense undergrowth to the disorienting fog, had tested their resilience and determination. Yet, through it all, Mystic had remained by his side, a constant source of comfort and support.

Mystic, sensing the tension in the air, stayed close to Finn, her warm body pressed against his leg. Finn reached down and ran his fingers through her soft fur, finding solace in the simple gesture. Together, they gazed into the dancing flames, the hypnotic movement offering a momentary escape from the uncertainties that surrounded them.

The fog seemed to thicken, its tendrils snaking through the trees and enveloping the campsite in an otherworldly shroud. The forest grew eerily silent, the usual nocturnal sounds conspicuously absent. Finn felt a sense of unease creeping up his spine, but he tried to brush it off, attributing it to the strange atmosphere that had followed them throughout the day.

A CHANGE IN THE ATMOSPHERE became increasingly apparent. The once gentle breeze picked up, morphing into gusts that rustled the leaves and swayed the branches of the surrounding trees. Finn, attuned to the shifts in his environment, noticed the wind's growing intensity and the sudden drop in temperature that accompanied it.

Mystic, too, seemed to sense the impending change. She grew restless, her ears twitching at the slightest sound and her body tensing as if in anticipation of an unseen threat. Finn, concerned by his companion's behavior, scanned the darkening sky, searching for any signs of the approaching storm.

In the distance, a low rumble echoed through the forest, the first hint of the thunder to come. The sound, muffled by the dense foliage and the thick fog, seemed to come from all directions at once, disorienting and unsettling. Finn's heart raced as he realized the storm was drawing closer, its arrival imminent.

As if to confirm his fears, a flash of lightning illuminated the fog, casting an eerie glow across the campsite. The sudden burst of light was followed by another, louder crack of thunder, causing Mystic to press closer to Finn's side, seeking comfort in his presence.

Finn sprang into action, his survival instincts taking over. He quickly set about securing their tent, double-checking the stakes and ensuring the rainfly was taut and ready to withstand the impending downpour. He gathered their gear, stowing it safely within the confines of the tent, and made sure their food supplies were protected from the elements.

As he worked, the wind continued to howl, its force growing stronger with each passing minute. The trees swayed and creaked, their branches straining against the invisible onslaught. The fog, once a mere inconvenience, now seemed to take on a more sinister quality, as if concealing untold dangers within its swirling depths.

THE STORM UNLEASHED its full fury upon the forest, the wind howled through the trees with a deafening roar, its force clearing away the once-thick fog and replacing it with a torrential downpour. The rain lashed against the tent, the relentless pounding of the droplets creating a cacophony that drowned out all other sounds.

Inside the tent, Finn and Mystic huddled together, seeking comfort in each other's presence as they tried to stay dry and warm. The small space offered little protection from the storm's onslaught, and Finn could feel the chill seeping into his bones despite his best efforts to insulate himself with his sleeping bag.

The tent shook violently, its fabric straining against the wind's force. Finn watched with growing concern as the poles bent and flexed, threatening to snap under the pressure. He feared that at any moment, the tent might collapse, leaving them exposed to the storm's full wrath.

Outside, the forest had transformed into a scene of chaos. The once-peaceful surroundings were now a maelstrom of wind and rain, the trees swaying dangerously as they were battered by the elements. Finn could hear the ominous creaking of the trunks and the sharp snapping of branches as they gave way under the strain.

The storm's intensity showed no signs of abating, and Finn realized that they were in for a long and challenging night. He pulled Mystic closer, finding solace in her warmth and the steady rhythm of her breathing. Together, they braced themselves for whatever the storm might bring, knowing that they would have to rely on each other to weather this unexpected trial.

The wind continued to howl as the rain pounded against the tent, Finn's thoughts turned to the dangers that lurked beyond the flimsy shelter of the tent. The snapping branches and creaking trees served as a constant reminder of the storm's destructive power, and he couldn't help but wonder what other challenges the night might hold in store for them.

THE STORM RAGED ON, the wind's ferocity reached a crescendo, and with a sickening crack, the tent's poles finally gave way. The fabric collapsed around Finn and Mystic, leaving them exposed to the elements. Finn scrambled to his feet, his heart pounding as he realized the gravity of their situation.

The rain pelted down on them, soaking through their clothes in a matter of seconds. Finn knew they had to act fast. He quickly gathered their essential gear, stuffing it into his backpack with trembling hands. Mystic, sensing the urgency, stayed close to his side, her ears flattened against her head as the wind whipped around them.

With no time to waste, Finn and Mystic dashed out into the storm, leaving the ruined tent behind. The wind buffeted them from all sides, making it difficult to maintain their balance. The rain obscured their vision, turning the once-familiar forest into a treacherous labyrinth of shadows and shifting shapes.

Finn's mind raced as he tried to recall any nearby landmarks or features that could provide them with shelter. He knew that every second they spent exposed to the storm increased the risk of hypothermia or injury. Mystic pressed close to his leg, her presence a comforting reminder that he wasn't alone in this ordeal.

As they stumbled through the undergrowth, Finn's eyes darted from one potential refuge to another, desperation mounting with each passing moment. Just when he began to lose hope, a flash of lightning illuminated a small, rocky overhang nestled against a hillside. It wasn't much, but it offered a glimmer of protection from the relentless wind and rain.

Finn and Mystic made a beeline for the overhang, their feet slipping on the muddy ground as they scrambled towards safety. As they drew closer, Finn's heart leapt with a mixture of relief and apprehension. The overhang was shallow, barely deep enough to accommodate them both, but it was their only option.

They huddled together under the rocky shelf, their breaths coming in short, ragged gasps as they tried to catch their breath. Finn's mind reeled with the realization of how close they had come to disaster. The storm continued to rage around them, the wind howling like a wounded beast, but for the moment, they were safe.

FINN AND MYSTIC WERE huddled under the rocky overhang, the storm continued to rage around them with unrelenting fury. The wind howled through the trees, and the rain pounded against the ground, creating a deafening cacophony that drowned out all other sounds. Finn's heart raced as he realized the precariousness of their situation, knowing that they were far from safety and at the mercy of the elements.

Acting quickly, Finn reached into his backpack and pulled out an emergency blanket, a thin but essential piece of gear that could mean the difference between life and death in a situation like this. With trembling hands, he unfolded the blanket and draped it over Mystic and himself, creating a small cocoon of warmth and protection against the biting wind and chilling rain.

Mystic pressed close to Finn, her body shivering as the cold seeped into her fur. Finn ran his hands over her, checking for any injuries or signs of distress. To his relief, she seemed unharmed, but the look in her eyes conveyed the same fear and uncertainty that gripped his own heart. He pulled her closer, offering comfort and reassurance through his touch and soft words.

They sat there, listening to the storm's relentless assault on the forest, Finn's mind raced with worries and doubts. What if the storm didn't let up? What if they were stuck here for hours, or even days? The thought of hypothermia crept into his mind, a silent and deadly threat that could claim them both if they weren't careful.

Finn tried to push those dark thoughts aside and focus on the present. They had shelter, albeit a small and cramped one, and they had each other. He knew that their bond, forged through countless adventures and trials, would be their greatest strength in the face of this adversity.

The minutes ticked by, each one feeling like an eternity as the storm raged on. Finn and Mystic remained huddled together, their breaths mingling in the small space, as they waited for any sign of the tempest's abatement. Despite the fear and uncertainty that gripped them, a small flicker of hope refused to be extinguished in Finn's heart. They had faced challenges before, and they would face this one too, together, no matter what the storm threw at them.

AT LAST, THE STORM'S fury finally began to wane, an unsettling calm descended upon the ravaged forest. The wind's howling diminished to a whisper, and the relentless rain dwindled to a gentle patter against the leaves. In the aftermath of nature's onslaught, an eerie stillness pervaded the once-lively woods.

Finn and Mystic emerged from their cramped shelter beneath the rocky overhang, their bodies stiff and chilled from the prolonged exposure to the elements. As they stepped out into the open, their eyes widened at the sight of the devastation that surrounded them.

The forest floor was a chaotic mess of fallen trees and broken branches, the once-clear paths now obscured by a tangled web of debris. The canopy above, which had previously provided a comforting shelter, was now a patchwork of gaping holes, allowing the gray light of the overcast sky to filter through in irregular patterns.

Finn's heart sank as he surveyed the damage, realizing the challenges that lay ahead. Navigating through this altered landscape would be no easy feat, and the thought of finding their way back to their original campsite seemed daunting in the face of such upheaval.

Mystic, too, seemed to sense the gravity of their situation. Her ears were pressed flat against her head, and her tail hung low as she sniffed the air, trying to make sense of the unfamiliar scents that now mingled with the earthy aroma of the rain-soaked forest.

Finn took a deep breath, trying to quell the rising apprehension in his chest. He knew that they couldn't afford to let fear or uncertainty cloud their judgment. They had to focus on the task at hand and find a way to reorient themselves in this transformed wilderness.

With a gentle pat on Mystic's head, Finn began to pick his way through the debris, his eyes scanning the surroundings for any familiar landmarks or signs that could guide them back to their original path. The forest, once a comforting and familiar presence, now felt alien and unpredictable, with each step revealing new obstacles and challenges.

As they moved deeper into the woods, the eerie quiet was occasionally broken by the groan of a tree settling or the rustle of leaves disturbed by a passing breeze. These sounds, once a natural part of the forest's symphony, now took on a sinister edge, as if the very trees were warning them of the dangers that lurked in the shadows.

Finn's mind raced as he tried to recall the lessons his father had taught him about navigation and survival in the wilderness. He knew that panic was his greatest enemy, and that he needed to remain calm and focused if they were to find their way back to safety.

FINN AND MYSTIC PUSHED forward through the storm-ravaged forest, their determination to find their way back to the original campsite never wavered. The once-familiar landscape had been transformed into a labyrinth of fallen trees, tangled vines, and deep puddles, making navigation a daunting task. However, Finn refused to let the challenges deter him.

With the map in hand, Finn carefully studied the contours of the land, trying to reconcile the altered terrain with the landmarks he had memorized. He knew that every decision he made could either lead them closer to safety or further into the heart of the wilderness. Mystic, too, played a crucial role in their journey, her keen senses guiding them through the maze of debris.

The journey was arduous, with each step requiring careful consideration. Finn had to navigate around fallen trees, some of which were so large that they blocked entire paths. He climbed over slippery logs, ducked under low-hanging branches, and waded through knee-deep water, all the while keeping a watchful eye on Mystic to ensure her safety.

Despite the physical and mental strain, Finn remained focused on their goal. He knew that giving up was not an option, and that they had to keep moving forward, no matter how long it took. Mystic's unwavering loyalty and trust in him provided a source of strength, reminding him that he was not alone in this struggle.

As they pressed on, the forest slowly began to reveal familiar sights. A distinctive rock formation, a peculiar twist in the creek's path, and a gnarled old tree that Finn had used as a landmark all signaled that they were getting closer to their destination. With each recognition, Finn's heart swelled with hope, and his pace quickened, eager to reach the safety of their original campsite.

Finally, after hours of grueling trekking, they emerged into the clearing where they had first set up camp. The sight of the familiar space, even in its disheveled state, brought a wave of relief washing over Finn. They had made it back, battered and exhausted, but alive and together.

FINN AND MYSTIC FINALLY reached their original campsite, a wave of relief washed over them. The familiarity of the clearing, even in its disheveled state, was a welcome sight after the grueling trek through the storm-ravaged forest. They paused for a moment, catching their breath and allowing the realization of their achievement to sink in.

Finn dropped his backpack and sank to the ground, his legs trembling from the exertion. Mystic, too, flopped down beside him, her tongue lolling out as she panted heavily. Finn reached for his water bottle and took a long, grateful swig before offering some to Mystic. As the cool liquid soothed their parched throats, Finn felt a renewed sense of determination rising within him.

With their thirst quenched, Finn turned his attention to assessing their situation. He rummaged through his backpack, taking stock of their remaining supplies. His heart sank as he realized that they were running dangerously low on food and water. The unexpected detour and the challenges of the storm had depleted their resources faster than he had anticipated.

Finn knew that they couldn't afford to linger at the campsite for too long. They needed to plan their journey back home, and the sooner they started, the better their chances of making it safely. He reached for the CB radio, hoping to establish contact with his parents and inform them of their situation.

Switching on the device, Finn couldn't help but feel a twinge of uncertainty. Without a compass to guide them, navigating the forest would be even more challenging. The storm had left its mark on the landscape, with fallen trees and muddy trails obscuring the once-familiar paths. Finn knew that they would have to rely on their wits, Mystic's instincts, and the lessons he had learned from his father to find their way back.

FINN TOOK A DEEP BREATH, his gaze fixed on the southern horizon. With the sun as his guide and the knowledge imparted by his father, he knew that heading due south was their best chance of reaching Loblolly Springs. He glanced down at Mystic, who stood beside him, her eyes alert and ears perked up. She seemed to sense the importance of their journey and the challenges that lay ahead.

With a nod of determination, Finn adjusted his backpack and set off into the forest, Mystic trotting faithfully by his side. The absence of his compass weighed heavily on his mind, but he refused to let it deter him. He had to trust in his own abilities and the lessons he had learned.

As they navigated through the dense undergrowth, Finn kept a keen eye on the position of the sun, using it as a reference point to maintain their southward direction. He also took note of the moss growing on the trees, remembering his father's teachings about how it tended to grow more prominently on the north side of the trunks.

The storm's aftermath was evident throughout the forest. Fallen branches littered the ground, and the once-clear paths were now obscured by debris. Finn and Mystic had to tread carefully, climbing over splintered wood and navigating around waterlogged sections of the trail.

Despite the obstacles, they pressed on, their determination fueling each step. Finn's mind raced with thoughts of home, of his parents' worried faces, and of the warm embrace that awaited him. He knew that every mile they covered brought them closer to safety.

Mystic remained vigilant, her nose twitching as she sniffed the air for any signs of danger. Her presence brought Finn a sense of comfort and reassurance, knowing that he had a loyal companion by his side.

The challenges of navigating without a compass became increasingly apparent. The storm had altered the landscape, making once-familiar landmarks difficult to recognize. Finn paused occasionally, scanning his surroundings and trying to reconcile his mental map with the changed terrain.

FINN AND MYSTIC JOURNEYED southward, their path was suddenly obstructed by an unexpected obstacle. The once-gentle creek that meandered through the forest had transformed into a swollen, raging torrent due to the recent storm. The water churned and frothed, its turbulent surface reflecting the frustration that welled up inside Finn.

He stood at the edge of the creek, assessing the situation with a furrowed brow. The current was too strong to risk crossing, and the water level had risen significantly, making it impossible to simply wade through. Finn knew that attempting to traverse the creek would be foolish and dangerous.

With a heavy sigh, Finn made the decision to find a way around the creek. He scanned the surrounding forest, searching for an alternative route. The dense underbrush and tangled vegetation seemed to mock him, presenting yet another challenge to overcome.

Undeterred, Finn and Mystic plunged into the thick foliage, determined to find a path forward. The underbrush tugged at their clothes and scratched at their skin, making every step a struggle. Progress was slow, and the air hung heavy with humidity, adding to their discomfort.

Finn relied on his navigational skills, using the sun's position and the moss on the trees to maintain their bearings. He refused to let the setback deter him from reaching their destination. Mystic, ever faithful, remained close by his side, her keen senses alert for any signs of danger.

As they pushed through the dense vegetation, Mystic suddenly perked up, her nose twitching with interest. She took the lead, guiding Finn through the underbrush with a sense of purpose. Finn trusted her instincts and followed closely behind, hopeful that she had picked up on a safer route.

The foliage gradually thinned, and they emerged into a small clearing. Finn's heart leaped with relief as he realized that Mystic had led them around the swollen creek. The sound of rushing water could still be heard in the distance, but they had successfully navigated the obstacle.

Finn took a moment to catch his breath and offer Mystic a grateful pat on the head. The challenges of the journey were far from over, but with Mystic by his side and his own determination fueling him, Finn knew they would find a way to overcome whatever lay ahead.

FINN AND MYSTIC CONTINUED their journey through the storm-ravaged forest, they came upon an unexpected sight. A normally dry stream bed had transformed into a swollen, rushing torrent due to the heavy rainfall. The water surged and swirled, carving a new path through the dense underbrush.

He approached the edge of the stream cautiously, his eyes widening in surprise at the sheer volume of water before him. The once-familiar landscape had been altered, presenting a new challenge in their quest to find their way back home.

With a determined set to his jaw, Finn assessed the situation. He knew that attempting to wade through the fast-moving water would be foolish and dangerous. The depth of the stream was uncertain, and the current looked strong enough to sweep them off their feet.

Finn's gaze swept along the banks of the stream, searching for a way to cross safely. His eyes landed on a cluster of fallen trees nearby, their trunks lying haphazardly across the forest floor. An idea sparked in his mind, and he quickly set to work.

Selecting a sturdy fallen tree that spanned a narrow section of the stream, Finn carefully maneuvered it into position. He tested its stability, ensuring that it could support their weight. Mystic watched intently, her tail wagging with anticipation.

Once satisfied with his makeshift bridge, Finn gestured for Mystic to cross first. The loyal dog stepped tentatively onto the fallen tree, her paws finding firm footing on the rough bark. With a few surefooted steps, she successfully made it to the other side of the stream.

Finn took a deep breath, steeling himself for his own crossing. He placed one foot on the tree trunk, testing his balance. The water rushed beneath him, its roar filling his ears. Slowly, he inched his way forward, arms outstretched for stability.

Halfway across, Finn's foot slipped on the slick bark, and he teetered precariously over the swirling water. His heart raced as he fought to regain his balance, the stream churning hungrily below. With a surge of determination, he managed to right himself and continue his cautious progress.

Finally, Finn stepped knee deep water on the other side of the stream, a wave of relief washing over him. Mystic bounded over to him, her tail wagging enthusiastically. Finn patted her head, grateful for her companionship and the successful crossing.

SUDDENLY, A RUSTLING in the underbrush ahead caught their attention. Finn's hand instinctively reached for Mystic's collar, gently signaling for her to halt. They stood motionless, their eyes fixed on the source of the disturbance.

From the shadows of the dense foliage, a group of wild boars emerged, their bristly coats glistening in the dappled sunlight that filtered through the canopy. The animals moved with a purposeful stride, their snouts low to the ground as they foraged for sustenance.

Finn's breath caught in his throat as he assessed the situation. Wild boars were known for their unpredictable nature and potential for aggression if provoked. He knew that any sudden movement or noise could trigger a dangerous confrontation.

With a slow, deliberate motion, Finn crouched down, bringing himself closer to Mystic's level. The loyal dog remained perfectly still, her ears pricked forward and her body poised in a state of heightened awareness. Finn could sense the tension radiating from her, a mirror of his own apprehension.

The wild boars continued their foraging, seemingly unaware of the human and canine presence nearby. Finn's mind raced as he considered their options. Attempting to navigate around the animals could prove risky, as any unexpected encounter could startle them into defensive behavior.

Instead, Finn made the decision to wait it out. He gently placed a hand on Mystic's back, a silent reassurance that they would remain still and patient until the boars moved on of their own accord. Mystic leaned into his touch, her warmth and steadiness a comforting presence amidst the uncertainty.

Time seemed to stretch on indefinitely as they watched the wild boars, each minute feeling like an eternity. Finn's muscles ached from the prolonged stillness, but he refused to budge, unwilling to risk disturbing the delicate balance of the moment.

Finally, after what felt like an age, the wild boars began to meander away, their interest in the area apparently satisfied. Finn released a slow, measured breath, the tension gradually dissipating from his body. Mystic, too, relaxed, her tail giving a tentative wag as the immediate danger passed.

FINN AND MYSTIC MOVED on from the area where they had encountered the wild boars, a new challenge now presented itself. The trail they had been following, already obscured by the aftermath of the storm, seemed to have vanished entirely. The once familiar markers and landmarks were nowhere to be seen, leaving them disoriented and uncertain of their direction.

He felt a rising sense of anxiety as he surveyed the surroundings, trying to reconcile their current position with his mental map of the forest. The realization that they were lost settled heavily in his chest, but he refused to let panic overtake him. He knew that he had to rely on the skills his father had taught him and the unwavering support of his loyal companion, Mystic.

Taking a deep breath to calm his nerves, Finn began to employ the natural navigation techniques he had learned. He observed the position of the sun, noting its angle and the shadows it cast upon the forest floor. He recalled his father's lessons on how the sun's movement could provide a rough indication of direction, and he used this knowledge to orient himself.

Next, Finn turned his attention to the trees around them. He searched for the telltale signs of moss growth, knowing that moss often thrived on the north side of tree trunks in the northern hemisphere. By identifying the consistent pattern of moss on the trees, he could establish a general sense of north and south.

Despite these efforts, the path forward remained elusive. Finn realized that their best course of action was to retrace their steps, to backtrack to the last recognizable landmark they had encountered. With Mystic by his side, he began to carefully navigate their way back, scanning the forest for any familiar features that could guide them.

As they moved through the undergrowth, Finn's eyes fell upon a sight that brought a glimmer of hope: a muscadine vine, its lush green leaves and twisted tendrils standing out amidst the foliage. The vine triggered a memory of his father's teachings, a crucial piece of knowledge that could aid them in their current predicament.

Finn recalled his father's words, explaining how muscadine vines could serve as a source of drinkable water in times of need. With their water supplies running low, Finn carefully approached the vine, using his knife to make a small incision. Clear, cool water trickled out, and he and Mystic took turns quenching their thirst, grateful for the vine's life-sustaining gift.

Refreshed and with renewed determination, Finn and Mystic pressed on, their senses heightened and their minds focused on finding the correct path. Mystic's keen sense of smell proved invaluable, as she began to pick up the faint scent of their previous trail. With her nose to the ground, she guided Finn through the forest, following the invisible traces of their earlier passage.

FINN AND MYSTIC TRUDGED through the forest, every step felt heavier than the last, their muscles aching from the prolonged exertion and the challenges they had faced. Yet, beneath the weariness, a fierce determination burned within them. They were so close to home, to the safety and comfort of Loblolly Springs, and they refused to let fatigue stand in their way.

His mind was focused on the goal, his thoughts a mantra of encouragement. "Just a little further," he whispered to himself and to Mystic, who walked steadily by his side. The bond between the boy and his loyal dog had only grown stronger throughout their ordeal, a testament to the unwavering companionship they shared.

As they navigated the familiar terrain, landmarks began to appear, like beacons of hope guiding them home. The distinctive shape of a boulder they had passed on their outward journey, the gnarled trunk of an ancient oak tree—each recognizable feature boosted their morale, reassuring them that they were on the right path.

Finn's hand reached for the CB radio, a lifeline to the outside world. With a press of the button, he spoke into the device, his voice tired but filled with relief. "Mom, Dad, it's Finn. We're getting close to Loblolly Springs. We'll be home soon." The static crackled in response, but Finn knew his message had been received. He could almost picture the expressions of joy and relief on his parents' faces.

The final stretch of their journey was not without its challenges. The terrain grew steeper, the underbrush denser, as if the forest was testing their resolve one last time. Finn and Mystic pushed through, their breaths coming in labored gasps, their hearts pounding in their chests. They climbed over fallen logs, navigated around thorny bushes, and forded shallow streams, each obstacle a testament to their unyielding spirit.

And then, as if by some miracle, the forest began to thin. The trees became more scattered, the sunlight filtering through the canopy with increasing intensity. Finn's heart leaped with recognition as he spotted the familiar outskirts of Loblolly Springs. They had made it.

AS FINN AND MYSTIC emerged from the forest, the familiar sights and sounds of Loblolly Springs enveloped them. The weight of their journey seemed to lift from their shoulders as they made their way through the quiet streets, their steps quickening with each passing moment. The anticipation of reuniting with their family propelled them forward, the exhaustion of their adventure momentarily forgotten.

From a distance, Finn spotted his parents, Ethan and Clara, waiting anxiously on the front porch of their home. As soon as they caught sight of Finn and Mystic, their faces lit up with a mixture of relief and joy. They rushed forward, their arms outstretched, ready to embrace their son and his loyal companion.

Finn found himself wrapped in the warm, comforting arms of his parents, their tears of happiness mingling with his own. Mystic, not to be left out, wagged her tail enthusiastically, her bark echoing through the air as she celebrated their safe return.

Inside the house, Finn recounted the details of their adventure to his eager parents. He spoke of the challenges they had faced, the clues they had uncovered, and the mysterious allure of the Mycelium Haven. Ethan and Clara listened intently, their eyes widening with each twist and turn of the tale.

Finn shared his experiences with his parents, he couldn't help but reflect on the profound bond he had forged with Mystic throughout their journey as he looked back. The trust, the companionship, and the unwavering support they had provided each other had been the cornerstone of their success. Finn realized that their adventure had not only brought them closer to the secrets of the forest but had also strengthened the connection between a boy and his dog.

The Thornwood family celebrated the safe return of Finn and Mystic, their laughter and tears intermingling as they savored the moment of reunion. They marveled at the courage and resilience displayed by the young adventurer and his faithful companion, their hearts swelling with pride.

Chapter 7

The sun began its descent painting the sky in hues of orange and pink. Finn and Mystic found themselves back in the comfort of their home. The exhaustion from their long night and day in the forest, with little to no sleep, was evident in their weary eyes and sluggish movements.

Finn's parents, Ethan and Clara, were eager to hear about their son's adventure. They sat at the kitchen table, listening intently as Finn recounted the details of his journey, sipping on ice-cold water to quench his thirst. He spoke of the challenges they had faced, the clues they had uncovered, and the mysterious allure of the Mycelium Haven. Ethan and Clara's eyes widened with each twist and turn of the tale, their hearts filled with a mixture of concern and pride for their brave son.

As Finn shared his experiences, he couldn't help but reflect on the profound bond he had forged with Mystic throughout their journey. The trust, the companionship, and the unwavering support they had provided each other had been the cornerstone of their success. Finn realized that their adventure had not only brought them closer to the secrets of the forest but had also strengthened the connection between a boy and his dog.

After the long and animated conversation, Finn excused himself to clean up and refresh himself. The warm water of the shower cascaded over his tired muscles, washing away the dirt and grime of the forest. He emerged feeling rejuvenated, ready to enjoy a hearty meal with his family.

The Thornwoods gathered around the dinner table, the aroma of a home-cooked meal filling the air. Finn savored every bite, his hunger finally satisfied after the long and arduous journey. Mystic, too, was not forgotten. Finn made sure to fill her bowl with her favorite food, watching as she eagerly devoured her meal.

Finn bid his parents goodnight and retired to his room, with Mystic following close behind. The comfort of his own bed was a welcome respite after the hard ground of the forest floor. Finn's eyes grew heavy, and he drifted off into a peaceful slumber, the events of the past few days replaying in his dreams. It was great to be home, surrounded by the love and warmth of his family.

HIS EYES FLUTTERED open, the first rays of the morning sun filtering through his bedroom window. He glanced at the clock, realizing it was still early, long before his father's usual departure for work. Beside him, Mystic stirred, her tail thumping gently against the bed.

Finn's mind wandered to the truffles they had collected during their two-day adventure in the forest. Seven in total, small but significant. A sense of accomplishment washed over him, but it was tinged with a hint of uncertainty. He had no clear recollection of the exact locations where they had found the truffles, but he had faith in Mystic's keen sense of smell to guide them back if needed.

With a newfound sense of purpose, Finn made his way downstairs, Mystic following close behind. He found his father, Ethan, in the kitchen, preparing his morning coffee. Finn took a deep breath and approached him, ready to share his plans for the day.

"Dad, I wanted to talk to you about something," Finn began, his voice steady despite the slight nervousness he felt. Ethan turned to face his son, his eyes attentive and encouraging.

Finn explained how he had lost his compass during their adventure in the forest. He recounted how he had relied on the skills his father had taught him, using the sun's position and the moss on the trees to navigate their way back home. Ethan listened intently, a mix of concern and pride evident on his face.

"I was thinking," Finn continued, "I'd like to ride my bike into town today. I want to sell the truffles we found to Chef Jacques. And with the money, I can buy a new compass and some other camping supplies we might need for future adventures."

Ethan considered his son's proposal for a moment, his brow furrowed in thought. Finn held his breath, waiting for his father's response. After what seemed like an eternity, Ethan nodded, a smile spreading across his face.

"I think that's a great idea, Finn," Ethan said, placing a hand on his son's shoulder. "I'm proud of how you handled yourself out there, using the skills we've practiced together. And it's smart to reinvest in the gear you need for your future explorations."

Finn's face lit up, his heart brimming with gratitude and excitement. He understood that his father's support was invaluable, and having his approval only strengthened his resolve to carry on with his forest adventures.

FINN'S HEART RACED with anticipation as he prepared for his journey into town. The seven truffles, a mix of Périgord and Bianchetto varieties, were carefully packed in an insulated container, their earthy aroma filling the room. Finn couldn't help but smile as he thought about the potential financial gain from this sale, a significant contribution to his college fund and a relief to his family's financial burden.

As he secured the container in his backpack, Finn's mind wandered to the memories of his truffle hunting adventures with Mystic, his loyal companion. The bond between the boy and his dog had grown stronger with each foray into the forest, and Finn knew that Mystic's keen sense of smell had been instrumental in their success.

With a final check of his gear, Finn set off on his bike, the cool morning air whipping through his hair as he pedaled towards town. The familiar roads stretched out before him, but today, they seemed to hold a new promise, a path towards his dreams.

His thoughts turned to Chef Jacques, the culinary maestro who had previously praised the quality of the truffles Mystic had found. The chef's encouragement had been a driving force behind Finn's determination to continue his truffle hunting endeavors, and he hoped that this new batch would impress the chef just as much.

The sign for "Le Chêne Doré" came into view, and Finn felt a flutter of nerves in his stomach. He dismounted his bike, taking a moment to compose himself before entering the restaurant. The delicate clinking of cutlery and the soft murmur of conversation greeted him as he stepped inside, the aroma of delectable dishes wafting through the air.

Chef Jacques emerged from the kitchen, his face lighting up as he spotted Finn. The chef's warm greeting put Finn at ease, and he carefully presented the container of truffles, watching as Chef Jacques examined each one with a discerning eye.

The chef's expression transformed into one of pure delight as he inspected the truffles, confirming their high quality and authenticity. Finn felt a surge of pride as Chef Jacques praised his skill and dedication, recognizing the effort that had gone into finding such exquisite specimens.

"THESE ARE TRULY EXCEPTIONAL, Finn," Chef Jacques praised, his voice filled with admiration. "The Périgords are perfectly ripe, and the Bianchettos are of the highest grade. I can already envision the exquisite dishes I'll create with these."

Finn's heart swelled with pride at the chef's words, knowing that his hard work and dedication had paid off. Chef Jacques, recognizing the value of the truffles and the effort behind their discovery, made a generous offer.

"For truffles of this caliber, I'm willing to pay top dollar," the chef declared, naming a figure that exceeded Finn's expectations. "Your skill and perseverance in finding these are truly commendable."

His eyes widened as he processed the offer, a mixture of surprise and elation washing over him. The amount Chef Jacques proposed would make a significant contribution to his college fund and ease the financial burden on his family.

With a grateful smile, Finn accepted the offer, his voice filled with appreciation. "Thank you, Chef Jacques. Your support means the world to me."

The chef returned the smile, his eyes twinkling with a hint of excitement. "Finn, I must say, I'm thoroughly impressed by your abilities. If you continue to find truffles of this quality, I would be more than happy to establish a regular partnership with you. Whenever you have a new batch, please bring them directly to me."

Finn's heart leaped at the prospect of a continued collaboration with the renowned chef. The idea of having a reliable buyer for his future truffle finds filled him with a sense of security and motivation.

"I would be honored, Chef Jacques," Finn replied, his voice brimming with enthusiasm. "I'll keep searching the forest with Mystic, and we'll do our best to bring you more exceptional truffles."

With a firm handshake, the transaction was complete, and a new partnership was forged. Finn left the restaurant with a lighter heart and a heavier wallet, the weight of the bills in his pocket a tangible reminder of his success.

The sun seemed to shine a little brighter, and the world felt full of possibilities. Finn's determination to continue his truffle hunting adventures surged through him, fueled by the knowledge that he and Mystic had a promising future ahead in uncovering the hidden treasures of Loblolly Springs.

FINN'S STEPS WERE LIGHT and his heart was soaring. The weight of the money in his pocket, a staggering $207 from his first truffle hunt, filled him with an overwhelming sense of accomplishment and excitement for the future. The world seemed to shine a little brighter, and the possibilities felt endless.

With a spring in his step, Finn made his way to his favorite store, Wester-Auto. The shop was a treasure trove of goods, ranging from auto parts and appliances to sporting equipment, guns, ammo, bows, fishing rods, and camping gear. It was a haven for outdoor enthusiasts and adventurers like Finn.

As he stepped inside, Finn's eyes sparkled with determination. He was on a mission to find the best compass available, a tool that would guide him through the wilderness and ensure he never lost his way again. He browsed the shelves, carefully examining each option, weighing their features and quality.

After much deliberation, Finn settled on a top-of-the-line compass, one that promised unparalleled accuracy and durability. He also picked up a fire starting kit, water purification tablets, a folding camp saw, and other essential items that would enhance his future truffle hunting expeditions.

With his purchases in hand, Finn couldn't resist the temptation to treat himself. Despite the early hour, he found himself drawn to the local Dairy Queen. The aroma of burgers and the promise of a cool, creamy shake were too enticing to pass up.

Finn entered the DQ, a grin plastered on his face. He placed his order, eagerly anticipating the delicious meal that awaited him. As he waited, he couldn't help but reflect on the incredible journey he had embarked upon with Mystic by his side.

When his order was ready, Finn collected his shake and burger, the perfect reward for a successful day. With his new gear and a satisfied appetite, he set off towards home, ready to share his triumphs with his family and plan his next adventure in the enchanting forest of Loblolly Springs.

AS FINN PEDALED HOME from Wester-Auto, the weight of his new compasses in his backpack filled him with a sense of security and preparedness. Never again would he venture into the forest without a reliable means of navigation. The harrowing experience of being lost in the fog-shrouded wilderness had taught him a valuable lesson, one he would never forget.

At the edge of town, Finn spotted a tall, sprawling oak tree, its branches extending like a canopy, offering a welcome respite from the sun. He steered his bike towards the shade, the leaves rustling gently in the breeze as he approached. With a smooth motion, he dismounted and leaned his bike against the sturdy trunk.

Finn unzipped his backpack, eager to examine his new acquisitions. He carefully removed the boxes containing his two compasses: a high-end sighting compass and a thumb compass. The sighting compass was a marvel of engineering, with a mirrored base and a precise bezel for taking accurate bearings. The thumb compass, small and compact, was designed for quick reference and easy access during his adventures.

Finn realized there was no better time than the present to familiarize himself with his new tools. He unboxed both compasses, holding them reverently in his hands. The weight of the sighting compass felt reassuring, its polished surface glinting in the sunlight that filtered through the leaves.

With a sense of purpose, Finn began to practice using the compasses, immersing himself in the task. He aligned the sighting compass with a distant landmark, a towering Arkansas white oak on a far-off ridge, peering through the mirror to get a precise reading. The sharpness of the reflection and the clarity of the bezel markings filled him with confidence. The thumb compass, clipped to his pocket, provided a quick reference as he turned and oriented himself, its needle swinging smoothly to point north. Each movement was deliberate, as he cross-referenced the compasses against the topographical map of the Loblolly Springs forest, ensuring that he could navigate this vast wilderness with accuracy. The forest, with its rolling hills and winding streams, seemed to welcome his newfound skills, as if acknowledging the young explorer's determination and respect for its secrets.

He set a course for home, using both compasses to guide his way. He imagined navigating through the dense underbrush of Loblolly Springs forest, the compasses serving as his unwavering guides. With each minute, he grew more confident in his ability to find his way, no matter the challenges that lay ahead.

FINN SAT AT THE KITCHEN table with his mother, Clara, recounting his successful day in town. The aroma of freshly brewed coffee filled the air as Clara listened intently to her son's adventures.

"And then, Chef Jacques was so impressed with the truffles Mystic and I found," Finn said, his eyes sparkling with pride. "He bought them all and even said he'd be interested in more if we find them."

Clara smiled warmly, her heart swelling with joy at her son's accomplishment. "That's wonderful, Finn. Your hard work and dedication are really paying off."

Finn nodded, his fingers tracing the edges of his new compasses, which lay on the table before him. "I used some of the money to buy these," he explained, holding up the sighting compass for his mother to see. "Top-of-the-line equipment. I'll never get lost in the woods again."

Clara reached out and gently squeezed Finn's hand, her eyes reflecting a mix of concern and admiration. "I'm so proud of you, Finn. But please, always remember to be careful out there. The forest can be unpredictable."

"I know, Mom," Finn assured her, his voice filled with confidence. "But I've learned so much, and with these compasses and Mystic by my side, I feel ready for anything."

As the conversation lulled, Finn's thoughts drifted to the upcoming discussion with his father, Ethan. He glanced at the clock, anticipation building in his chest. Ethan's shift at the wildlife research center would be ending soon, and Finn couldn't wait to share his plans for another camping trip in the woods.

Clara, sensing her son's excitement, smiled knowingly. "Your father will be thrilled to hear about your success, Finn. And I'm sure he'll be more than happy to discuss your next adventure."

Finn grinned, his mind already racing with the possibilities. Two nights in the forest, just him, Mystic, and the untamed wilderness of Loblolly Springs. It was a thrilling prospect, a chance to put his newfound skills and equipment to the test.

As the minutes ticked by, Finn and Clara continued to chat, their conversation drifting from Finn's truffle hunting to Clara's day at the school where she taught. The bond between mother and son was evident in their easy banter and the way they listened attentively to each other's stories.

THE FRONT DOOR OPENED, and Ethan Thornwood stepped into the warm embrace of his home, the scent of Clara's cooking wafting through the air. Finn, barely able to contain his excitement, rushed to greet his father, his new compasses clutched in his hands.

Clara smiled at her husband, her eyes filled with love and contentment. "Welcome home, dear," she said, wiping her hands on her apron as she stepped out of the kitchen. "Dinner will be ready soon."

Ethan grinned, placing a gentle kiss on his wife's cheek before turning his attention to Finn. "So, how was your day, son? Any exciting adventures to report?"

Finn's face lit up, his words tumbling out in an enthusiastic rush. "Dad, you won't believe it! I sold the truffles Mystic and I found to Chef Jacques at Le Chêne Doré. He was so impressed, and he paid me $207 for them!"

Ethan's eyebrows shot up, his expression a mix of surprise and pride. "That's incredible, Finn! I'm so proud of you and Mystic. You've really taken this truffle hunting business to the next level."

Finn beamed, his chest swelling with pride. "And that's not all, Dad. Look what I bought with the money." He held out the sighting and thumb compasses, their polished surfaces glinting in the light.

Ethan took the compasses, turning them over in his hands with an appreciative nod. "These are top-notch, Finn. You made a wise investment. These will serve you well in the forest."

As Clara disappeared back into the kitchen, Finn leaned in closer to his father, his voice dropping to a conspiratorial whisper. "Dad, I have a plan. I want to spend two nights in the woods with Mystic, at the first campsite we found. With these new compasses and the skills you've taught me, I know I'm ready."

Ethan considered his son's words, his brow furrowing slightly. "Two nights, huh? That's a big step, Finn. But I trust you, and I know you and

Mystic make a great team. Let's talk more about it over dinner, and we'll make sure you're fully prepared for the trip."

Finn nodded, his heart racing with anticipation. The prospect of spending two nights in the heart of Loblolly Springs, just him and Mystic, was both thrilling and daunting. But with his father's guidance and his own growing skills, he knew he was ready for the challenge.

THE THORNWOOD FAMILY gathered around the dinner table, the aroma of Clara's home-cooked meal filled the air. Ethan, his mind still on Finn's upcoming camping trip, decided to share some of his wilderness wisdom with his son.

"Finn," Ethan began, "if you want to ensure a hot, clean-burning campfire, you should consider building a Dakota fire hole."

Finn looked up from his plate, his curiosity piqued. "A Dakota fire hole? What's that, Dad?"

Ethan smiled, always eager to pass on his knowledge. "It's a type of fire pit that's designed to be efficient and low-profile. You dig two holes in the ground, connecting them with a tunnel. The first hole is where you build your fire, and the second acts as a chimney, drawing air into the fire."

Clara listened intently, her eyes flickering between her husband and son as they discussed the intricacies of campfire building.

"The Dakota fire hole is great because it burns hotter and cleaner than a regular campfire," Ethan continued. "The air is drawn in through the tunnel, providing plenty of oxygen to the fire. This means you get a more complete burn, with less smoke."

Finn nodded, absorbing the information. Then, a thought occurred to him. "But wouldn't this use more wood than a normal fire pit?"

Ethan chuckled, shaking his head. "Actually, it's quite the opposite. Because the fire burns more efficiently, you end up using less wood overall. Plus, the heat is concentrated, so you can cook food or boil water more quickly."

Finn's eyes widened, impressed by the ingenuity of the Dakota fire hole. He could already picture himself digging the holes, carefully constructing the tunnel, and watching as the fire roared to life.

Clara, seeing the excitement on her son's face, smiled warmly. "It sounds like you've got a lot to teach Finn, Ethan. I'm sure he'll be a pro at building Dakota fire holes in no time."

Ethan grinned, reaching across the table to ruffle Finn's hair. "I have no doubt about that. Our boy's a quick learner, and with Mystic by his side, they'll be unstoppable in the wilderness."

As the family continued their meal, the conversation flowed easily, filled with laughter and love. Finn's mind, however, was already wandering to the forests of Loblolly Springs, eager to put his newfound knowledge to the test.

Chapter 8

L ong before first light, Finn was already wide awake, his mind buzzing with anticipation for the journey ahead. He moved quietly through the house, careful not to wake his parents as he gathered his supplies.

Mystic, ever the faithful companion, watched intently as Finn methodically packed his backpack. Her tail wagged with excitement, sensing the adventure that awaited them.

Finn double-checked his list, ensuring he had everything he needed. This time, he was determined to be prepared for anything the wilderness might throw their way. He carefully selected an assortment of high-calorie foods, including energy bars, trail mix, and dried fruits. These would provide the sustenance they needed to keep their strength up during long days of trekking through the forest.

For Mystic, Finn packed three days' worth of dog food, ensuring that his loyal friend would have plenty to eat. He also included extra water and a collapsible bowl for her to drink from.

For himself, Finn made sure to pack enough instant soup packs to last three days, with a few extras just in case. He knew that these quick and easy meals would be a welcome comfort after a long day of hiking.

As he finished packing, Finn paused for a moment, his hand resting on the worn fabric of his backpack. He could feel the weight of responsibility settling on his shoulders, but it was a burden he was more than willing to bear. This was his chance to prove himself, to show that he had what it took to navigate the wilderness and uncover the secrets of Loblolly Springs.

With a deep breath, Finn shouldered his backpack and turned to Mystic. "You ready, girl?" he whispered, scratching behind her ears.

Mystic's eyes shone with anticipation, and she let out a soft bark in response.

Together, they made their way out of the house, the cool morning air nipping at their skin. As they set off towards the forest, Finn could feel his heart pounding with excitement. This was the beginning of a new adventure, and he was ready to embrace whatever challenges lay ahead.

FINN AND MYSTIC HAD ventured deep into the heart of Loblolly Springs forest, the young adventurer knew that navigation would be key to their success. He scanned the terrain, searching for a suitable spot to consult his map and chart their course.

A small clearing caught Finn's eye, its flat expanse of dirt providing the perfect surface for map reading. He knelt down, carefully unfolding the map and laying it out before him. With a practiced hand, Finn oriented the map due north, aligning it with the cardinal directions.

Reaching into his pocket, Finn retrieved his new compass—a sleek, reliable tool that would guide them through the wilderness. He held it steady, watching as the needle quivered before settling on magnetic north. With a few deft movements, Finn set their course, plotting a path that would lead them directly to their first campsite.

Satisfied with his calculations, Finn meticulously folded the map and stowed it away in his backpack. He then turned his attention to the thumb compass, a compact device that would serve as their primary guide for the journey ahead.

Finn felt a surge of confidence coursing through his veins. The weight of the thumb compass on his wrist was a constant reminder of his newfound navigational skills, a testament to the lessons he had learned from his father.

Finn and Mystic moved through the uncharted territory of Loblolly Springs forest, the terrain grew increasingly treacherous. The dense underbrush and tangled vines obscured the path, making navigation a formidable challenge. Determined to reach their destination, Finn made the bold decision to take a shortcut through an area unmarked on his map.

At first, the shortcut seemed promising, with the forest floor relatively clear of obstacles. However, as they pressed on, the ground beneath their feet became loose and unstable. Suddenly, Finn's foot slipped on a patch of loose gravel, sending him tumbling down a steep slope.

Mystic's urgent barks filled the air as Finn desperately grasped for a hand hold, his hands scrabbling against the rocky terrain. By sheer luck, his fingers caught hold of a jagged rock jutting out from the hillside, halting his descent. Pain seared through his palm as the sharp edges of the rock tore into his skin, leaving a bloody gash in their wake.

Finn clung to the rock, his heart pounding in his chest as he assessed his precarious situation. The path ahead was far more treacherous than he had anticipated, with loose rocks and hidden drop-offs threatening to send him plummeting further down the slope.

Mystic whined anxiously from above, her keen senses alerting her to the danger that lay ahead. Finn knew that they needed to re-calibrate their route immediately, lest they risk further injury or becoming hopelessly lost in the unforgiving wilderness.

With a grunt of effort, Finn hauled himself back up the slope, his injured hand throbbing with every movement. Once he reached stable ground, he quickly retrieved the first aid kit from his backpack and set about bandaging his wound. The white gauze stood out starkly against his dirt-stained skin, a reminder of the perils that lurked in the forest.

The hours passed swiftly as Finn and Mystic navigated the forest, their footsteps falling into a steady rhythm on the soft earth. The sun climbed higher in the sky, its warm rays filtering through the canopy of leaves above.

To their delight, the journey proved uneventful, a welcome respite from the challenges they had faced in previous expeditions. Finn's mastery of the compass was evident in the ease with which they traversed the terrain, avoiding the pitfalls and obstacles that had once hindered their progress.

As the sun approached high noon, familiar landmarks began to emerge from the greenery, signaling their proximity to the first campsite. Finn's heart swelled with pride as he recognized the telltale signs—a distinctive rock formation, a gnarled oak tree, a babbling brook that wound its way through the undergrowth.

They had made excellent time, arriving at their destination well before noon. Finn couldn't help but marvel at the efficiency of their travel, a testament to the power of proper planning and the invaluable guidance of his new compass.

FINN'S FIRST TASK WAS to erect the tent, a sturdy shelter that would protect them from the elements. He searched the area, retrieving the tent stakes he had carefully crafted during their last overnight stay in this very spot. The memory of that stormy night was still fresh in his mind—the howling winds, the driving rain, and the sense of accomplishment that had come with weathering the tempest.

With practiced movements, Finn began to assemble the tent, his hands working deftly as he threaded the poles through the fabric and secured them in place. Mystic watched attentively, her tail wagging with anticipation as she sensed the excitement in the air.

Finn's thoughts drifted back to that fateful night, remembering how he had fashioned the tent stakes from sturdy branches, using his knife to whittle them to the perfect size and shape. Those stakes had proven their worth, holding fast against the fury of the storm and keeping the tent firmly anchored to the ground.

Now, as he drove the stakes into the soft earth, Finn felt a sense of pride and satisfaction. He had learned so much since that first camping trip, honing his skills and growing more confident with each passing day. The tent stakes were a testament to his resourcefulness and ingenuity, a symbol of the lessons he had learned in the heart of the forest.

With the tent securely in place, Finn stepped back to admire his handiwork. The shelter stood tall and proud, its green fabric blending seamlessly with the surrounding foliage. It was a sight that filled him with a sense of accomplishment, a tangible reminder of how far he had come.

FINN TURNED HIS ATTENTION to the next task at hand: constructing a Dakota fire pit. He had learned about this efficient and low-profile fire pit from his father, Ethan, and was eager to put his knowledge to the test.

Finn began by digging two holes in the ground, each about a foot deep and a foot wide, with a small tunnel connecting them at the base. He carefully removed the dirt, piling it neatly to the side. Mystic watched with curiosity, her nose twitching as she caught the scent of the freshly turned earth.

Next, Finn lined the holes with rocks, creating a sturdy foundation for his fire pit. He selected flat, dry stones from the surrounding area, fitting them snugly together like pieces of a puzzle. As he worked, he felt a sense of satisfaction, knowing that his efforts would result in a fire that would burn efficiently and provide warmth and light throughout the night.

With the Dakota fire pit complete, Finn turned his attention to creating a protective cover for the pit. He knew that the weather in Loblolly Springs could be unpredictable, and he wanted to ensure that his fire would remain lit even in the event of rain.

Finn gathered several large branches from the surrounding trees, carefully selecting ones that were sturdy and relatively straight. He arranged them in a conical shape over the fire pit, with the tips of the branches meeting at the top to form a peak. He then covered the framework with smaller branches and leaves, creating a dense, waterproof canopy.

Stepping back to admire his work, Finn felt a sense of pride and accomplishment. The Dakota fire pit and its protective cover stood as a testament to his growing skills and knowledge of the wilderness.

HE PRESSED THE BUTTON on his CB radio, holding it close to his mouth as he spoke. "Mom, it's Finn. I've got the camp all set up, and Mystic and I are about to head out to search for truffles."

Clara's voice crackled through the speaker, warm and comforting despite the distance. "That's great, honey. How's everything going so far?"

"Really well," Finn replied, his enthusiasm evident in his tone. "I used the Dakota fire pit technique Dad taught me, and I think it's going to work perfectly. We're planning to search for truffles until just before sundown, and then we'll check in with you again before bedding down for the night."

"Sounds like a solid plan," Clara said, her voice filled with a mix of pride and concern. "Just remember to stay safe out there, and don't push yourself too hard. You've got plenty of time to find those truffles."

Finn smiled, touched by his mother's unwavering support. "I will, Mom. I promise. I've got my compass, my map, and Mystic by my side. We'll be careful."

"I know you will, sweetheart. Your father and I are so proud of you, you know that, right?"

"I do," Finn said softly, feeling a warmth spread through his chest. "Thanks, Mom. I love you."

"I love you too, Finn. Stay safe, and we'll talk again soon."

With that, the conversation ended, and Finn clipped the CB radio back onto his belt. He turned to Mystic, who had been patiently waiting by his side, her tail wagging with anticipation.

"Alright, girl," Finn said, reaching down to scratch behind her ears. "Let's go find some truffles."

Together, the boy and his loyal dog set off into the forest, their hearts filled with determination and the spirit of adventure. The sun filtered through the canopy of leaves above, coating the ground with patches of golden light. Finn consulted his map and compass, plotting their course towards map grid M45.

As they walked, Finn couldn't help but feel a sense of gratitude for the opportunity to be out here, in the heart of nature, pursuing his dreams. He knew that whatever challenges lay ahead, he had the skills, the knowledge, and the companionship to face them head-on.

FINN AND MYSTIC SET off from their campsite, heading due west towards map grid M45. The forest enveloped them, the towering trees creating a cathedral-like canopy overhead. Shafts of sunlight pierced through the leaves, dappling the forest floor with golden patches. The air was crisp and clean, filled with the earthy scents of moss, bark, and damp soil.

He consulted his compass regularly as they walked, ensuring they stayed on course. He scanned the ground, searching for any signs of the elusive truffles. Mystic trotted ahead, her nose to the ground, her tail wagging with purpose.

The terrain began to change as they progressed, the soft, loamy soil giving way to a rockier, more uneven landscape. Finn navigated carefully, mindful of the loose stones and gnarled roots that threatened to trip him up.

Suddenly, Mystic paused, her body stiffening as she sniffed the air. Finn watched her intently, his heart quickening with anticipation. The dog circled a spot near the base of a large oak tree, her nose working furiously.

Finn approached, kneeling beside her. He brushed aside the fallen leaves and twigs, revealing a small patch of disturbed soil. With gentle fingers, he probed the earth, his breath catching in his throat as he felt the unmistakable texture of a truffle.

Carefully, he extracted the precious fungus, holding it up to the light. It was a beautiful specimen, its surface marbled with shades of brown and black. Finn grinned, feeling a surge of pride and excitement.

As he placed the truffle in his bag, Mystic gave a soft bark, her tail wagging with renewed energy. Finn ruffled her fur affectionately, praising her for her keen senses.

They continued their search, moving deeper into the forest. The sun began to sink lower in the sky, casting long shadows across the ground. Finn checked his watch, realizing they had covered a significant distance.

Mystic froze once more, her nose twitching. Finn followed her gaze, his eyes widening as he spotted a small cluster of mushrooms nestled beneath a fallen log.

He approached cautiously, his heart pounding as he recognized the distinctive shape and color of Bianchetto truffles. With trembling hands, he harvested the precious fungi, marveling at their delicate aroma.

THE DENSE UNDERBRUSH had now thinned out, revealing a more open woodland floor carpeted with fallen leaves and patches of lush, green moss. The canopy above remained thick, filtering the sunlight into a soft, emerald glow that bathed the forest in an enchanting atmosphere.

Finn consulted his map and compass, confirming they were now at the edge of grid O45, heading towards N45. He scanned the surroundings, his eyes searching for any signs of the elusive truffles or the telltale trees that often harbored them.

Mystic, ever the eager truffle hunter, darted ahead, her nose pressed to the ground as she zigzagged through the underbrush. Her tail wagged with excitement, a clear indication that she was hot on the scent of something promising.

Finn followed close behind, his own senses heightened as he looked for any disturbances in the soil or the presence of specific plants known to grow near truffles. As they progressed, he noticed a change in the forest's composition. The towering oaks and hickories gave way to a grove of hazelnut trees, their trunks slender and their leaves a vibrant green.

Mystic suddenly paused, her body rigid with anticipation. She sniffed the base of a particularly large hazelnut tree, her tail quivering with excitement. Finn hurried to her side, his heart racing as he knelt down to examine the spot that had captured Mystic's attention.

With gentle fingers, he brushed aside the fallen leaves and twigs, revealing a patch of loose, dark soil. The unmistakable aroma of truffles wafted up to his nostrils, causing a surge of excitement to course through his veins.

Carefully, Finn began to dig, using a small trowel to loosen the earth around the precious fungi. Mystic watched intently, her nose twitching as she caught the scent of their quarry.

As Finn worked, he uncovered not one, but three perfectly formed Bianchetto truffles nestled together in the rich soil. Each one was about the size of a golf ball, their surfaces slightly rough and marbled with shades of cream and pale brown.

Finn gently extracted the truffles, holding them up to the dappled light that filtered through the hazelnut leaves. He marveled at their beauty and rarity, knowing that each one represented a significant step towards his goal of paying for college.

With a smile of satisfaction, Finn carefully placed the truffles in his collection bag, giving Mystic an affectionate pat on the head. Together, they continued their journey westward, deeper into grid N45, their spirits high and their determination unwavering.

Finn relied on Mystic's keen sense of smell to guide them towards their prized quarry—the elusive truffles. The determined duo weaved through the underbrush, their eyes and noses alert for any signs of the valuable fungi.

Suddenly, Mystic's tail began to wag with increased fervor, and she darted towards the base of a towering oak tree. Finn followed close behind, his heart racing with anticipation. As they approached the tree, Mystic began to dig frantically at the soft, damp soil, her paws working with precision and purpose.

Finn knelt beside his faithful companion and gently brushed away the loose earth, revealing a marbled truffle nestled beneath the surface. Its distinctive aroma wafted up to his nostrils, confirming the authenticity of their find. With a smile of satisfaction, Finn carefully extracted the truffle and held it up to the filtered sunlight, admiring its unique beauty.

However, their moment of triumph was short-lived. As Finn pocketed the truffle, a sudden rustling in the nearby underbrush caught their attention. Mystic's ears perked up, and her body tensed, sensing potential danger.

To their surprise, a nest of baby raccoons emerged from the foliage, their tiny eyes blinking in the dappled light. Finn's heart melted at the sight of the adorable creatures, but his joy quickly turned to alarm as a protective mother raccoon appeared, hissing and baring her teeth.

The mother raccoon advanced towards Finn and Mystic, her eyes filled with maternal fury. Finn, realizing the gravity of the situation, quickly backed away, gently tugging on Mystic's collar to urge her to retreat. Mystic, usually curious and friendly, understood the threat and obediently followed Finn's lead.

As they cautiously distanced themselves from the raccoon family, the mother raccoon lunged forward, her sharp teeth narrowly missing Finn's leg. Finn's heart pounded in his chest as he and Mystic hurriedly moved to another area, putting a safe distance between themselves and the protective mother.

Once they were out of harm's way, Finn and Mystic paused to catch their breath, their hearts racing from the close encounter. The incident served as a stark reminder of the unpredictable nature of the forest and the importance of respecting the wildlife that called it home.

FINN AND MYSTIC PRESSED on through the heart of grid N45, the forest seemed to grow more ancient and mysterious with each step. The trees here were taller, their trunks thicker and gnarled with age. The canopy above was so dense that only the most determined rays of sunlight could penetrate, casting a perpetual twilight on the forest floor.

The terrain became more challenging, with rocky outcrops and steep inclines that tested Finn's endurance and agility. Mystic, however, navigated the obstacles with ease, her four paws finding purchase on even the most treacherous surfaces.

As they climbed a particularly steep ridge, Finn paused to catch his breath and survey the surroundings. It was then that he noticed something peculiar in the distance. Through the trees, he caught a glimpse of what appeared to be a stone structure, its weathered surface almost entirely obscured by the dense foliage.

Intrigued, Finn and Mystic made their way towards the hidden edifice. As they drew closer, the structure came into clearer view. It was an ancient stone building, its walls crumbling and overgrown with moss and ivy. The architecture was unlike anything Finn had ever seen before, with intricate carvings and symbols adorning the weathered stone.

The entrance to the structure was a massive wooden door, its surface worn smooth by the passage of time. Rusted hinges creaked as Finn pushed against it, revealing a dimly lit interior.

As they stepped inside, Finn's eyes adjusted to the gloom. The room was circular, with a high, domed ceiling that disappeared into the shadows above. The walls were lined with shelves, each one filled with ancient books and scrolls. In the center of the room stood a large stone table, its surface covered in strange, arcane symbols and diagrams.

But what caught Finn's attention most was the far wall of the room. There, embedded in the stone, was a large, intricately designed lock. It was made of a dark, tarnished metal, with gears and cogs that seemed to move and shift of their own accord.

Finn approached the lock, he realized with a start that it was the perfect size and shape for the old, rusted key he had found on their previous adventure. With trembling fingers, he retrieved the key from his pocket and held it up to the lock.

FINN INSERTED THE RUSTED key into the ancient lock, he felt a sense of anticipation and trepidation. The key slid into the mechanism with surprising ease, as if it had been waiting for this moment for centuries. With a deep breath, Finn began to turn the key, feeling the resistance of the ancient tumblers within.

At first, nothing seemed to happen. But then, a soft clicking sound emanated from deep within the lock. Finn's heart raced as he continued to turn the key, each click becoming louder and more distinct. Mystic, sensing the importance of the moment, stood alert by Finn's side, her ears perked and her eyes fixed on the lock.

With a final, resounding click, the lock surrendered its secrets. Finn watched in amazement as the gears and cogs began to move, their ancient mechanisms coming to life after countless years of dormancy. The entire wall seemed to shudder as the lock disengaged, and a hidden seam appeared in the stone, outlining a previously invisible compartment.

Finn's hands trembled as he reached out to the newly revealed opening. His fingers found purchase on the edges of the compartment, and with a gentle tug, he pulled it open, revealing the secrets within.

Inside the compartment, Finn discovered a small, ornate wooden box. The box was intricately carved with symbols and patterns that matched those on the stone table in the center of the room. The wood was dark and rich, with a patina that spoke of great age and importance.

With reverent hands, Finn lifted the box from its resting place and carried it to the stone table. Mystic followed closely, her curiosity piqued by the strange object. As Finn set the box down on the table, he noticed that it, too, had a lock – a smaller version of the one on the wall, with the same intricate gears and cogs.

Finn's mind raced with possibilities. What could be inside this ancient box? What secrets did it hold? And why had it been hidden away in this mysterious, forgotten place? He knew that whatever lay within could hold the key to unlocking the mysteries of Loblolly Springs and perhaps even the legendary Mycelium Haven.

HE STOOD BEFORE THE ancient wooden box, his heart raced with anticipation. The intricate carvings on its surface seemed to whisper secrets from a bygone era, beckoning him to uncover the mysteries within. With trembling hands, Finn reached for the rusted key that had opened the hidden compartment and inserted it into the lock on the box.

To his surprise, the key fit perfectly, as if it had been crafted specifically for this purpose. Finn took a deep breath and turned the key, feeling the resistance of the ancient mechanism. Mystic watched intently, her tail wagging with excitement as she sensed the significance of the moment.

With a soft click, the lock released its hold on the box. Finn carefully lifted the lid, his eyes widening as he beheld the contents within. Nestled inside the box was a meticulously folded piece of parchment, its edges worn and yellowed with age. The parchment had a distinct aroma, a blend of musty paper and the faint scent of the earth.

Finn delicately removed the parchment from the box, his fingers trembling with a mix of excitement and reverence. As he unfolded the fragile document, he realized that it was a map – an ancient, hand-drawn map of Loblolly Springs and the surrounding forest.

The map was unlike any Finn had ever seen. The lines were intricate and precise, depicting the contours of the land with remarkable detail. Symbols and markings adorned the map, hinting at hidden paths, secret groves, and long-forgotten landmarks. The ink had faded in some places, but the overall integrity of the map remained intact.

As Finn studied the map, his eyes were drawn to a particular area marked with a peculiar symbol – a intertwined network of lines resembling the delicate threads of a mycelium network. The symbol was situated deep within the heart of the forest, far from any known trails or landmarks.

Finn's heart raced as he realized the significance of his discovery. This ancient map, hidden away for centuries, could hold the key to unlocking the secrets of the legendary Mycelium Haven. The intertwined symbol on the map seemed to call out to him, beckoning him to embark on a journey into the unknown depths of Loblolly Springs.

FINN CAREFULLY SET the ancient map aside, his attention was drawn to the next object nestled within the wooden box. It was a book, its leather cover worn and weathered by the passage of time. The book had a substantial weight to it, as if it carried the wisdom of ages within its pages.

Finn gently lifted the book from the box, his fingers brushing against the rough texture of the leather. The cover was adorned with intricate embossed patterns, reminiscent of the symbols he had seen on the stone table and the map. The book's spine creaked softly as he opened it, revealing pages that were thick and slightly discolored, bearing the marks of time.

As he turned the pages, Finn noticed that the book was written in an unfamiliar language, its script flowing and elegant, yet incomprehensible to his untrained eyes. The ink had faded in some places, but the majority of the text remained legible. Illustrations accompanied the words, depicting strange plants, fungi, and what appeared to be diagrams of underground networks.

Finn's heart raced with excitement as he realized that this book could hold invaluable knowledge about the Mycelium Haven and the secrets of the forest. He carefully flipped through the pages, his eyes scanning the foreign words and illustrations, hoping to glean any information that could aid him in his quest.

He delved deeper into the book, Finn noticed that certain pages had been marked with thin ribbons, as if someone had deliberately highlighted passages of particular importance. The ribbons were made of a delicate, shimmering material that seemed to catch the light in an almost ethereal way.

Finn's curiosity was piqued by the marked pages, and he made a mental note to investigate them further. He knew that deciphering the ancient language would be a challenge, but he was determined to unravel the mysteries contained within the book.

Alongside the book, Finn discovered a small, intricately carved wooden box. It was no larger than the palm of his hand and had a hinged lid that opened smoothly. Inside the box, nestled on a bed of soft, dark velvet, was a small, polished stone.

The stone was unlike anything Finn had ever seen before. It was a deep, rich burgundy color, shot through with veins of shimmering gold. As he picked it up, Finn noticed that the stone was warm to the touch, almost as if it pulsed with a hidden energy.

FINN HELD THE ENIGMATIC stone in his hand, he couldn't help but wonder about its significance. The stone's warmth seemed to pulse against his skin, as if it were alive with a hidden energy. Questions raced through his mind: Where did this stone come from? Who had placed it here, nestled within the ancient book? What role did it play in the greater mystery surrounding the Mycelium Haven?

Finn turned the stone over in his palm, examining its smooth surface and the intricate veins of gold that ran through its burgundy depths. It was unlike any stone he had ever seen before, and he couldn't shake the feeling that it held a purpose beyond mere aesthetics.

As he pondered the stone's origins and importance, Finn suddenly felt a strange sensation wash over him. It was as if the stone was responding to his thoughts, its warmth intensifying ever so slightly. The golden veins within the stone seemed to shimmer and dance, catching the light in a mesmerizing display.

Finn's breath caught in his throat as he watched the stone's transformation. The warmth emanating from it grew, spreading up his arm and throughout his body. It was a comforting sensation, like being enveloped in a gentle embrace.

Suddenly, the stone began to emit a soft, pulsing light. It was a warm, golden glow that cast shadows on the walls of the ancient room. Finn's eyes widened in amazement as the light grew brighter, illuminating the stone table and the intricate carvings that adorned its surface.

As the light from the stone intensified, Finn noticed that the symbols on the table seemed to respond to its presence. They began to shimmer and shift, as if they were coming to life before his very eyes. The ancient language that had once been incomprehensible started to morph, the characters rearranging themselves into patterns that Finn could almost understand.

Finn's heart raced with excitement and trepidation as he witnessed the stone's power firsthand. He knew that he was on the cusp of a great discovery, one that could unlock the secrets of the Mycelium Haven and change the course of his life forever.

Mystic, who had been watching the scene unfold with curious eyes, let out a soft whine, as if sensing the significance of the moment. Finn glanced at his faithful companion, a smile tugging at the corners of his mouth. Together, they stood in the presence of something extraordinary, a key to the mysteries that lay ahead.

FINN HELD THE ENIGMATIC stone in his hand, and marveled at its unique appearance and the warmth that seemed to radiate from its core. The stone's burgundy hue was shot through with delicate veins of gold, creating a mesmerizing pattern that caught the light and shimmered with an otherworldly beauty.

Finn's curiosity was piqued by the stone's unusual qualities, and he felt a strong desire to give it a name, to acknowledge its significance in his journey. With a thoughtful expression, he lifted the stone to eye level and spoke softly, "I will name you 'Glimmerstone' for now."

The name felt right on his tongue, capturing the essence of the stone's captivating appearance and the mysterious energy that seemed to pulse within it. Finn carefully placed the newly christened Glimmerstone into his pants pocket, ensuring its safety by zipping the pocket securely. He didn't want to risk losing such a precious and potentially powerful object.

As Finn patted his pocket, feeling the reassuring weight of the Glimmerstone, something extraordinary happened. To his utter amazement, the stone responded to his touch, sending a gentle vibration through the fabric of his pants and into his skin.

Finn's eyes widened in disbelief as he felt the stone's reaction. It was as if the Glimmerstone had heard his words and acknowledged its new name, forming a connection with him in that moment. The sensation was unlike anything Finn had ever experienced before, and it sent a shiver of excitement and wonder down his spine.

He quickly reached into his pocket and retrieved the Glimmerstone, holding it up to examine it more closely. The stone's surface seemed to shimmer and dance with an inner light, the golden veins pulsing in rhythm with Finn's own heartbeat. It was as if the stone had come alive in his hands, responding to his presence and his intentions.

Finn's mind raced with possibilities as he contemplated the implications of the Glimmerstone's response. What other secrets did this ancient artifact hold? How might it guide him on his quest to uncover the mysteries of the Mycelium Haven? The thought of the adventures that lay ahead filled Finn with a sense of purpose and determination.

FINN CAREFULLY PLACED the Book of Tones back into the wooden box, a sense of reverence filled the air. The ancient tome seemed to hold untold secrets, and Finn couldn't help but feel a mix of excitement and responsibility as he closed the lid. With the rusted key in hand, he secured the box, ensuring its contents were protected from prying eyes.

He then returned the locked box to the hidden compartment, his movements precise and deliberate. The compartment itself was a marvel, blending seamlessly into the structure's walls. As he closed the panel, Finn marveled at the ingenuity of those who had come before him, creating such an intricate and secure hiding place.

With a satisfying click, Finn locked the compartment, sealing away the precious artifacts. He knew that this was the safest place he could imagine for now, a sanctuary where the secrets of the past could remain undisturbed until the time was right.

Finn's mind raced with excitement as he thought about showing his dad what he had discovered. Ethan Thornwood's love for history and his deep connection to the forest would make him the perfect person to share this incredible find with. Finn could already picture the look of amazement and pride on his father's face when he revealed the hidden structure and its treasures.

With a renewed sense of purpose, Finn turned to Mystic, his faithful companion. The dog's tail wagged eagerly, sensing the adventure that lay ahead. Together, they left the hidden structure behind, stepping back into the lush embrace of the forest.

As they walked, Finn's thoughts remained on the Book of Tones and the secrets it might hold. He couldn't shake the feeling that this discovery was just the beginning, a tantalizing glimpse into a larger mystery waiting to be unraveled.

But for now, Finn and Mystic had a more immediate task at hand. They needed to continue their truffle hunt, scouring the forest floor for the elusive and valuable fungi. With their heightened senses and keen instincts, the pair moved through the undergrowth, their eyes and noses attuned to any sign of the prized delicacies.

The forest seemed to come alive around them, the sunlight filtering through the canopy and casting shadows on the ground. The earthy scent of the soil mingled with the sweet aroma of wildflowers, creating a heady perfume that filled their nostrils.

Finn and Mystic pressed on, their determination and curiosity driving them forward. The hidden structure and its secrets would have to wait, but Finn knew that they would return, ready to unlock the mysteries that lay within.

Chapter 9

Finn, with the enigmatic Glimmerstone securely nestled in his pocket, consults the map grid and sets a course back to his first campsite. The ancient Book of Tones remains safely locked away in the hidden structure, its secrets waiting to be unveiled at a later time.

As Finn and his loyal companion Mystic navigate eastward through the dense forest, the afternoon sun casts shadows across their path. The terrain proves challenging, with gnarled roots and dense underbrush impeding their progress. Finn, however, remains undeterred, his mind buzzing with the implications of his recent discoveries.

Mystic, ever vigilant, trots ahead, her keen senses alert for any signs of danger or potential truffle spots. The duo moves in sync, their bond strengthened by their shared adventures and the secrets they now carry.

As they traverse a particularly rocky section of the forest, Finn feels the Glimmerstone pulse warmly against his leg, as if responding to the energy of the ancient woods around them. Its presence serves as a constant reminder of the mysteries that lie ahead, fueling Finn's determination to unravel the secrets of the Mycelium Haven.

The quarter-mile journey back towards the campsite feels longer than usual, the weight of knowledge and anticipation hanging in the air. Finn's thoughts drift between the present moment and the future, imagining the look on his father's face when he reveals the hidden structure and the artifacts within.

Mystic, sensing Finn's preoccupation, nudges his hand with her nose, bringing him back to the present. Finn smiles, grateful for her grounding presence, and together they press on, the first campsite drawing ever closer with each step.

AS FINN AND MYSTIC continue their eastward journey towards the first campsite, the enigmatic Glimmerstone nestled in Finn's pocket pulses warmly once more. The sensation catches Finn off guard, causing him to halt in his tracks. He glances down at his pocket, curiosity etched on his face as he wonders what the stone might be trying to communicate.

Finn's eyes scan the surrounding forest, searching for any clues that might explain the Glimmerstone's sudden activity. The ancient trees stand tall and silent, their branches swaying gently in the breeze, offering no obvious answers to the mystery at hand.

Beside him, Mystic suddenly becomes alert, her nose twitching as she catches a scent in the air. Without hesitation, she begins to dig at the base of a large oak tree, her paws working frantically to unearth something hidden beneath the soil.

Finn watches in amazement as Mystic's efforts reveal a large, rare truffle nestled in the earth. The truffle's pungent aroma fills the air, mingling with the earthy scent of the forest floor. Finn's eyes widen with excitement as he realizes the significance of the find.

Reaching into his pocket, Finn retrieves the map of Loblolly Springs. He carefully studies the grid, determining their current location to be approximately halfway between the hidden structure and the first campsite. With a nod of satisfaction, Finn makes a mental note of their position, committing the coordinates to memory.

As he tucks the map back into his pocket, Finn's fingers brush against the Glimmerstone once more. The stone's warmth seems to have subsided, leaving Finn to ponder the connection between its pulsing energy and the discovery of the rare truffle.

Finn gently retrieves the Pecan Truffle from the ground, marveling at its size and unique appearance. He carefully places it in his backpack, ensuring its safety for the remainder of their journey. With a grateful pat on Mystic's head, Finn signals for them to continue their trek towards the campsite, his mind buzzing with questions about the Glimmerstone's mysterious ways.

AS FINN AND MYSTIC continue their journey through the lush forest of Loblolly Springs, they find themselves navigating a dense honeysuckle thicket. The sweet fragrance of the delicate white and yellow flowers fills the air, creating an enchanting atmosphere. Finn pushes through the tangled vines, his hands brushing against the soft petals as he forges a path for himself and his loyal companion.

Suddenly, a rustling sound catches their attention. Finn freezes, his senses heightened as he scans the surrounding vegetation for any signs of movement. Mystic, too, becomes alert, her ears perked and her body tense, ready to react to any potential threat.

From the depths of the thicket, a massive black bear emerges, her fur glistening in the sunlight that filters through the canopy. Finn's heart races as he realizes the gravity of the situation. The mother bear, fiercely protective of her cubs, fixes her dark eyes on the intruders, a low growl rumbling from her throat.

Finn's mind races, trying to recall the survival techniques his father had taught him for such encounters. He knows that running is not an option, as it would only trigger the bear's predatory instincts. Instead, he slowly reaches for his backpack, hoping to find something that might help them escape unscathed.

As if sensing Finn's distress, the Glimmerstone in his pocket begins to pulse with a warm, comforting energy. The stone's vibrations intensify, sending a tingling sensation through Finn's body. Suddenly, a soft, golden light emanates from the stone, enveloping Finn and Mystic in a protective aura.

The mother bear, momentarily startled by the unexpected luminescence, takes a step back. Her growl subsides, replaced by a curious tilt of her head as she regards the glowing duo before her. The Glimmerstone's light seems to communicate a message of peace and non-aggression, assuring the bear that Finn and Mystic mean no harm to her or her cubs.

As if understanding the stone's silent communication, the mother bear relaxes her stance. She turns her attention back to her cubs, who have been watching the encounter with wide, innocent eyes. With a gentle nudge, she ushers them deeper into the thicket, away from the perceived threat.

Finn releases a breath he didn't realize he was holding, his heart still pounding in his chest. He looks down at Mystic, who has remained calm and steady throughout the ordeal, her trust in Finn and the Glimmerstone unwavering. The stone's light gradually fades, returning to its normal, pulsing state.

FINN METHODICALLY PACKS up the campsite, his mind already racing ahead to the journey home and the revelations he plans to share with his father. With each item he secures in his backpack, the weight of the Glimmerstone in his pocket serves as a constant reminder of the extraordinary discoveries he and Mystic have made in the depths of Loblolly Springs forest.

As he works, Finn's thoughts drift to the ancient tome and the intricate map that now lie hidden in the stone structure. The symbols and illustrations swirl in his mind, tantalizing him with the promise of even greater secrets waiting to be uncovered. He can hardly contain his excitement at the prospect of delving deeper into the mysteries of the Mycelium Haven.

Mystic, ever the loyal companion, watches Finn with attentive eyes, her tail wagging in anticipation of their next adventure. She seems to sense the significance of their findings, and her presence brings a sense of comfort and confidence to Finn as he prepares for the journey ahead.

With the campsite cleared and their belongings packed, Finn retrieves the grid map from his pocket. He unfolds the worn paper, his fingers tracing the lines and symbols that have become increasingly familiar to him over the course of their explorations. Using his compass, Finn carefully plots their route back home, taking into account the terrain and landmarks they've encountered along the way.

The map and compass work in tandem, guiding Finn's hand as he charts a course through the forest. He double-checks his calculations, ensuring that they have the most direct and efficient path back to Loblolly Springs. The sun hangs low in the sky, painting the forest in a warm, golden light, and Finn knows they must make good time to reach home before darkness falls.

With a final glance around the campsite, Finn shoulders his backpack and calls Mystic to his side. The two set off into the forest, their steps sure and purposeful as they navigate the winding trails and dense undergrowth. The Glimmerstone pulses in Finn's pocket, as if urging them forward, and Finn can't help but feel a sense of destiny propelling them towards the next chapter of their adventure.

As they walk, Finn's mind is already racing ahead to the moment he'll sit down with his father and share the incredible tales of their journey. He can imagine the look of wonder and pride on Ethan's face as he recounts the discovery of the ancient artifacts and the secrets they hold. Together, father and son will pore over the map and the Book of Tones, piecing together the clues that will lead them deeper into the heart of the Mycelium Haven.

FINN AND MYSTIC NAVIGATED through the familiar landscape of Loblolly Springs forest, their steps sure and steady as they made their way back home. The trek had become almost second nature to them now, with landmarks etched into Finn's mind serving as guideposts along the way.

They passed a towering oak tree, its gnarled branches reaching out like welcoming arms, marking the halfway point of their journey. The bubbling brook, its clear waters dancing over smooth stones, signaled a change in direction. Finn's eyes scanned the surroundings, spotting the open grassy areas where they had paused for rest on previous adventures.

As they continued, the majestic cottonwood trees stood sentinel, their leaves rustling in the gentle breeze. Finn's gaze fell upon a large tree stump, a natural seat where he and Mystic had shared a snack and a moment of reflection during past expeditions. Each landmark held a memory, a testament to the bond they had forged in the heart of the forest.

The Glimmerstone pulsed gently in Finn's pocket, its warmth a constant reminder of the extraordinary discoveries that awaited them. The ancient tome and the intricate map, safely hidden away in the stone structure, beckoned to Finn, promising untold secrets and adventures yet to come.

As the sun began its descent, painting the sky in a vibrant array of oranges and pinks, Finn and Mystic quickened their pace. The familiar sights and sounds of Loblolly Springs grew closer with each step, guiding them back to the comfort and safety of home.

Just as the last rays of sunlight disappeared behind the horizon, Finn and Mystic emerged from the forest's edge. The sight of their house, nestled amidst the tranquil surroundings of their hometown, brought a smile to Finn's face. They had made it back, their journey complete for now.

With a contented sigh, Finn reached down and patted Mystic's head, silently thanking her for her unwavering companionship. Together, they strode towards the welcoming lights of home, eager to share their tales with Finn's family and to begin planning their next foray into the mysteries of the Mycelium Haven.

AS FINN ENTERED THE warm, inviting atmosphere of his home, the aroma of a hearty meal wafted through the air. His parents, Ethan and Clara Thornwood, had just settled down at the dining table, their faces a mix of surprise and delight at their son's unexpected arrival.

Finn quickly hung up his coat and made his way to the kitchen sink, washing his hands thoroughly. The cool water refreshed his skin, washing away the traces of his recent adventure in the forest. With a quick glance at his reflection in the mirror, he smoothed his tousled hair and joined his parents at the table.

Ethan, his eyes filled with curiosity, looked at Finn and asked, "Finn, why are you home? We didn't expect you back so soon."

Finn smiled, his excitement barely contained as he pulled out a chair and sat down. "I have so much to tell you," he began, his voice brimming with enthusiasm. "Mystic and I made some incredible discoveries in the forest."

Clara, her maternal instincts kicking in, reached out and gently touched Finn's hand. "Is everything alright, dear? You look like you've been through quite an adventure."

Finn nodded, his eyes sparkling with the promise of the tales he was about to share. "Everything is more than alright, Mom. In fact, it's extraordinary."

Ethan leaned forward, his interest piqued by his son's words. "Well, don't keep us in suspense, Finn. Tell us all about it."

As the family settled into their meal, Finn began to recount the events of his journey, starting with the ancient stone structure hidden deep within the forest. He described the intricate carvings, the mysterious symbols, and the hidden compartment that held the ancient tome and the intricately detailed map.

Ethan and Clara listened intently, their eyes widening with each revelation. They marveled at the Glimmerstone, its warm glow and pulsating energy a testament to the extraordinary nature of Finn's discoveries.

Finn's vivid descriptions of his forest adventure unfolded, the cozy dining room began to take on a different ambiance. It felt as though the mundane boundaries of their home began to blur and soften, making way for the enchanting imagery Finn was painting with his words. In the minds of Ethan and Clara, the walls of the room seemed to dissolve, being replaced by the towering trees and lush undergrowth of Loblolly Springs forest. Every detail Finn spoke of—the intricate carvings of the stone structure, the enigmatic symbols, and the thrilling discovery of the Glimmerstone—came alive in the flickering candlelight that adorned the dining table.

The subtle, wavering light created shadows that danced along the walls and ceiling, mirroring the movement of rustling leaves and the whisper of ancient secrets hidden within the forest. It was as if the Thornwood family was no longer seated in their dining room but standing amidst the very wilderness that Finn had explored. The atmosphere was charged with a blend of excitement and mystery, highlighting the incredible nature of Finn's discoveries and deepening the bond of shared wonder between him and his parents. This enchanting moment filled the room with a palpable sense of awe, bringing Finn's extraordinary adventure to life within the warmth and comfort of their home.

FINN'S CAPTIVATING tale came to an end, the enchanting atmosphere that had enveloped the Thornwood dining room began to dissipate. The shadows that had danced along the walls, mimicking the rustling leaves and whispers of the forest, slowly faded back into the warm, familiar glow of the candlelight. The room seemed to settle back into its mundane reality, the boundaries of the walls once again solid and tangible.

Ethan Thornwood sat back in his chair, his eyes wide with a mix of amazement and disbelief. He ran a hand through his hair, trying to process the incredible story his son had just shared. "How is this possible?" he exclaimed, his voice filled with wonder. "It seemed as if I was there, it seemed so real. I can't wrap my mind around what just happened."

Clara Thornwood, equally astounded, reached out and grasped Finn's hand, her touch gentle and reassuring. She searched her son's face, seeking confirmation that the extraordinary tale he had just recounted was indeed true. "Finn, my dear, that was... it was as if we were right there with you, in the heart of the forest, discovering those ancient secrets alongside you."

Finn, his eyes shining with the excitement of his adventure, nodded eagerly. "I know, it's hard to believe, but it's all true. The Glimmerstone, the ancient tome, the map—it's all real. And it feels like it's just the beginning of something even greater."

Ethan leaned forward, his curiosity piqued by the mention of the Glimmerstone. "May I see it, Finn? The Glimmerstone?"

Finn reached into his pocket and carefully retrieved the enchanted stone. As he placed it on the table, the Glimmerstone began to pulse with a soft, warm light, its burgundy and gold hues casting a mesmerizing glow across the room. The Thornwoods gazed at the stone, each of them feeling a strange, inexplicable connection to its energy.

Clara, her voice filled with a mix of awe and concern, looked at her son. "Finn, this is... it's incredible. But I can't help but worry about what this all means. The forest, the ancient secrets, the Glimmerstone—it's a lot for someone so young to carry."

Ethan, sensing his wife's unease, placed a comforting hand on her shoulder. "Clara, our son has proven himself to be brave, resourceful, and wise beyond his years. I have no doubt that he is destined for great things, and these discoveries are just the beginning of his journey."

A SENSE OF NORMALCY settled over the household as the Thornwoods finished their evening meal. Clara, ever the diligent caretaker, began clearing the table and tidying up the kitchen. The clinking of dishes and the running of water provided a soothing background noise, a familiar soundtrack to the end of another day.

Meanwhile, Ethan and Finn stepped outside, the cool evening air greeting them as they made their way to the porch swing. The wooden planks creaked gently beneath their weight as they sat down, the swing swaying slightly with their movement. Ethan draped his arm across the back of the swing, his fingers brushing against the weathered wood, worn smooth by countless evenings spent in quiet contemplation.

Finn, his mind still buzzing with the excitement of his recent discoveries, turned to his father. "Dad, when can I show you the Book of Tones?" he asked, his voice filled with eagerness. "I can't wait for you to see it. The ancient language, the illustrations of the underground networks—it's like nothing I've ever seen before."

Ethan, his curiosity piqued by his son's enthusiasm, smiled warmly. "I'd love to see it, Finn. How about we plan a trip back to the forest this weekend? We can go together, and you can show me everything you've found—the ancient stone structure, the hidden compartment, and of course, the Book of Tones."

Finn's eyes lit up at the prospect of sharing his discoveries with his father. "That would be perfect, Dad! I can't wait to show you everything. And maybe, with your knowledge of history and archaeology, we can start to unravel some of the mysteries surrounding the Mycelium Haven."

Ethan nodded, his mind already racing with the possibilities. "I have a feeling that this is just the beginning of a grand adventure, Finn. The secrets hidden within that ancient tome and the power of the Glimmerstone—it's all pointing towards something extraordinary."

FINN AND HIS DAD SAT in the porch swing, their conversation lulled into a comfortable silence. The chirping of crickets and the distant hooting of an owl filled the night air, a symphony of nature's tranquility. Finn's mind, however, was far from tranquil. It buzzed with questions and possibilities, all centered around the enigmatic Glimmerstone and the legendary Mycelium Haven.

He reached into his pocket, his fingers brushing against the smooth surface of the stone. As he held it in his palm, Finn couldn't help but wonder if the Glimmerstone held the key to locating the elusive truffle paradise. Could this ancient artifact, with its pulsing energy and mysterious connection to the forest, guide him to the heart of Mycelium Haven?

As if in response to Finn's unspoken question, the Glimmerstone began to react. It pulsed with a gentle warmth, the burgundy hue deepening as the golden veins shimmered in the moonlight. Finn's eyes widened in surprise, his breath catching in his throat as he watched the stone come to life in his hand.

The pulsing intensified, the warmth spreading from the stone and into Finn's palm, up his arm, and throughout his body. It was a sensation unlike anything he had ever experienced before—a gentle, guiding force that seemed to beckon him towards an unknown destination.

Ethan, noticing his son's sudden change in demeanor, leaned closer. "Finn, what's happening? Is everything alright?"

Finn, his voice filled with a mix of awe and excitement, held out the Glimmerstone for his father to see. "Dad, look! The stone... it's responding to something. I think it might be trying to show me the way to Mycelium Haven."

Ethan's eyes widened as he took in the sight of the pulsing, shimmering stone. He had never seen anything quite like it before, and the historian in him was immediately intrigued by the possibilities it presented.

"This is incredible, Finn," Ethan breathed, his voice filled with wonder. "If the Glimmerstone is indeed reacting to the location of Mycelium Haven, then we may be on the verge of a groundbreaking discovery."

ETHAN'S EYES SPARKLED with the thrill of adventure as he turned to Finn, a grin spreading across his face. "You know what, Finn? I've got six weeks of vacation saved up. Why wait for the weekend when we can start our journey now? Let's pack up and head out to the first camp at first light."

Finn's heart leaped with excitement at his father's words. The prospect of embarking on this adventure with his dad, of unraveling the mysteries of the Glimmerstone and Mycelium Haven together, filled him with a sense of purpose and anticipation.

"Really, Dad? That's amazing! I can't wait to get started," Finn exclaimed, his eyes shining with enthusiasm.

As they sat there, the porch swing creaking gently beneath them, Finn suddenly remembered his encounter with the black bear in the forest. He turned to his father, his expression growing serious.

"Dad, there's something else I need to tell you about my trip," Finn began, his voice low and earnest. "When Mystic and I were navigating through a honeysuckle thicket, we came across a black bear mother and her cubs."

Ethan's brow furrowed with concern, but he remained silent, allowing his son to continue.

"I was scared at first, remembering all the survival techniques you taught me," Finn admitted. "But then, something incredible happened. The Glimmerstone in my pocket started glowing, and it seemed to signal peace to the bear. She just looked at us for a moment, and then retreated with her cubs, leaving us unharmed."

Ethan's eyes widened in astonishment as he listened to Finn's story. The idea that the Glimmerstone could possess such protective powers was both thrilling and unnerving.

"That's incredible, Finn," Ethan breathed, his mind racing with the implications of his son's encounter. "It seems that the Glimmerstone may have even more secrets and abilities than we initially thought."

ETHAN AND FINN METICULOUSLY gathered the necessary supplies for their overnight stay at the first camp. With practiced efficiency, they packed their backpacks, ensuring they had all the essentials: sleeping bags, a tent, a portable stove, and enough food and water to sustain them during their adventure.

Finn carefully placed the Glimmerstone in a secure pocket of his zippered pants pocket, its presence a constant reminder of the mysteries that awaited them in the depths of Loblolly Springs forest.

Ethan, too, couldn't help but feel a sense of anticipation, his mind buzzing with the possibilities of what they might uncover.

Despite the late hour, neither Ethan nor Finn found it difficult to rise before the first light. The excitement of their impending journey had them up and ready, their energy palpable as they joined Clara in the kitchen for breakfast.

Clara, ever the supportive mother, had prepared a hearty meal to fuel their adventure. The aroma of freshly brewed coffee mingled with the scent of sizzling bacon and eggs, creating a warm and inviting atmosphere in the Thornwood household.

As they sat around the table, Ethan and Finn eagerly discussed their plans, their voices animated with the thrill of the unknown. Clara listened intently, her eyes shining with a mixture of pride and concern for her adventurous husband and son.

"You two be careful out there," Clara said, her tone gentle yet firm. "And don't forget to check in with me on the CB radio, just so I know you're safe."

Ethan reached across the table, giving his wife's hand a reassuring squeeze. "Don't worry, Clara. We'll be cautious, and we'll make sure to keep in touch. You know Finn and I, we're a pretty good team out there."

Finn nodded in agreement, his mouth full of scrambled eggs. He swallowed quickly, adding, "And we've got Mystic with us, too. She's the best adventure companion anyone could ask for."

As if on cue, Mystic's tail thumped against the floor, her eyes bright and eager, ready to embark on another journey with her beloved humans.

With breakfast finished and their backpacks loaded, Ethan and Finn prepared to set off, their hearts filled with a sense of purpose and the promise of adventure. They hugged Clara tightly, savoring the warmth and love of their family before stepping out into the cool morning air, ready to face whatever challenges and discoveries the forest had in store for them.

Chapter 10

The mid-morning sun filtered through the dense canopy of Loblolly Springs forest as Finn and his father, Ethan, arrived at their first campsite. The air was crisp with the hint of autumn, a reminder that the cooler nights of mid-September were fast approaching in Arkansas.

With practiced efficiency, the father-son duo set up camp, their movements synchronized and purposeful. Ethan pitched the tent while Finn gathered dry firewood, ensuring they would have a warm and comforting fire to combat the chilly evening ahead.

Once the campsite was established, Finn and Ethan set off towards the hidden structure, their steps filled with anticipation. Mystic, Finn's loyal canine companion, trotted alongside them, her tail wagging with excitement.

The journey through the forest was an adventure in itself, with the trio navigating through the dense undergrowth and over fallen logs. The earthy scent of moss and decaying leaves filled their nostrils, a reminder of the vibrant ecosystem that surrounded them.

About a quarter of a mile into their westward trek, Finn suddenly stopped in his tracks. A peculiar sensation emanated from the Glimmerstone, safely tucked away in his zippered pants pocket. The stone began to vibrate and warm up, its energy palpable even through the fabric.

Finn's brow furrowed as he reached into his pocket, his fingers closing around the enigmatic stone. He held it out, watching as it pulsed with an inner light, its surface warm to the touch.

"Dad, the Glimmerstone... it's acting strange," Finn said, his voice tinged with both curiosity and concern. "It's never done this before."

Ethan moved closer, his eyes widening as he observed the stone's unusual behavior. "What do you think it means, Finn?" he asked, his mind racing with possibilities.

Finn shook his head, uncertain. "I don't know, but we should investigate. It could be a sign of danger, or maybe it's reacting to something nearby... like truffles or another clue to the Mycelium Haven."

With a determined nod, Finn and Mystic began to search the immediate area, their senses heightened and their movements cautious. Ethan joined in, his eyes scanning the forest floor for any signs of what might have triggered the Glimmerstone's reaction.

WHILE FINN, ETHAN, and Mystic searched the immediate area, the Glimmerstone's vibrations intensified, its warm light pulsing in a steady rhythm. Finn held the stone out in front of him, using it as a compass to guide their way.

The trio moved slowly, their eyes scanning the forest floor for any signs of what might have triggered the Glimmerstone's reaction. Suddenly, the stone's light began to flicker, its vibrations becoming more urgent.

Finn's heart raced as he followed the stone's guidance, moving towards a dense thicket of underbrush. As he approached, the Glimmerstone's light grew brighter, illuminating a small, almost imperceptible path through the foliage.

With a deep breath, Finn pushed through the bushes, Ethan and Mystic close behind. As they emerged on the other side, they found themselves in a small, hidden clearing.

In the center of the clearing stood an ancient, gnarled oak tree, its trunk twisted and weathered with age. The Glimmerstone's light pulsed even brighter, drawing Finn towards the tree.

As he approached, Finn noticed a small, almost invisible symbol carved into the bark. It was the same symbol he had seen in the ancient tome and on the map - the mark of the Mycelium Haven.

Finn's hand trembled as he reached out, his fingers tracing the intricate lines of the symbol. As he did, the Glimmerstone suddenly grew warm, its light spreading out from Finn's hand and illuminating the entire symbol.

There was a soft click, and a hidden compartment within the tree trunk swung open, revealing a small, ornate wooden box. Finn carefully lifted the box from its resting place, his heart pounding with anticipation.

As he opened the lid, Finn's eyes widened in amazement. Inside, nestled on a bed of soft, green moss, was a single, perfect truffle. But this was no ordinary truffle - it was larger than any Finn had ever seen, its surface a rich, deep black with delicate white veins running through it.

Ethan and Mystic moved closer, their eyes fixed on the extraordinary find. They knew, without a doubt, that they were one step closer to uncovering the secrets of the Mycelium Haven.

FINN GENTLY CRADLED the extraordinary truffle in his hands, Ethan's eyes widened with a mix of awe and realization. "This is no ordinary truffle, Finn," he breathed. "I think we should call it the Mycelium Royale."

Finn looked up at his father, his own expression mirroring the older man's wonder. "Mycelium Royale," he repeated, feeling the weight of the name on his tongue. "It's perfect."

Ethan placed a hand on his son's shoulder, his gaze intense. "Finn, this find could change everything for you. If this truffle is as rare and valuable as it seems, it could have huge implications for your future education."

Finn's heart raced at the thought. He had always dreamed of attending college, but the financial burden had seemed insurmountable. Now, with the Mycelium Royale in his hands, those dreams suddenly felt within reach.

But as the initial excitement began to fade, a new question arose. What should they do with the truffle now?

Finn and Ethan exchanged a thoughtful look, both grappling with the same dilemma. The Mycelium Royale was an incredible discovery, but they knew they couldn't rush into any decisions.

After a moment of contemplation, Ethan spoke. "I think we should return it to the box for now," he said, his voice measured. "We can leave it as we found it until we have a better understanding of what we're dealing with."

Finn nodded, seeing the wisdom in his father's words. Carefully, he placed the Mycelium Royale back into the ornate wooden box, nestling it once again on its bed of soft moss.

As he closed the lid, Finn made a mental note of their approximate location. He would log this spot, marking it with the name they had given to the extraordinary truffle.

With the Mycelium Royale safely stored away, Finn and Ethan turned their attention back to their original goal. The hidden structure still awaited them, its secrets yet to be uncovered.

With renewed determination, they set off once again, the Glimmerstone guiding their way through the dense forest. The discovery of the Mycelium Royale had only fueled their desire to unravel the mysteries of the Mycelium Haven.

FINN AND ETHAN LEFT the ancient oak behind, the Glimmerstone in Finn's pocket continued to pulse with a gentle warmth, guiding them through the dense underbrush of the forest. The terrain began to change as they moved from the soft, loamy soil of grid O45 to the more challenging landscape of grid M45.

The ground beneath their feet became rockier, with jagged stones and gnarled roots threatening to trip them at every step. Mystic, ever the faithful companion, navigated the obstacles with ease, her keen senses helping her avoid the pitfalls that lay hidden beneath the fallen leaves.

Finn and Ethan, however, had to move with more caution. They picked their way carefully through the undergrowth, using sturdy branches as walking sticks to maintain their balance. The air around them grew cooler as they progressed, the dense canopy overhead blocking out much of the sun's warmth.

As they walked, Ethan kept a watchful eye on their surroundings, his years of experience in the forest serving him well. He pointed out the different types of trees they passed, sharing his knowledge with Finn, who listened with rapt attention.

"See that tree there, with the deeply furrowed bark?" Ethan said, indicating a tall, stately tree to their right. "That's a black walnut. Its wood is prized for furniture making."

Finn nodded, making a mental note of the tree's characteristics. He had always been fascinated by his father's vast understanding of the natural world, and he relished every opportunity to learn from him.

They continued on, the Glimmerstone's pulsing growing stronger with each step. Finn could feel it vibrating against his leg, as if it were eager to reach their destination.

As they neared grid M45, the forest around them seemed to shift. The trees grew older, their trunks thicker and their branches more gnarled. There was a sense of ancient presence here, as if the very earth itself held secrets long forgotten.

Finn and Ethan exchanged a glance, both feeling the weight of the moment. They knew they were close to the hidden structure now, and the anticipation was palpable.

With the Glimmerstone as their guide, they pressed on, ready to uncover the mysteries that lay ahead.

A MOVEMENT IN THE distance caught Ethan's eye. He turned south, spotting an opening in the forest that revealed a small, tranquil pool fed by a narrow creek. The shoreline was lush with cattails, their tall, slender stalks swaying gently in the breeze.

Intrigued, Ethan approached the water's edge, his boots sinking slightly into the damp soil. He knelt down and began to dig around the base of a particularly large cattail, carefully extracting its roots. Finn watched with curiosity as his father worked, his hands deftly separating the plant from the earth.

With the cattail in hand, Ethan returned to Finn's side, holding up the plant for his son to see. "Cattails are a versatile plant," he explained, his voice filled with the enthusiasm of a seasoned naturalist. "Nearly every part of it is edible, from the young shoots to the pollen."

Ethan began to clean the cattail, stripping away the outer layers to reveal the tender, white core. He handed a piece to Finn, who tentatively took a bite. The taste was mild and slightly nutty, with a texture reminiscent of cucumber.

"The roots are rich in starch," Ethan continued, "and can be boiled or roasted. In a survival situation, cattails can be a valuable source of food."

Finn nodded, impressed by his father's knowledge. He made a mental note to remember the location of the pool, should they ever need to return.

With their impromptu foraging lesson complete, Finn and Ethan returned to their path, heading west towards the hidden structure. The Glimmerstone pulsed steadily in Finn's pocket, its warmth a constant reminder of their mission.

As they neared their destination, the forest seemed to grow quieter, as if holding its breath in anticipation. Even Mystic, usually eager to explore every new scent and sound, stayed close to Finn's side, her ears pricked forward.

At last, they arrived at the hidden structure, its ancient stone walls covered in a thick blanket of moss and vines. Finn stepped forward, the Glimmerstone's pulsing growing stronger with each step. He could feel its energy resonating with the structure, as if the two were somehow connected.

With Mystic at his side, Finn led the way, his heart pounding with excitement and trepidation. Ethan followed close behind, his eyes scanning the surroundings for any signs of danger. Together, they entered the hidden structure, ready to face whatever mysteries lay within.

FINN INSERTED THE RUSTED key into the lock of the hidden compartment, his hands trembling slightly with anticipation. With a soft click, the lock yielded, and the door swung open, revealing the wooden box within. Finn carefully removed the box, its surface smooth and cool beneath his fingertips.

He carried the box over to the stone table, where Ethan stood waiting, his eyes alight with curiosity. Finn set the box down gently and produced the second key from his pocket. The key slid into the lock with ease, and with a turn, the box opened, revealing the Book of Tones nestled inside.

Finn lifted the book from its resting place, marveling at its weight and the intricate embossing on its leather cover. He placed it reverently on the table, running his fingers over the ancient symbols.

Ethan moved to stand beside his son, his gaze fixed on the tome before them. Together, they began to thumb through the pages, each one filled with strange script and detailed illustrations.

The pages were thick and slightly brittle with age, but the ink remained clear and vibrant. The script was unlike anything they had ever seen, a complex system of swirls and dots that seemed to dance across the page.

As they turned the pages, Finn and Ethan found themselves drawn into the book's mysteries. The illustrations depicted sprawling underground networks, intricate webs of fungi that seemed to pulse with life. There were drawings of plants and trees, their roots intertwined with the mycelium below.

Certain pages were marked with delicate ribbons, their colors faded but still distinct. Finn paused at one of these pages, his eyes widening as he took in the image before him. It was a detailed rendering of a truffle, its surface marbled with shades of white and brown.

Beside the illustration was a series of symbols, their meaning obscure. Finn traced his finger over the script, wondering what secrets it held.

Ethan leaned in closer, his brow furrowed in concentration. "I've never seen anything like this," he murmured, his voice filled with wonder. "It's like a whole new language."

Finn nodded, his mind racing with possibilities. He knew that the Book of Tones held the key to unlocking the secrets of Mycelium Haven, but deciphering its contents would be no easy task.

FINN PONDERED THE ENIGMATIC symbols and illustrations within the Book of Tones, a sudden thought struck him. He reached into his zippered pocket and retrieved the Glimmerstone, its surface warm and pulsing with energy.

The stone seemed to respond to Finn's touch, its vibrant burgundy hue intensifying as he held it aloft. Ethan watched, transfixed, as the stone's golden veins began to shimmer, casting a soft light across the ancient pages.

Finn's heart raced as he brought the Glimmerstone closer to the book, its warmth seeping into his fingers. As the light from the stone washed over the cryptic script, something extraordinary began to happen.

The symbols on the page started to shift and change, their lines and swirls rearranging themselves before Finn and Ethan's astonished eyes. Slowly, the incomprehensible text began to morph into something more familiar, the strange characters transforming into recognizable letters and words.

Finn's breath caught in his throat as he watched the metamorphosis unfold, the secrets of the Book of Tones revealing themselves with each passing second. Ethan leaned in closer, his eyes wide with wonder as the ancient language yielded to the power of the Glimmerstone.

As the transformation neared its completion, Finn and Ethan exchanged a look of pure astonishment. The book that had once seemed an impenetrable mystery now lay open before them, its contents accessible and ready to be explored.

With trembling hands, Finn set the Glimmerstone down on the table, its light still illuminating the pages. He and Ethan bent over the book, their eyes scanning the newly revealed text, eager to uncover the secrets that had been hidden for so long.

The air in the ancient structure seemed to hum with energy, the weight of the discovery hanging heavy in the air. Finn and Ethan knew that they stood on the precipice of something extraordinary, the key to unlocking the mysteries of Mycelium Haven now within their grasp.

FINN AND ETHAN TURNED to the first chapter of the Book of Tones, their eyes were drawn to the title: "The History of Mycelium Haven." The ancient pages seemed to whisper secrets of a long-forgotten past, inviting them to uncover the truth behind the legendary truffle paradise.

The chapter began with the origins of Mycelium Haven, revealing how ancient truffle hunters had first discovered this hidden gem deep within the heart of the forest. These intrepid explorers had stumbled upon a lush, secret grove where the earth was rich with the scent of truffles, and the trees seemed to hum with an otherworldly energy.

Finn's eyes widened as he read about the key figures who had played crucial roles in the preservation and growth of Mycelium Haven. These individuals, whose names were etched in history, had dedicated their lives to protecting the haven and nurturing its precious bounty. Some were skilled truffle hunters, while others were wise sages who understood the delicate balance of nature.

Ethan, his curiosity piqued, focused on the legends and myths surrounding Mycelium Haven. These stories, passed down through generations, blended fact and fiction, weaving together elements of fantasy and reality. Some spoke of guardian spirits that watched over the haven, while others told of magical creatures that roamed the forest, drawn to the power of the truffles.

As they read on, Finn and Ethan discovered tales of ancient rituals performed by the truffle hunters, ceremonies meant to honor the land and ensure a bountiful harvest. The descriptions were so vivid that they could almost hear the chanting of the hunters and smell the earthy aroma of the truffles.

The chapter also hinted at the existence of hidden paths and secret chambers within Mycelium Haven, known only to a select few. Finn's heart raced at the thought of uncovering these mysteries, his mind already conjuring images of what they might find.

Ethan, his brow furrowed in concentration, absorbed every word, marveling at the depth of knowledge contained within the pages. He knew that this was no ordinary book, but rather a key to unlocking the secrets of the forest and the true potential of Mycelium Haven.

Reaching the end of the chapter, Finn and Ethan exchanged a look of wonder and excitement. They knew that they held in their hands a treasure trove of information, a guide that could lead them deeper into the heart of the haven and closer to the truth behind its existence.

FINN AND ETHAN TURNED the page, their eyes fell upon the title of the next chapter: "Truffle Hunter's Guide." Finn's heart skipped a beat, knowing that this section held the key to becoming a master truffle hunter. Ethan, sensing his son's excitement, smiled and nodded, encouraging him to dive into the wealth of knowledge that lay before them.

The first section, "Truffle Identification," caught Finn's attention immediately. He marveled at the detailed descriptions and intricate illustrations of various truffle species, each one more fascinating than the last. The book showcased rare and valuable varieties, their shapes, colors, and textures so vividly depicted that Finn felt as if he could reach out and touch them.

Ethan, equally intrigued, pointed out a particularly rare specimen, the Mycelium Royale, which they had recently discovered. The illustration in the book matched their find perfectly, confirming the significance of their discovery.

Finn's eyes widened at the "Hunting Techniques" section. Here, the book revealed proven methods and strategies for locating and harvesting truffles. The author's words were like a gentle mentor, guiding Finn through the art of truffle hunting.

The book emphasized the importance of understanding the forest, reading the signs of nature, and working in harmony with the environment. Finn absorbed every word, committing the techniques to memory, eager to put them into practice on their next truffle hunting adventure.

Ethan, ever the pragmatist, focused on the "Seasonal Tips" section. He knew that timing was crucial in truffle hunting, and the book provided invaluable insights into the best times of the year to search for these elusive delicacies.

The chapter explained how different truffle species thrived in specific seasons, influenced by factors such as temperature, humidity, and rainfall. Ethan made mental notes, already planning future expeditions based on the information provided.

As they continued to thumb through the pages, Finn and Ethan found themselves lost in the world of truffle hunting. The book was more than just a guide; it was a treasure map, leading them to the hidden gems of the forest.

FINN AND ETHAN TURNED to the next section of the Book of Tones, they found themselves immersed in the "Botanical Compendium." The pages were filled with vivid illustrations and detailed descriptions of the diverse flora that thrived within the Mycelium Haven.

Ethan, with his background in biology, was immediately drawn to the "Medicinal Plants" subsection. He marveled at the extensive knowledge contained within the pages, detailing plants with healing properties and precise instructions on how to use them.

One plant in particular caught his eye—the Moonlight Moss. The book described its ability to soothe inflammation and promote rapid healing when applied as a poultice. Ethan carefully studied the illustration, committing the moss's distinct silver-green hue and delicate structure to memory.

Finn, on the other hand, found himself intrigued by the "Toxic Flora" portion of the compendium. The book warned of dangerous plants to avoid, providing clear identifying features to help navigate the forest safely.

The Crimson Nightshade, with its deep red berries and glossy leaves, was highlighted as a particularly lethal plant. The book cautioned that even a small amount of its juice could cause severe illness or worse. Finn made a mental note to steer clear of this plant during their future adventures.

As they delved further into the compendium, a section on "Magical Plants" caught their attention. The pages described rare flora with mystical properties and their potential uses.

The Whispering Willow, a tree with shimmering, silver-veined leaves, was said to enhance intuition and provide guidance to those who sought its wisdom. The book instructed readers to brew a tea from its leaves and sip it under the light of a full moon to unlock its magical potential.

Finn and Ethan exchanged a glance, their eyes sparkling with wonder and curiosity. The idea of magical plants added a new layer of enchantment to their quest for the Mycelium Haven.

They continued to explore the Botanical Compendium, Finn and Ethan found themselves not only gaining valuable knowledge but also developing a deeper appreciation for the incredible diversity and power of the flora that surrounded them.

FINN AND ETHAN CONTINUED reading the Book of Tones, they turned to a section titled "Maps and Navigation." The pages were filled with intricate maps and detailed navigational aids that promised to guide them through the mysteries of the Mycelium Haven.

The first subsection, "Annotated Maps," contained ancient maps that depicted hidden paths, significant landmarks, and key locations within the forest. The maps were adorned with intricate symbols and cryptic annotations, hinting at secrets waiting to be uncovered.

Finn's eyes widened as he traced his finger along a particularly detailed map, noticing a winding path that seemed to lead to a hidden grove deep within the forest. Ethan leaned in closer, studying the symbols and trying to decipher their meaning.

As they flipped through the pages, they discovered a section on "Star Charts." The book provided celestial navigation guides relevant to the region, showing how to orient oneself using the stars and constellations visible in the night sky above the Mycelium Haven.

Ethan, with his knowledge of astronomy, was fascinated by the star charts. He pointed out familiar constellations and explained to Finn how they could be used to determine direction and location when navigating the forest at night.

The final subsection, "Compass Techniques," caught Finn's attention. The book provided detailed instructions on using natural elements for navigation, such as the position of the sun, the growth of moss on trees, and the direction of prevailing winds.

Finn eagerly read through the techniques, committing them to memory. He knew that these skills would be invaluable during their explorations of the Mycelium Haven, especially if they found themselves in unfamiliar territory.

They studied the maps and navigational aids, Finn and Ethan felt a growing sense of excitement and anticipation. The Book of Tones was not only a source of knowledge but also a key to unlocking the secrets of the forest.

With each page they turned, they felt more equipped and prepared for the adventures that lay ahead. The maps and navigational techniques provided a sense of direction and purpose, guiding them towards their ultimate goal of discovering the true wonders of the Mycelium Haven.

FINN AND ETHAN CONTINUED their exploration of the Book of Tones, they turned to a section titled "Mystical Rituals and Spells." The pages were filled with ancient incantations, intricate diagrams, and detailed instructions for performing various rituals and spells.

Finn's eyes widened as he read the first subsection, "Protection Spells." The book described incantations and rituals designed to safeguard oneself or a companion from harm. One particular spell caught his attention—a ritual that involved drawing a protective circle using sacred herbs and reciting an ancient chant to create an invisible shield around the caster.

Ethan, intrigued by the next subsection, "Nature's Aid," carefully studied the rituals meant to summon the aid or goodwill of forest creatures. The book explained how to communicate with the spirits of the trees, how to request guidance from the wise old owls, and how to earn the trust of the woodland animals.

As they delved deeper into the section, Finn discovered a subsection titled "Unlocking Secrets." The spells within were thought to reveal hidden or concealed items or paths within the Mycelium Haven. One spell described how to use the Glimmerstone to illuminate invisible trails, while another explained how to decipher the language of the ancient trees to uncover long-forgotten secrets.

Finn and Ethan exchanged excited glances as they realized the potential of the rituals and spells. They knew that mastering these mystical arts could provide them with invaluable tools for their journey through the Mycelium Haven.

Ethan, ever the cautious one, reminded Finn that they should approach the rituals and spells with respect and caution. He emphasized the importance of understanding the consequences and responsibilities that came with wielding such power.

Finn nodded in agreement, his eyes still sparkling with excitement. He knew that the knowledge contained within the Book of Tones was not to be taken lightly. With great power came great responsibility, and he was determined to use the rituals and spells wisely.

They continued on to the section on mystical rituals and spells, Finn and Ethan felt a sense of awe and reverence. The ancient wisdom contained within the pages seemed to whisper secrets from a time long past, promising to guide them through the challenges that lay ahead in their quest to uncover the mysteries of the Mycelium Haven.

FINN AND ETHAN TURNED to the next section of the Book of Tones, their eyes widened with fascination. The title "Alchemical Recipes" glimmered on the ancient page, promising a world of mystical potions and elixirs.

Finn's fingers traced the intricate illustrations that adorned the pages, depicting various herbs, roots, and fungi. The recipes were divided into three categories: Healing Potions, Enhancement Elixirs, and Truffle Enhancers.

The Healing Potions section caught Ethan's attention. He carefully studied the recipes that utilized natural ingredients to heal various ailments. One potion, made from the essence of the Moonlight Moss and the nectar of the Whispering Willow, promised to mend broken bones and soothe painful wounds. Another, concocted from the petals of the Crimson Nightshade and the sap of the ancient oak, claimed to cure even the most severe illnesses.

Finn, on the other hand, was drawn to the Enhancement Elixirs. These mixtures were designed to temporarily heighten senses or physical abilities. One elixir, made from the crushed leaves of the Silverthorn plant and the powdered scales of a dragon's tail, promised to grant the drinker superhuman strength. Another, brewed from the essence of the Firefly Fungus and the pollen of the Ghostly Orchid, claimed to enhance one's vision, allowing them to see in complete darkness.

But it was the Truffle Enhancers that truly captured their imagination. These potions were said to attract truffles or enhance their growth in a specific area. One recipe called for the essence of the Mycelium Royale truffle, combined with the nectar of the Honeysuckle and the crushed leaves of the Truffle Oak. The book claimed that by sprinkling this potion on the roots of a tree, one could encourage the growth of the rarest and most valuable truffles.

Ethan and Finn exchanged excited glances, their minds racing with the possibilities. They knew that mastering the art of alchemy could provide them with invaluable tools for their journey through the Mycelium Haven. The healing potions could keep them safe from harm, the enhancement elixirs could give them an edge in their quest, and the truffle enhancers could lead them to the most elusive and sought-after truffles in the forest.

ETHAN AND FINN TURNED the page, they found themselves immersed in the section titled "Ancestral Wisdom." The ancient parchment seemed to hold a reverent air, as if the words themselves carried the weight of generations past.

The first part of the section was dedicated to "Proverbs and Sayings." Ethan's eyes were drawn to a particular adage: "The forest whispers to those who listen." He read it aloud, his voice barely above a whisper, and Finn nodded in agreement. They both understood the truth in those words, having experienced the forest's secrets firsthand.

Another saying caught Finn's attention: "A true hunter respects the balance of nature." It resonated with him deeply, reminding him of the responsibility that came with their quest for truffles. He silently vowed to always hunt with respect and gratitude for the forest's bounty.

As they delved deeper into the section, they encountered "Lessons Learned." These were accounts of past experiences and the wisdom gained from them. One story told of a young truffle hunter who got lost in the forest and was guided back to safety by a wise old oak tree. The lesson was clear: the forest itself could be a guide and protector to those who treated it with respect.

Another tale spoke of a hunter who became greedy and took more than he needed from the forest. As a result, the truffles disappeared, and the hunter was left with nothing. Ethan and Finn exchanged a meaningful glance, understanding the importance of balance and moderation in their own truffle hunting endeavors.

The final part of the section contained "Philosophical Insights." These were reflections on the interconnectedness of all life and the importance of harmony with nature. One passage spoke of the Mycelium Haven as a living, breathing entity, with the truffles as its heart and the trees as its lungs. It emphasized the delicate balance that existed within the haven and the role of the truffle hunters as guardians of that balance.

Another insight compared the journey of a truffle hunter to the growth of a tree. It spoke of the patience, perseverance, and resilience required to thrive in the face of challenges. Finn felt a sense of kinship with this passage, recognizing his own growth and the obstacles he had overcome in his quest for truffles.

As they finished reading the section, Ethan and Finn felt a renewed sense of purpose and connection to the ancient wisdom of the Mycelium Haven. They knew that by embracing these teachings, they could become not just skilled truffle hunters, but also true stewards of the forest and its secrets.

AS ETHAN AND FINN TURNED to the next section of the Book of Tones, their eyes widened with intrigue. The title "Secret Societies" seemed to leap off the page, promising a glimpse into a hidden world within the Mycelium Haven.

The first part of the section delved into the "Origins" of the secret society. Ethan read aloud about a group of ancient truffle hunters who had banded together to protect the haven from those who sought to exploit its bounty. These founding members were described as wise, courageous, and deeply attuned to the forest's rhythms.

Finn's attention was drawn to the "Current Members" section. It contained profiles of the present-day guardians of the Mycelium Haven. Each guardian was assigned a specific role, such as the "Keeper of the Spores," the "Whisperer of the Trees," and the "Guardian of the Glimmerstone." Finn couldn't help but wonder if he and his father might one day join their ranks.

As they delved deeper into the section, they discovered the "Rituals and Codes" that governed the secret society. Ethan marveled at the intricate ceremonies described, such as the "Rite of the Truffle Moon," where new members were initiated under the light of a full moon, their faces painted with the juice of a rare truffle.

The code of conduct was equally fascinating. It emphasized the importance of secrecy, loyalty, and respect for the forest. Members were sworn to protect the Mycelium Haven at all costs, even if it meant sacrificing their own lives. Finn felt a shiver run down his spine at the gravity of such a commitment.

Reading on, they learned about the society's hierarchical structure and the way knowledge was passed down from one generation to the next. Only the most trusted and proven members were granted access to the deepest secrets of the Mycelium Haven.

Ethan and Finn exchanged a glance, both feeling a mix of awe and trepidation. The existence of this secret society added a new layer of depth and mystery to their quest for truffles. They couldn't help but wonder if their own journey might somehow intersect with the path of these ancient guardians.

ETHAN AND FINN TURNED to the next section of the Book of Tones, their eyes fell upon the title "Environmental Stewardship." The words seemed to shimmer with a sense of purpose, beckoning them to delve into the wisdom contained within.

The first part of the section focused on "Sustainable Foraging." Ethan's eyes scanned the pages, absorbing the techniques for harvesting truffles without harming the delicate ecosystem of the Mycelium Haven. The book emphasized the importance of taking only what was needed and leaving the rest to flourish. Finn leaned in closer, eager to learn how to be a responsible truffle hunter.

As they turned the page, the section on "Conservation Efforts" caught their attention. The book detailed various projects and methods for protecting endangered species and habitats within the haven. Ethan's brow furrowed as he read about the rare Crimson-Capped Mushroom and the efforts to preserve its dwindling population. Finn's heart swelled with a newfound sense of responsibility to safeguard the forest's treasures.

The final part of the section was dedicated to "Educational Outreach." The book emphasized the importance of passing on the knowledge of environmental stewardship to future generations. It outlined programs designed to teach young people about the wonders of the Mycelium Haven and the role they could play in preserving it. Finn's mind raced with ideas for how he could share his own experiences and inspire others to care for the forest.

As they closed the book, Ethan and Finn sat in contemplative silence. The weight of the knowledge they had gained settled upon their shoulders, but it was a burden they were eager to bear. They knew that their quest for truffles was no longer just about personal gain; it was about being guardians of the Mycelium Haven and ensuring its survival for generations to come.

Ethan placed a hand on Finn's shoulder, a silent acknowledgment of the responsibility they now shared. Finn met his father's gaze, his eyes shining with determination. Together, they knew they would not only seek out the treasures of the forest but also protect them with every fiber of their being.

AS ETHAN AND FINN DELVED deeper into the Book of Tones, they turned to a section titled "Hidden Treasures and Artifacts." The pages seemed to crackle with anticipation, as if the book itself was eager to reveal its secrets.

The first part of the section focused on "Treasure Locations." Ethan's eyes widened as he scanned the pages, taking in the intricate maps and cryptic clues that promised to lead them to buried or hidden treasures within the Mycelium Haven. One map depicted a winding path through a dense grove of ancient oaks, with a peculiar symbol marking a spot at the base of a twisted tree. Finn leaned in closer, his finger tracing the path, already imagining the adventure that awaited them.

The next part of the section was dedicated to "Artifact Descriptions." The pages were filled with detailed accounts of ancient artifacts, each with its own rich history and significance. Ethan's gaze was drawn to an illustration of a golden amulet, adorned with intricate engravings of mushrooms and vines. The description spoke of its power to enhance the wearer's connection to the forest and guide them to the most bountiful truffle patches. Finn's eyes sparkled with wonder as he read about a carved wooden staff, said to have been wielded by the first guardian of the Mycelium Haven.

They turned to the final part of the section, "Unlocking Instructions," Ethan and Finn's excitement grew. The pages revealed a series of puzzles and codes that guarded the hidden treasures of the forest. One puzzle required the alignment of celestial bodies, while another spoke of a sequence of mushroom species that needed to be identified. Finn's mind raced with the possibilities, eager to put his knowledge and skills to the test.

Ethan and Finn looked at each other, their eyes filled with a shared sense of adventure and purpose. They knew that the treasures and artifacts described in the Book of Tones were not merely objects of value, but keys to unlocking the deeper mysteries of the Mycelium Haven. With the Glimmerstone pulsing gently in Finn's pocket, they felt a renewed sense of determination to uncover the secrets that lay hidden within the forest.

Chapter 11

E than and Finn stood inside the hidden structure, their eyes locked on the ancient map that Finn had discovered. The parchment crinkled beneath their fingers as they traced the intricate lines and symbols, searching for clues that might lead them to the legendary Mycelium Haven.

Finn's finger landed on a specific point on the map, tapping it with excitement. "Look, Dad! Map Grid K47. That's where we need to go."

Ethan leaned in closer, studying the area Finn had pointed out. He nodded, a smile tugging at the corners of his mouth. "You're right, Finn. If the Mycelium Haven is anywhere, it's got to be there."

They spread the map out on the stone table, the Glimmerstone's soft glow illuminating the worn parchment. Ethan retrieved his compass from his backpack and placed it on the map, aligning it with the cardinal directions.

"Okay, let's see," Ethan murmured, his brow furrowed in concentration. "To get from Map Grid M45 to K47, we need to head southwest." He traced a line with his finger, following the compass needle. "That's a heading of 225 degrees."

Finn's eyes sparkled with anticipation, the thrill of the impending adventure coursing through his veins. He carefully folded the map and tucked it into his backpack, ensuring its safety.

Before leaving, Finn took one last look around the hidden structure. He secured the wooden box containing the Book of Tones back in its compartment, making sure it was well-hidden. With a nod of satisfaction, he joined his father and Mystic at the entrance.

Ethan placed a hand on Finn's shoulder, a gesture of reassurance and pride. "Ready, Finn?"

Finn grinned, his eyes meeting his father's. "Ready as I'll ever be, Dad."

With Mystic leading the way, her tail wagging with excitement, the trio stepped out of the hidden structure and into the lush forest of Loblolly Springs. Finn pulled out his compass, double-checking their heading. The needle pointed southwest, guiding them towards Map Grid K47 and the secrets that awaited them.

As they walked, the forest seemed to whisper to them, the leaves rustling in anticipation. The Glimmerstone pulsed gently in Finn's pocket, as if sensing the importance of their journey. Ethan, Finn, and Mystic strode forward, their hearts filled with determination and the promise of discovery.

ETHAN AND FINN TREKKED through the lush forest of Loblolly Springs, their progress was steady but measured. The terrain beneath their feet shifted from soft, loamy soil to rocky outcroppings, challenging their pace. Mystic, their faithful companion, navigated the undergrowth with ease, her keen senses guiding them through the dense foliage.

The canopy above them was a tapestry of green, with shafts of sunlight filtering through the leaves, casting dappled shadows on the forest floor. Towering oaks and hickories stood as silent sentinels, their branches reaching skyward. The air was filled with the gentle rustling of leaves and the distant chirping of birds.

As they ventured deeper into the forest, the landscape began to change. The undergrowth grew thicker, with tangles of wild blackberry bushes and clusters of delicate ferns. Ethan pointed out the distinctive leaves of a sassafras tree, explaining its medicinal properties to an attentive Finn.

Wildlife stirred around them, their presence marked by fleeting glimpses and soft rustles in the brush. A whitetail deer bounded across their path, its tawny coat flashing in the dappled light. Finn's eyes widened in wonder as a pileated woodpecker hammered away at a decaying tree trunk, its crimson crest a splash of color amidst the green.

Consulting their map, Ethan determined that they had covered approximately half a mile, placing them in Map Grid N46. The terrain here was a mix of gentle slopes and rocky outcrops, with occasional clearings that offered a momentary respite from the dense foliage.

As they paused to catch their breath, Finn's gaze was drawn to a patch of vibrant wildflowers, their delicate petals a riot of color against the forest floor. He knelt down, marveling at the intricate details of a ladyslipper orchid, its pink and white blooms a testament to nature's artistry.

Ethan, ever the knowledgeable guide, identified a stand of shagbark hickory trees, their distinctive bark peeling away in long, narrow strips. He shared with Finn the importance of these trees to the forest ecosystem, providing food and shelter for countless creatures.

The terrain of Map Grid N46 presented a tapestry of challenges for Ethan and Finn as they navigated the ever-shifting landscape of Loblolly Springs. The forest seemed to test their resolve at every turn, with obstacles both natural and unexpected.

They were now in a particularly dense section of the forest, the ground suddenly fell away, revealing a steep ravine that plunged into shadowy depths. The chasm stretched before them, a seemingly impassable barrier in their path. Ethan and Finn exchanged a look of concern, their eyes searching for a way across.

It was Finn who spotted the fallen tree, its trunk spanning the width of the ravine like a makeshift bridge. The ancient oak had succumbed to the forces of nature, its once-mighty form now serving as a precarious pathway to the other side.

Finn approached the fallen tree with caution, testing its stability with a tentative foot. The trunk held firm, offering a glimmer of hope. With a deep breath, Finn began to traverse the narrow bridge, his arms outstretched for balance.

Each step was a calculated risk, a dance between courage and caution. Finn's heart raced as he navigated the uneven surface, the ravine yawning beneath him. Mystic followed close behind, her paws finding purchase on the rough bark.

Finn's voice was a soothing presence, guiding Mystic paw by paw across the fallen tree. The dog's trust in her human companion was unwavering, a bond forged through countless adventures.

Ethan watched with bated breath as Finn and Mystic made their way across the ravine. The weight of responsibility hung heavy on his shoulders, a reminder of the dangers that lurked in the forest. When it was his turn to cross, Ethan's steps were measured and deliberate, a testament to his experience and wisdom.

With the ravine behind them, Ethan and Finn pressed onward, their determination renewed by the successful crossing. However, the forest had more trials in store.

As they ventured deeper into Map Grid N46, the undergrowth grew denser, the foliage more unforgiving. Thorny blackberry bushes rose up before them, their tangled branches forming a formidable barrier.

The thorns tore at their clothes, leaving small scratches on exposed skin. Ethan and Finn exchanged a knowing look, recognizing the need for patience and meticulous planning to navigate the thicket.

With each step, Ethan and Finn felt a growing sense of anticipation, the Glimmerstone pulsing gently in Finn's pocket. The secrets of the Mycelium Haven lay ahead, waiting to be discovered. As they pressed onward, the forest seemed to whisper its encouragement, urging them forward on their quest for knowledge and adventure.

ETHAN AND FINN CONTINUED their journey through the Loblolly Springs forest, the terrain began to evolve once more. The gentle slopes and rocky outcrops of Map Grid N46 gradually gave way to a more level landscape, punctuated by the occasional gurgling stream.

Consulting their map, Ethan determined that they had traveled approximately half a mile past N46, placing them squarely in Map Grid M45. The forest here was characterized by its lush undergrowth, with dense thickets of rhododendron and mountain laurel flanking their path.

Finn's keen eyes spotted a flash of movement in the brush, and he pointed excitedly as a red fox darted across their trail. Its russet coat gleamed in the dappled sunlight, and Mystic's ears perked up at the sight, her tail wagging with curiosity.

As they pressed onward, the sound of running water grew louder, and they soon found themselves on the banks of a small creek. The water was crystal clear, its surface broken by the occasional ripple as a brook trout darted beneath the surface.

Ethan knelt down, cupping his hands to bring the cool, refreshing water to his lips. He pointed out a cluster of cattails growing along the water's edge, explaining to Finn that the roots and young shoots were edible, a valuable source of sustenance for those who knew where to look.

The forest floor was a tapestry of green, with patches of sphagnum moss and delicate ferns covering the rich, loamy soil. Finn's gaze was drawn to a cluster of chanterelle mushrooms, their golden caps a bright contrast against the earthy hues of the forest floor.

As they continued their trek, the trees began to thin, revealing a small clearing. The sun's rays bathed the area in a warm, golden light, and a gentle breeze carried the sweet scent of honeysuckle. Finn closed his eyes for a moment, savoring the tranquility of the scene.

Ethan consulted the map once more, tracing their route with his finger. "We're making good time," he said, a note of satisfaction in his voice. "If we keep this pace, we should reach the heart of Map Grid M45 within the next half hour."

Finn nodded, his eyes sparkling with anticipation. The Glimmerstone pulsed gently in his pocket, as if in response to his growing excitement. With Mystic leading the way, they set off once more, the secrets of the Mycelium Haven drawing ever closer.

AS ETHAN AND FINN TRAVERSED the lush landscape of Map Grid M45, their destination—the legendary Mycelium Haven—loomed ever closer. The forest around them was alive with the sounds of nature, a symphony of birdsong and the rustling of leaves in the gentle breeze.

Finn, his brow furrowed in concentration, suddenly came to a halt. He reached into his pocket, pulling out the worn map that had guided their journey thus far. Ethan paused beside him, watching as his son carefully unfolded the parchment.

"Let's double-check our route," Finn said, his eyes scanning the intricate lines and symbols. "We want to make sure we're on the right path to Map Grid K47."

Ethan nodded, peering over Finn's shoulder at the map. Together, they traced their progress, comparing the landmarks they had passed with those depicted on the parchment. The Glimmerstone pulsed gently in Finn's pocket, as if offering its own guidance.

Finn's finger came to rest on a small clearing marked on the map, a landmark they had passed mere minutes ago. "We're here," he said, tapping the spot. "And if we continue southwest, we should reach the edge of Map Grid K47 within the next mile or so."

Ethan smiled, pride evident in his eyes. "Good navigating, son," he said, clapping Finn on the shoulder. "Let's check the compass to make sure we're staying on course."

Finn reached into his pack, pulling out the compass he had purchased with the proceeds from his truffle sales. The instrument gleamed in the dappled sunlight, its needle pointing steadily southwest.

"Looks like we're right on track," Finn said, holding the compass up for his father to see. "If we keep following this bearing, we should be at the doorstep of the Mycelium Haven in no time."

Ethan grinned, his own excitement mirroring that of his son. "Then let's not waste any more time," he said, adjusting his pack on his shoulders. "The secrets of the haven await."

With renewed determination, Finn folded the map, tucking it carefully back into his pocket. Mystic, who had been patiently waiting beside them, let out a soft bark, as if urging them onward.

Together, the trio set off once more, their footsteps carrying them ever closer to the heart of the Mycelium Haven. The forest seemed to whisper its encouragement, the Glimmerstone pulsing in time with their heartbeats as they ventured deeper into the unknown.

AS ETHAN, FINN, AND Mystic ventured deeper into the heart of Loblolly Springs forest, the landscape began to shift and change around them. Leaving behind the lush vegetation of Map Grid M45, they crossed an invisible boundary into the uncharted territory of Map Grid N46.

The terrain here was a mix of gentle slopes and rocky outcrops, with occasional clearings that offered a momentary respite from the dense foliage. The trees grew taller and more ancient, their gnarled trunks and sprawling canopies hinting at the secrets they had witnessed over the centuries.

Finn paused to consult the map once more, the Glimmerstone pulsing gently in his pocket as if guiding their way. "We're in Map Grid N46 now," he said, tracing their route with his finger. "The haven should be just a few more miles to the southwest."

Ethan nodded, his eyes scanning the surrounding forest with a mixture of wonder and caution. "Stay alert," he said, his voice low. "We don't know what kind of creatures or challenges we might encounter as we get closer to the Mycelium Haven."

As if on cue, a rustling in the underbrush caught their attention. Mystic's ears perked up, her body tensing as she stared intently into the foliage. But the sound faded as quickly as it had come, leaving them once again in the quiet stillness of the forest.

They pressed on, the ground beneath their feet becoming softer and more spongy with each step. The air grew heavy with the scent of damp earth and decaying leaves, a testament to the rich, fertile soil that nourished the forest's abundance.

Finn's eyes widened as they entered a particularly dense patch of undergrowth, the vines and creepers twisting and twining around the trees like a living tapestry. He reached out to touch a delicate, purple flower that bloomed amidst the greenery, marveling at its beauty.

"Careful," Ethan warned, gently pulling Finn's hand away. "Some of these plants can be poisonous. It's best not to touch anything unless we're sure it's safe."

Finn nodded, chastened but still filled with a sense of wonder at the forest's myriad mysteries. As they continued their journey, the Glimmerstone pulsed more insistently, as if urging them forward towards their ultimate goal.

With each step, they drew closer to the secrets of the Mycelium Haven, the ancient forest guiding their way like a silent, watchful guardian.

ETHAN, FINN, AND MYSTIC were now at Map Grid N46, the landscape changing, it was taking on an ancient and lush appearance. The trees grew to colossal sizes, their trunks wide and their canopies stretching high into the sky, filtering the sunlight into a soft, emerald glow.

The forest floor became pristine, as if untouched by the passage of time. The usual debris of fallen leaves and twigs was replaced by a carpet of soft, verdant moss in some areas, while other patches were blanketed with a light layer of golden leaves. The air hummed with the vibrant energy of life, and the rich scent of earth and wildflowers filled their nostrils.

The abundance of wildlife became increasingly apparent. Squirrels darted between the trees, their bushy tails flicking as they leaped from branch to branch. A herd of deer emerged from the foliage, their gentle eyes watching the trio curiously before bounding away into the depths of the forest.

The undergrowth was a kaleidoscope of color, with enormous wildflowers blooming in shades of purple, yellow, and white. Their petals seemed to dance in the gentle breeze, attracting a myriad of pollinators. Honeybees buzzed from flower to flower, their legs laden with golden pollen, while hummingbirds hovered in midair, their iridescent feathers glinting in the sunlight.

Finn marveled at the beauty surrounding them, his eyes wide with wonder. "It's like we've stepped into another world," he breathed, his voice hushed with reverence.

Ethan nodded, a smile playing at the corners of his mouth. "The closer we get to the Mycelium Haven, the more the forest seems to come alive. It's as if it's welcoming us, guiding us to our destination."

Mystic, too, seemed enchanted by the forest's magic. Her tail wagged with excitement as she sniffed at the wildflowers, her nose twitching with curiosity.

They continued their journey towards Map Grid K47, the Glimmerstone pulsed with increasing intensity, its warm glow seeming to resonate with the very heartbeat of the forest. With each step, they drew closer to the secrets of the Mycelium Haven, the ancient trees and vibrant wildlife bearing witness to their quest.

A FLICKER OF DOUBT crossed Finn's mind. He turned to his father, his brow furrowed with concern. "What are the odds of us being right, maybe this is the wrong direction, we have been walking for quite a while now," he said, his voice tinged with uncertainty.

Ethan, ever the optimist, smiled reassuringly at his son. "Only one way to find out, keep going," he said, his tone filled with determination and a hint of excitement.

Finn nodded, his resolve strengthened by his father's unwavering confidence. With Mystic leading the way, her tail wagging with enthusiasm, the trio pressed onward, their footsteps muffled by the soft, mossy ground.

As they continued their journey, the landscape began to shift, transforming into something almost otherworldly. The trees grew taller, their trunks thicker and more gnarled, their branches intertwining to create a canopy that filtered the sunlight into a soft, ethereal glow. The air became thick with the scent of rich, loamy soil and the sweet perfume of exotic flowers.

Finn's eyes widened as he took in the breathtaking beauty that surrounded them. The forest floor was carpeted with a vibrant array of wildflowers, their petals shimmering in hues of amethyst, sapphire, and emerald. Delicate ferns unfurled their fronds, their leaves a lush, vivid green that seemed to pulse with life.

The fauna, too, seemed to have undergone a transformation. Butterflies with wings of iridescent gold and silver fluttered through the air, their flight patterns intricate and mesmerizing. Birds with plumage of the most brilliant colors perched on the branches, their melodic songs filling the air with an enchanting symphony.

Ethan and Finn exchanged a look of awe, their hearts racing with anticipation. Could this be the edge of the Mycelium Haven? The very thought sent a thrill down their spines, and they quickened their pace, eager to uncover the secrets that lay ahead.

The Glimmerstone in Finn's pocket pulsed with an intensity they had never felt before, its warmth spreading through his body like a gentle, guiding force. The forest seemed to whisper to them, beckoning them forward, inviting them to discover the wonders that awaited them in the heart of the Mycelium Haven.

THE FOG GREW THICKER, enveloping them in a ghostly embrace. The dense mist swirled around their feet, obscuring the path ahead and making navigation increasingly difficult.

Finn paused, his brow furrowed as he studied the map in his hands. According to their calculations, they should be in the vicinity of map grid K47, where the legendary Mycelium Haven was rumored to be hidden. However, the landscape before them showed no signs of the truffle-rich paradise they sought.

Ethan placed a reassuring hand on his son's shoulder. "We must be close," he said, his voice filled with determination. "The Book of Tones mentioned cryptic puzzles and clues that would guide us to the haven. Perhaps we need to look beyond the obvious."

Finn nodded, his mind racing as he recalled the ancient symbols and rituals described in the book. He wished they had brought the tome with them, but it was safely stored in the hidden structure they had discovered earlier.

They pressed on, Mystic suddenly stopped, her nose twitching as she caught a scent on the breeze. She let out a low growl, her body tense and alert. Finn and Ethan exchanged a wary glance, their hands instinctively reaching for the Glimmerstone in Finn's pocket.

The stone pulsed with a soft, comforting warmth, its light piercing through the fog like a beacon. Finn held it aloft, the burgundy and gold veins shimmering in the diffused light. As he did so, a strange pattern emerged on the forest floor, a series of interlocking circles and symbols that seemed to dance in the mist.

Ethan's eyes widened in recognition. "Those symbols," he whispered, his voice filled with awe. "They were in the Book of Tones, remember? They were part of a ritual to reveal hidden paths."

Finn's heart raced with excitement as he knelt down, tracing the symbols with his fingertips. As he did so, the Glimmerstone began to vibrate, its light growing brighter and more intense. Suddenly, the fog parted, revealing a narrow, winding path that had been hidden from view.

Mystic barked excitedly, her tail wagging as she bounded forward, eager to explore the newly revealed trail. Finn and Ethan followed close behind, their hearts filled with anticipation and wonder.

The forest around them seemed to come alive, the trees whispering ancient secrets and the earth thrumming with a deep, primal energy. They knew they were close to uncovering the mysteries of the Mycelium Haven, and with each step, their resolve grew stronger.

Chapter 12

Nearing the Haven
Finn, Ethan, and Mystic rested in a small clearing, the tranquility of the forest was shattered by the unmistakable sounds of people approaching through the dense foliage. Mystic's ears perked up, and a low growl rumbled in her throat, alerting her companions to the potential danger.

Finn crept towards the edge of the clearing, peering through the bushes to investigate the source of the disturbance. His eyes widened as he caught sight of a group of rough-looking men carrying rifles, their appearance and demeanor leaving no doubt that they were poachers, likely seeking to exploit the forest's resources for their own gain.

The poachers moved with purpose, their course set directly towards the clearing where Finn, Ethan, and Mystic had taken refuge. Finn's heart raced as he realized the imminent threat, his mind scrambling to formulate a plan of action.

Suddenly, the Glimmerstone nestled within Finn's pouch began to glow, its burgundy and gold veins pulsing with an otherworldly light. A warm, comforting energy emanated from the stone, enveloping Finn, Ethan, and Mystic in a protective aura. The air around them shimmered, as if a veil of invisibility had been draped over their forms.

The poachers drew closer, their heavy footsteps crunching against the forest floor. As they neared the clearing, they paused, confusion etched upon their faces as they scanned the area. It was as if an unseen force had obscured Finn, Ethan, and Mystic from their sight, rendering them invisible to the untrained eye.

Finn held his breath, his hand instinctively reaching for the Glimmerstone, feeling its reassuring warmth against his palm. He realized, with a surge of relief and awe, that the ancient artifact was shielding them from detection, its power cloaking their presence from the poachers' gaze.

THE POACHERS DISAPPEARED into the dense foliage, Finn, Ethan, and Mystic emerged from their concealed position, the Glimmerstone's protective aura fading as the immediate danger passed. The small clearing where they had intended to set up camp for the night now felt exposed and vulnerable, the tranquility shattered by the unwelcome intrusion.

Ethan, his brow furrowed with concern, turned to Finn. "We should find another spot to camp," he suggested, his voice low and cautious. "The poachers could return, and it's best we put some distance between us and this place."

Finn nodded in agreement, his hand instinctively reaching for the Glimmerstone in his pocket, its reassuring presence a reminder of the extraordinary powers at play in the forest. With Mystic at their side, the trio set off in search of a more secluded location, their senses heightened and their steps careful to avoid leaving any discernible tracks.

After a short trek through the dense underbrush, they stumbled upon a small, hidden glade, its perimeter sheltered by towering trees and thick, tangled vines. The soft, mossy ground and the gentle babbling of a nearby stream made it an ideal spot for their camp, offering both comfort and concealment.

Ethan wasted no time in setting up the tent, his practiced hands working efficiently to secure the shelter against the forest floor. Meanwhile, Finn busied himself with the task of digging a Dakota fire pit, his trowel carving deep into the earth to ensure that the flames would remain hidden from prying eyes.

Ethan's mind turned to the evening meal, it was best to conserve the food they had, especially when wild eatables were abundant. "Finn," he called out, his voice carrying across the glade, "let's gather some wild eatables to add to our dinner tonight. The forest provides for those who know where to look."

Finn looked up from his work, a smile spreading across his face at the prospect of foraging for their supper. With the Glimmerstone securely in his pocket and Mystic at his side, he felt a renewed sense of purpose and connection to the ancient wisdom of the forest.

THE CRISP MORNING AIR filled the dense Arkansas forest with an earthy scent, and the sun casting a golden hue through the canopy of leaves. Finn, Ethan, and Mystic's campsite nestled in a small clearing surrounded by towering trees, their tent set up near a babbling brook. A small campfire crackled with the remnants of their breakfast preparations.

Finn, excited and eager to start the day, checked his backpack, ensuring he had all the necessary tools for foraging: a field guide to wild edibles, a small trowel, a knife, and a collection bag. His father Ethan, a seasoned wildlife biologist, gave him last-minute tips on identifying safe plants.

"Remember, Finn," Ethan said, his voice carrying the wisdom of experience, "always cross-reference with the field guide and avoid anything unfamiliar. When in doubt, leave it out."

Finn nodded, absorbing his father's advice like a sponge. He knew the importance of caution when foraging in the wild.

Mystic, alert and ready, stood by their side, her nose twitching as she picked up various scents. She sensed the excitement in the air and was eager to join the adventure, her tail wagging in anticipation.

FINN, ETHAN, AND MYSTIC set out from their campsite, they followed a narrow trail that wound through the dense Arkansas forest. The path, lined with a carpet of fallen leaves, created a soft, rustling sound with each step they took. Finn, armed with his backpack full of foraging tools and the invaluable field guide, walked alongside his father, absorbing the tranquility of the surroundings.

The forest was alive with the sounds of nature. Birds chirped overhead, their melodies echoing through the canopy of leaves. The occasional rustle of foliage indicated the presence of small animals, scurrying about their daily routines. Squirrels darted from tree to tree, their bushy tails flicking as they moved, while a gentle breeze carried the distant call of a woodpecker.

The air was cool and invigorating, perfect for a day of foraging. It filled their lungs with the scent of pine and damp earth, refreshing their senses and invigorating their spirits. The morning dew clung to the leaves, glistening in the filtered sunlight that peeked through the branches.

Ethan, with his keen eye and wealth of knowledge, scanned the forest floor and the surrounding vegetation. He pointed out various plants and mushrooms, sharing tidbits of information with Finn. "See that cluster of mushrooms near the base of the oak tree?" Ethan asked, gesturing towards a group of tan-colored fungi. "Those are honey mushrooms, edible but easily confused with poisonous look-alikes."

Finn nodded, making a mental note of the mushrooms' appearance and location. He pulled out his field guide, flipping through the pages to find the corresponding entry. The book provided detailed descriptions and illustrations, aiding him in the identification process.

Mystic, ever the curious companion, trotted ahead of them, her nose to the ground as she explored the new scents. Her golden fur contrasted against the rich greens and browns of the forest, making her easy to spot. Every so often, she would pause and look back at Finn and Ethan, as if to ensure they were still following.

The trail became narrower, and the vegetation grew denser. The air hummed with the energy of life, and Finn felt a deep connection to the wilderness around him. With each step, he grew more excited about the foraging adventure that lay ahead, eager to discover the hidden treasures of the forest.

FINN, ETHAN, AND MYSTIC continued their foraging adventure, they came across a small pond nestled amidst the trees. The edges of the pond were lined with tall, slender stalks of cattails, their brown, cylindrical heads swaying gently in the breeze. Finn's eyes lit up with recognition as he approached the water's edge.

"Look, Mystic," Finn said, pointing to the cattails. "These are cattails, and they're edible!"

Mystic tilted her head, watching curiously as Finn carefully cut a few shoots with his foraging knife. Ethan joined them, nodding approvingly at Finn's find.

"Great spot, Finn," Ethan said. "Cattails are versatile plants. The roots, shoots, and even the pollen can be used in various dishes."

Finn examined the cattail shoots, explaining to Mystic the different parts of the plant that could be harvested. Ethan, ever mindful of the environment, reminded Finn of the importance of sustainable foraging.

"Remember, we only take what we need," Ethan said. "Leaving enough for the ecosystem to thrive is crucial."

Finn nodded, carefully placing the cattail shoots in his backpack. As they moved on, the forest canopy opened up, allowing sunlight to filter through and illuminate a sunny patch. There, a thicket of wild blackberry bushes thrived, their branches heavy with plump, dark berries.

Mystic's nose twitched as she caught the scent of the ripe fruit. Finn and Ethan approached the bushes, their mouths watering at the sight of the juicy berries. They carefully picked the ripest ones, their fingers stained with the sweet juice.

"Blackberries are not only delicious but also packed with nutrients," Ethan said, popping a berry into his mouth. "They're rich in antioxidants and vitamins."

Finn savored the burst of flavor as he bit into a berry, imagining the various recipes they could create with their harvest. Mystic watched curiously, occasionally sniffing at the berries, her tail wagging with interest.

They entered a grassy clearing dotted with bright yellow dandelions. Finn knelt down, his fingers gently plucking the tender leaves and flowers.

"You know, Mystic," Finn said, holding up a dandelion leaf, "many people consider dandelions as weeds, but they're actually valuable wild edibles."

Ethan nodded, a smile playing on his lips. "Dandelions have a long history of medicinal use," he said. "In fact, during World War II, dandelion roots were used as a coffee substitute when regular coffee was scarce."

Finn's eyes widened with interest, fascinated by the historical tidbit. He carefully gathered a handful of dandelion leaves and flowers, adding them to his growing collection of wild edibles.

FINN, ETHAN, AND MYSTIC decided to take a well-deserved break. They found a shaded area with a fallen log, its weathered surface providing a perfect seat amidst the tranquil surroundings.

Finn unslung his backpack and rummaged through its contents, his hand emerging with a water bottle. He unscrewed the cap and took a long, refreshing sip, the cool liquid soothing his throat. Mystic, her tongue lolling, looked up at Finn with hopeful eyes.

"Here you go, girl," Finn said, pouring some water into his cupped hand. Mystic lapped it up eagerly, her tail wagging in appreciation.

Ethan took a deep breath, inhaling the earthy scent of the forest. He turned to Finn, a thoughtful expression on his face.

"You know, Finn," Ethan began, "moments like these remind me of the importance of understanding and respecting nature."

Finn nodded, his eyes scanning the vibrant greenery around them. "It's amazing how everything in the forest is connected," he said, "like a big, intricate puzzle."

Ethan smiled, pride shining in his eyes. "Exactly. As a wildlife biologist, I've learned that every living thing has its role to play in the ecosystem. From the tiniest insect to the mightiest oak, each element is crucial to maintaining balance."

Finn listened intently, absorbing his father's words. "It's like the forest is one big family," he mused, "all working together to thrive."

"That's a beautiful way to put it," Ethan said, patting Finn's shoulder. "And it's our responsibility to be mindful of our impact on this family. We must tread lightly, take only what we need, and give back whenever we can."

Mystic lay contentedly at their feet, her golden fur illuminated with the sunlight filtering through the leaves. Her eyes were half-closed, a picture of serenity as she enjoyed the peaceful moment alongside her human companions.

Finn reached down and stroked Mystic's soft ears, feeling a deep sense of connection to the forest and all its inhabitants. With his father's wisdom and Mystic's loyal presence, he felt empowered to be a responsible steward of the natural world.

AFTER THEIR MOMENT of reflection, Finn and Ethan continued their foraging journey, with Mystic trotting happily alongside them. As they ventured deeper into the forest, they came across an old oak tree, its trunk gnarled and twisted with age.

Finn's keen eyes spotted a cluster of mushrooms growing at the base of the tree. He crouched down, carefully examining the fungi. Pulling out his field guide, he flipped through the pages, comparing the illustrations to the specimens before him.

"These look like chanterelles," Finn said, his voice tinged with excitement. "The guide says they're safe to eat, but we have to be careful. There are poisonous look-alikes."

Mystic sniffed at the mushrooms, her nose twitching with curiosity. Finn gently patted her head, "Remember, girl, not all mushrooms are good for you. We have to know which ones are safe."

Ethan knelt beside Finn, nodding approvingly. "You're right, son. When foraging for mushrooms, it's crucial to look for key characteristics." He pointed to the mushrooms' distinctive features, "See the wavy cap and the ridged underside? Those are telltale signs of chanterelles."

Finn carefully harvested a few of the mushrooms, placing them in his basket. They continued their walk, the sound of a nearby stream guiding their steps. As they approached the water's edge, a splash of color caught Finn's eye.

In a shaded area near the stream, a patch of delicate violets bloomed, their purple petals a vibrant contrast to the lush green foliage. Finn bent down, gently plucking a few of the flowers.

"I remember reading that violets are edible," Finn said, holding the flowers up to the dappled sunlight. "They can be used in salads or as a pretty garnish."

Ethan smiled, his eyes warm with admiration for his son's growing knowledge. "Violets have a long history of use in herbal medicine, too," he added. "They're rich in vitamins and antioxidants, making them a nutritious addition to our wild diet."

Finn carefully tucked the violets into his basket, marveling at the diverse bounty the forest had to offer. With Mystic by their side, Finn and Ethan continued their foraging adventure, their hearts filled with gratitude for the wilderness and the knowledge they shared.

AS THE SUN BEGAN ITS descent, Finn, Ethan, and Mystic retraced their steps back to their campsite. The trio walked in comfortable silence, each lost in their own thoughts about the day's foraging adventures.

Finn's heart swelled with a sense of accomplishment. He had learned so much from his father, absorbing the wisdom Ethan shared about the plants and fungi they encountered. The weight of his basket, filled with a diverse array of wild edibles, served as a tangible reminder of his growing knowledge and skills.

Ethan glanced at his son, a proud smile playing on his lips. "You did an excellent job today, Finn," he said, his voice warm with praise. "Your keen eye and careful attention to detail really shone through. You're becoming quite the forager."

Finn grinned, basking in his father's approval. "Thanks, Dad. I couldn't have done it without your guidance. You've taught me so much about the forest and its bounty."

Mystic trotted happily beside them, her golden fur catching the dappled sunlight. Her tail wagged in a steady rhythm, as if she, too, could sense the satisfaction and camaraderie that flowed between her human companions. The loyal dog had been a constant presence throughout their foraging journey, her keen senses and unwavering companionship adding an extra layer of comfort and security.

Finn's mind wandered to the future, imagining the delicious meals they could create with their foraged ingredients. He pictured himself and Ethan, working side by side in the kitchen, transforming the wild plants and mushrooms into nourishing dishes that celebrated the flavors of the forest.

The path wound through the trees, the sound of their footsteps mingling with the gentle rustling of leaves overhead. The air was filled with the earthy scent of the forest floor, a reminder of the rich ecosystem that surrounded them.

Ethan paused, his hand resting on the trunk of a large oak tree. "You know, Finn," he said, his voice taking on a reflective tone, "foraging is about more than just gathering food. It's a way of connecting with the land, of understanding the intricate web of life that exists all around us."

Finn nodded, his eyes shining with understanding. "I can feel it, Dad. When we're out here, it's like we're part of something bigger, something ancient and powerful."

FINN, ETHAN, AND MYSTIC arrived back at their campsite, the warm glow of the setting sun painted the sky in a breathtaking array of oranges and pinks. The trio, invigorated by their successful foraging expedition, eagerly set about preparing a meal that would showcase the bounty of the forest.

Ethan, with his years of experience in the wilderness, took the lead in the cooking process. He guided Finn in sorting through their foraged finds, selecting the best ingredients for their dinner. Together, they carefully washed the dandelion greens and violets, creating a vibrant and nutritious salad that celebrated the flavors of the wild.

Finn, eager to contribute, took charge of the blackberry compote. He gently simmered the ripe berries with a touch of water and a sprinkle of sugar, allowing their natural sweetness to intensify. The aroma of the bubbling compote filled the campsite, mingling with the earthy scent of the forest.

Meanwhile, Ethan skillfully sautéed the chanterelle mushrooms in a pan over the campfire. The golden mushrooms sizzled and released their rich, nutty aroma, promising a delectable addition to their meal. Finn watched intently, absorbing his father's techniques and committing them to memory.

As the cooking process neared completion, Finn turned his attention to Mystic. The loyal dog had been a constant companion throughout their foraging journey, and Finn wanted to show his appreciation. He rummaged through his backpack and retrieved a special treat he had packed just for her. Mystic's eyes lit up as Finn presented the reward, her tail wagging in anticipation.

With their meal prepared and Mystic happily munching on her treat, Finn and Ethan settled around the campfire. The flickering flames cast a warm, comforting glow over their faces as they savored the fruits of their labor. The instant soup, enhanced by the wild edibles they had gathered, took on a new depth of flavor, each spoonful a testament to the abundance of the forest.

As they ate, Finn and Ethan engaged in a heartfelt conversation, reflecting on the day's adventures and the importance of the knowledge they had gained. Ethan shared stories of his own foraging experiences, imparting wisdom and inspiration to his son. Finn listened intently, his heart swelling with a newfound appreciation for the natural world and the skills his father had passed down to him.

Mystic, her belly full and her spirit content, lay by the fire, her eyes reflecting the dancing flames. Her presence added to the sense of companionship and unity that permeated the campsite, a reminder of the unbreakable bond between the trio.

THE FOREST OF LOBLOLLY Springs settled into a peaceful twilight, and the campfire crackled softly, its warm glow casting flickering shadows across the faces of Finn, Ethan, and their loyal dog, Mystic. The sounds of the day faded, replaced by the gentle chirping of crickets and the distant hooting of an owl, signaling the arrival of the forest's nocturnal inhabitants.

Finn sat quietly, his eyes filled with a newfound appreciation for the wilderness that surrounded him. The day's foraging expedition had been more than just a search for sustenance; it had been a journey of discovery, a chance to deepen his connection with the natural world. He reflected on the knowledge his father had shared, the wisdom passed down through generations, and felt a profound sense of gratitude for the opportunity to learn and grow in the heart of the forest.

Ethan watched his son with a mixture of pride and contentment. He had witnessed Finn's transformation throughout their adventure, seeing him evolve from a curious young man to a skilled and respectful forager. Ethan's heart swelled with the knowledge that he had played a role in nurturing Finn's love for nature, guiding him on a path of understanding and harmony with the wilderness.

Mystic, ever the faithful companion, lay curled up beside them, her golden fur illuminated by the campfire's glow. She had been an integral part of their journey, a silent guardian and a symbol of the unbreakable bond between humans and the natural world. Her presence brought a sense of comfort and security, a reminder that they were never truly alone in the vast expanse of the forest.

As the night deepened and the stars began to emerge in the inky sky above, Finn, Ethan, and Mystic savored the tranquility of the moment. The forest, with its ancient trees and hidden wonders, had become more than just a backdrop to their adventure; it had become a part of them, a sanctuary where they could find solace, wisdom, and a profound connection to the earth.

Chapter 13

A storm approached, Finn and Ethan hastened their search for shelter. The sky darkened ominously, and the air grew heavy with the impending rain. Ethan, sensing the urgency of the situation, called out to his son, "Finn, we need to find shelter. This storm is coming in fast."

Rushing to find cover, Finn's keen eyes spotted an unusual formation of rocks at the base of a nearby hill. "Over there, Dad! Those rocks look like they might provide some shelter," he exclaimed, pointing towards the intriguing outcropping.

Without hesitation, they sprinted towards the rock formation, their feet pounding against the forest floor. As they drew closer, they discovered a narrow entrance partially obscured by dense foliage. Working together, they quickly cleared away the vines and overgrown vegetation, revealing the mouth of a cave just as the rain began to pour down in torrents.

Ethan ushered Finn and Mystic inside, seeking refuge from the raging storm. "This storm came out of nowhere," he remarked, catching his breath. "Let's take shelter in here and see what we've stumbled upon. Be careful where you step, Finn. Caves can be treacherous."

The flickering light of their lanterns illuminated the walls, revealing an astonishing sight. The cave walls were covered in ancient carvings, worn by time but still discernible. The intricate designs depicted scenes of early settlers in the forest, their truffle-hunting expeditions, and maps that seemed to point towards the elusive Mycelium Haven.

Ethan's eyes widened as he studied the carvings, his voice filled with awe. "These carvings must be hundreds of years old. They seem to tell the story of the Mycelium Haven and the people who first discovered it. This could be a significant find, Finn. We need to document everything we see here."

Finn nodded, his heart racing with excitement. The cave itself was damp and cool, with the sound of dripping water echoing throughout the chamber. The unexpected discovery of the ancient carvings added a new layer of mystery to their adventure, hinting at the rich history of the forest and the secrets it held.

ETHAN HELD THE LANTERN aloft, the flickering light danced across the cave walls, revealing the intricate carvings that had been hidden for centuries. The ancient etchings seemed to come to life, telling a story of the early settlers who had once traversed these very forests in search of the elusive truffles.

Finn stepped closer to the walls, his eyes wide with wonder as he took in the detailed images. The carvings depicted scenes of truffle hunters, their faces etched with determination as they scoured the forest floor. Some carried baskets filled with their precious finds, while others knelt beside trees, carefully digging at the roots.

"Look at this, Dad," Finn exclaimed, pointing to a particular section of the wall. "These carvings show a map of some sort. Could it be leading to the Mycelium Haven?"

Ethan moved closer, his brow furrowed in concentration as he studied the intricate lines and symbols. The map was unlike any he had seen before, with twisting paths and hidden markers that seemed to hint at a secret location deep within the forest.

"You might be right, Finn," Ethan said, tracing his fingers along the carved lines. "These early truffle hunters must have left clues for future generations to find. It's almost as if they knew the importance of preserving the knowledge of the Mycelium Haven."

They continued to explore the cave, the carvings revealed more and more of the settlers' story. They saw images of bountiful harvests, with baskets overflowing with prized truffles. There were also scenes of camaraderie, with the hunters gathered around campfires, sharing their tales and knowledge.

Mystic, ever curious, sniffed at the cave walls, her tail wagging with excitement. It was as if she, too, could sense the significance of their discovery.

Ethan and Finn moved from one section of the cave to another, their lantern casting a warm glow on the ancient artwork. They marveled at the skill and dedication of the early settlers, who had not only hunted for truffles but had also taken the time to record their experiences and leave a legacy for future generations.

"We have to document this, Finn," Ethan said, his voice filled with excitement. "These carvings could hold the key to unlocking the secrets of the Mycelium Haven. We need to study them carefully and see if we can decipher the map."

SOME OF THE CARVINGS depicted scenes of joyous celebration, with the settlers gathered around fires, their faces alight with laughter and camaraderie. These images likely represented the moments after successful truffle hunts, when the fruits of their labor were shared and enjoyed by all.

Other carvings, however, told a different story. They showed the challenges and hardships faced by the early hunters as they navigated the dense forests and battled the elements in search of their precious quarry. Scenes of hunters braving storms, crossing treacherous rivers, and facing wild animals served as a testament to their unwavering determination and resilience.

As Finn studied these carvings, he felt a deep connection to the past explorers. He understood their passion for the hunt and their drive to uncover the secrets of the forest. It was as if their spirits were still present in the cave, guiding him and Ethan on their own journey.

"This is incredible," Finn whispered, his voice filled with awe. "We're literally walking in the footsteps of history."

Ethan nodded, his eyes wide with wonder as he took in the ancient artwork. "These carvings are more than just a record of their lives, Finn. They're a testament to the human spirit and the desire to explore and discover."

Together, they moved from one section of the cave to another, their lantern illuminating the intricate details of the carvings. Each new image brought them closer to understanding the lives of the early truffle hunters and the secrets they had left behind.

Mystic, too, seemed to sense the significance of their find. She sniffed at the walls, her tail wagging with excitement as if she could pick up the scent of the long-gone hunters.

THE STORM RAGED ON outside the cave, Ethan pulled out his well-worn field notebook and began to carefully sketch the intricate carvings that adorned the rocky walls. His pencil moved with precision, capturing every detail of the ancient artwork. Beside each sketch, he jotted down notes about the symbols, the scenes depicted, and his initial interpretations.

"We need to document everything we find here," Ethan said, his voice echoing in the cavernous space. "This could be a significant piece of history, not just for us but for the entire town."

Finn nodded in agreement, his eyes wide with excitement. He pulled out his phone and began taking photographs of the carvings, making sure to capture every angle and detail. The flash of his camera illuminated the cave in brief bursts, casting eerie shadows on the walls. Finn suggested, "I would call this the Wisdom Cave", and that became it's name.

Despite the storm that continued to rage outside, Finn and Ethan felt safe and engrossed in their discovery. The Wisdom Cave had become a sanctuary, a place where they could unravel the mysteries of the past and connect with the early truffle hunters who had left their mark on these walls.

As they worked, the storm began to subside. The sound of the pounding rain and howling wind gradually faded, replaced by the gentle drip of water from the cave's entrance. Finn and Ethan, however, were now driven by a new sense of purpose. The cave and its carvings had given them valuable clues and a deeper connection to the Mycelium Haven.

They gathered their belongings and prepared to leave the cave, their minds racing with the possibilities that lay ahead. As they stepped outside, they were greeted by a transformed landscape. The rain had slowed to a gentle drizzle, and the sun was starting to peek through the clouds, casting a golden light on the forest.

Finn looked down at the map he had sketched based on the carvings in the cave. "We need to follow this map," he said, his voice filled with determination. "We're closer than ever to finding the Mycelium Haven."

FINN AND ETHAN EMERGED from the cave, the forest greeted them with a transformed landscape. The storm had passed, leaving behind a world glistening with raindrops and filled with the fresh scent of the earth. The golden light filtering through the clouds cast an enchanting glow on the trees, as if nature itself was celebrating their discovery.

Mystic, who had been patiently waiting by the cave entrance, bounded towards them, her tail wagging with excitement. She sensed the renewed energy in her human companions and was eager to continue their adventure.

Ethan took a deep breath, filling his lungs with the crisp, post-rain air. "Let's get camp setup for the night and plan our next move," he said, his voice filled with determination. "We have a lot to think about and even more to explore."

Finn nodded in agreement, his mind already racing with the possibilities that lay ahead. The ancient carvings in the cave had provided them with invaluable clues and a deeper connection to the Mycelium Haven. He couldn't wait to decipher the secrets hidden within the sketches and photographs they had taken.

They made their way in search for a new campsite, Finn and Ethan discussed the significance of their findings. They knew that the carvings held the key to unlocking the mysteries of the forest and the legendary truffle paradise. The thought of being on the cusp of such a monumental discovery filled them with a sense of purpose and excitement.

Mystic trotted alongside them, her golden fur glistening with raindrops. She seemed to share in their enthusiasm, as if she too understood the importance of their quest.

They now found themselves in a low, wet area where the air was thick with the scent of damp earth and decaying leaves. The ground under their feet was soft and squelched with each step.

Mystic, alert but cautious, stopped and sniffed the air, a low growl rumbling from her throat. Finn froze, his eyes widening as he took in their surroundings. "Dad," he whispered, clutching Ethan's arm. "Look."

Emerging from the underbrush were the unmistakable forms of wild pigs—boars and sows with their piglets—rooting for acorns. There were at least a dozen of them, and the moment Finn's voice reached their ears, the boars lifted their heads, their small, dark eyes narrowing in on the intruders.

Ethan quickly assessed the situation, his hand instinctively reaching for Finn's shoulder to steady him. "Finn," he murmured, "we need to back away slowly. No sudden movements."

As they began to retreat, one of the larger boars let out an aggressive snort, pawing the ground and flaring its tusks threateningly. Finn's heart pounded, and Mystic whimpered softly, sensing the danger.

In that tense moment, the Glimmerstone in Finn's pocket began to pulse and glow with an ethereal light. Finn felt its warmth spreading through his body, calming his racing heart and steadied his breathing. The stone pulsed in rhythm with his heartbeat, sending out gentle waves of light that seemed to shimmer and dance in the humid air.

Ethan noticed the glow and nodded to Finn. "Trust the Glimmerstone," he whispered, his voice filled with a new sense of calm.

The light from the Glimmerstone radiated outwards creating an invisible barrier between them and the wild pigs. The boars, sensing an unseen force, hesitated in their tracks. They sniffed the air, their aggressive stance relaxing as the light continued to diffuse through the misty forest.

Slowly, Ethan and Finn, with Mystic quietly at their side, began to move backward. The glowing barrier moved with them, keeping the pigs at a safe distance. It was as though the forest itself was guiding them, providing a safe passage through the perilous situation.

Once they had put enough distance between themselves and the pigs, the Glimmerstone's glow gradually faded, and the forest returned to its natural state. Finn let out a breath he hadn't realized he'd been holding and exchanged a relieved glance with Ethan.

Ethan placed a reassuring hand on Finn's shoulder. "That was incredible, son. The Glimmerstone truly is remarkable."

Finn nodded, still feeling the residual warmth of the stone in his pocket. "We did it," he said, his voice filled with a mixture of awe and gratitude.

Together, they continued their journey, more attuned to the power of the Glimmerstone and the secrets of the forest. They had faced a significant danger and emerged unscathed, their bond and determination stronger than ever.

With renewed determination, Finn and Ethan set their sights on the path ahead. They knew that the journey to the Mycelium Haven would be filled with challenges and obstacles, but they were ready to face them head-on. Armed with the knowledge gained from the ancient carvings and the unwavering support of each other and Mystic, they felt invincible.

The forest seemed to whisper its secrets to them as they walked, the leaves rustling in the gentle breeze. Finn and Ethan exchanged a knowing look, their hearts filled with anticipation for the adventures that awaited them. Together, they would unravel the mysteries of the Mycelium Haven and forge their own legacy in the annals of Loblolly Springs.

ETHAN AND FINN WORKED in tandem to set up their campsite with the ease that came from years of practice. Ethan focused on erecting the tent, his hands deftly assembling the poles and securing the fabric. Meanwhile, Finn took charge of creating the fire pit, carefully selecting a spot and digging two shallow holes with his trusty trowel. Mystic, ever vigilant, stood guard nearby, her keen senses attuned to the surrounding forest.

With the camp taking shape, Ethan and Finn set out to forage for wild edibles to complement their instant soup, a tradition they had established during their camping adventures. They made their way towards a small stream, their eyes scanning the undergrowth for any signs of nature's bounty.

Finn remained alert, not only for potential food sources but also for a dry firewood supply. He knew that a standing dead tree would be the best option, as it would have had time to dry out and would burn more efficiently.

Their foraging efforts proved fruitful, and they returned to the campsite with a handful of wild greens and mushrooms. Ethan set a pan of water to boil over the now-crackling fire, while Finn carefully cleaned and prepared their foraged finds.

Once the water reached a rolling boil, Ethan added the instant soup mix along with the wild edibles, stirring the pot with a contented smile. The aroma of the simmering soup filled the air, mingling with the earthy scent of the forest.

Finn retrieved Mystic's dry dog food from their supplies and poured it into her bowl. The loyal Labrador wagged her tail in appreciation, eagerly digging into her meal.

Ethan ladled the steaming soup into two bowls, ensuring a generous portion of the wild greens and mushrooms in each serving. He handed one to Finn, and they settled down near the fire, savoring the warmth and comfort of their campsite.

FINN STIRRED FROM HIS slumber, the first light of day was yet to break, the aroma of cooking breakfast gently rousing him. He emerged from the tent to find Ethan crouched by the fire, tending to a pot of simmering oatmeal. Beside him, a small griddle held a batch of biscuits, their golden-brown tops flecked with wild berries that Ethan had foraged from the surrounding forest.

He approached the fire, greeting his father with a smile. Ethan handed him a bowl of the steaming oatmeal, the wild berries adding a burst of color and natural sweetness to the hearty meal. They sat together, savoring the warmth and nourishment of the breakfast, as the rising sun painted the forest in a soft, golden glow.

With their hunger satiated, Finn and Ethan set about breaking camp. They worked efficiently, their movements synchronized from countless camping trips together. Finn doused the fire, ensuring that every ember was extinguished, while Ethan dismantled the tent, folding it neatly into its carrying case. They scanned the campsite, leaving no trace of their presence, respecting the wilderness that had sheltered them.

Mystic, eager for the day's adventure, bounded around the campsite, her tail wagging with anticipation. As Finn and Ethan shouldered their backpacks, the loyal Labrador took the lead, her nose twitching as she caught the scents of the forest.

With a shared nod, Finn and Ethan set off, following Mystic as she guided them southeast. Ethan estimated that they were about one half of a mile southeast of the hidden structure. The early morning light filtered through the canopy, casting dappled shadows on the forest floor. The air was crisp and invigorating, filled with the gentle rustling of leaves and the distant calls of birds.

As they walked, Finn couldn't help but feel a sense of excitement and wonder. Each step took them further into the unknown, promising new discoveries and adventures. With Mystic leading the way and Ethan by his side, Finn felt a profound connection to the forest and the mysteries it held.

The trio moved through the undergrowth, their senses attuned to the living world around them. Ethan pointed out various wild edible plants, sharing his knowledge with Finn, who absorbed every detail with rapt attention.

"Look here, Finn," Ethan said, picking a small plant with oval-shaped leaves and tiny white star-shaped flowers. "This is

Chickweed. You can eat the leaves, stems, and flowers. It's great raw in salads or even cooked as a leafy green."

Finn nodded, examining the plant closely. Mystic, too, seemed to be in her element, her keen senses guiding them through the wilderness with unwavering confidence.

Continuing their walk, Ethan stopped to show another find. "This is Dandelion," he explained, pointing to its bright yellow flowers and deeply toothed leaves. "The leaves can be used in salads, the flowers for making dandelion wine, and the roots as a coffee substitute."

Mystic sniffed around the plants with curiosity, her nose twitching as if to confirm Ethan's words.

A few steps further, Ethan bent down again. "And this here is Purslane. It has fleshy, spoon-shaped leaves and small yellow flowers. You can eat the leaves, stems, and flowers. It's excellent in salads or soups, and can also be cooked as a vegetable."

Finn marveled at the variety of edible plants the forest offered, feeling a deeper connection to the land with each new discovery. Mystic bounded ahead, her tail wagging with the thrill of the adventure.

"YOU KNOW HOW MUCH I love this forest and how much there is to discover here," Ethan continued. "But one of the most important rules of exploring is never to eat a wild plant unless you are absolutely certain of what it is."

Ethan reached into his backpack and pulled out a field guide, flipping to a section on local plants. "Look at this," he said, pointing to a picture of a plant with small, enticing berries. "This is a species of nightshade. The berries might look harmless, even tasty, but they're highly toxic. Eating just a few could make you very sick."

Finn nodded, absorbing the seriousness of his father's words. He knew Ethan wasn't trying to scare him, but rather protect him from the unseen dangers of the wild.

"Even experienced foragers can make mistakes," Ethan went on. "There are plants that look remarkably similar to each other, and sometimes the difference between what's safe to eat and what's dangerous is subtle. It's always better to be cautious."

Ethan closed the field guide and placed a reassuring hand on Finn's shoulder. "Remember, we have resources like books and experts who can help identify plants. When in doubt, it's better to bring a sample home and look it up, or better yet, ask someone who knows for sure."

Finn nodded again, feeling a deep respect for the wisdom his father was imparting. He resolved to be more careful and to always double-check before assuming any plant was safe to eat.

With a smile, Ethan stood up and ruffled Finn's hair. "Alright, explorer, let's keep going. There's a whole forest out there waiting for us."

As they continued their hike, Finn felt a renewed sense of responsibility and a deeper bond with his father, appreciating the balance of adventure and caution that Ethan had taught him.

ETHAN, FINN, AND MYSTIC continued their journey through the lush, vibrant forest of Loblolly Springs. The sun broke through the canopy, casting a mesmerizing play of light and shadow on the forest floor. The air was thick with the scent of earth and foliage, a testament to the rich, untamed wilderness that surrounded them.

Ethan's keen eyes spotted something unusual amidst the undergrowth. He paused, signaling for Finn and Mystic to halt. There, barely visible beneath the overgrown shrubs and vines, was an old, narrow path leading northwest, deeper into the heart of the woods.

He approached the path, Ethan's curiosity piqued. He brushed aside some of the foliage, revealing a trail that seemed to have been untrodden for years, perhaps decades. The path was narrow, just wide enough for a single person to pass through, and it wound its way through the dense forest, disappearing into the mysterious depths of the woods.

Finn joined his father, his eyes wide with excitement. "Where do you think it leads?" he asked, his voice hushed with anticipation.

Ethan studied the path, his brow furrowed in thought. "I'm not sure," he admitted. "This path isn't on any of our maps. It must be an old trail, perhaps used by the early settlers or the Native Americans who once lived in these woods."

Mystic, too, seemed intrigued by the discovery. She sniffed at the entrance of the path, her tail wagging with curiosity. It was as if the path itself was beckoning them, urging them to venture forth and uncover the secrets that lay hidden in the heart of the forest.

Finn looked up at his father, his eyes shining with the thrill of adventure. "Can we follow it?" he asked, barely able to contain his excitement.

Ethan hesitated for a moment, weighing the risks and rewards of venturing off their planned route. But the allure of the unknown, the promise of discovery, was too strong to resist. He nodded, a smile spreading across his face.

"Let's see where it takes us," he said, adjusting his backpack. "But we need to be careful. We don't know what we might encounter along the way."

Finn nodded solemnly, understanding the gravity of his father's words. Together, with Mystic leading the way, they stepped onto the old, overgrown path, ready to embrace the mysteries and adventures that awaited them in the depths of the Loblolly Springs forest.

SUDDENLY, THE PATH opened up into a hidden glade, a place so pristine and untouched that it felt as if time itself had forgotten its existence. The trio stopped, awestruck by the sight before them. The glade was a perfect circle, surrounded by towering, ancient trees that seemed to stand as silent guardians, their branches reaching up to embrace the sky. The ground was carpeted with a lush, verdant moss, so soft and inviting that it beckoned them to remove their shoes and feel its gentle caress beneath their feet.

In the center of the glade stood a single, majestic oak tree, its trunk gnarled and twisted with age, its leaves a vibrant green that seemed to pulse with life. The tree exuded an aura of wisdom and power, as if it held within its ancient heartwood the secrets of the forest itself.

Ethan and Finn exchanged a look of wonder, their eyes wide with the realization that they were on the brink of something truly significant. Mystic, too, seemed to sense the importance of the moment, her tail wagging slowly as she gazed up at the mighty oak.

Ethan approached the tree reverently, his hand outstretched to touch its rough, weathered bark. As his fingers made contact, he felt a gentle thrumming beneath his palm, as if the tree itself was acknowledging his presence. He closed his eyes, allowing the energy of the ancient oak to flow through him, filling him with a sense of peace and connection to the forest.

Finn, meanwhile, explored the edges of the glade, his keen eyes searching for any signs or clues that might shed light on the significance of this hidden sanctuary. He noticed strange, intricate symbols carved into the trunks of the surrounding trees, their meaning lost to time but their presence a testament to the importance of this place.

As they stood there, bathed in the golden light of the glade, Ethan, Finn, and Mystic knew that they were on the cusp of a great discovery. The hidden glade, with its ancient oak and mysterious symbols, held within it the promise of secrets long forgotten, of knowledge waiting to be uncovered. They could feel it in the very air around them, in the whispers of the leaves and the gentle rustling of the undergrowth. The trio exchanged a nod, silently agreeing to continue their exploration, ready to unravel the mysteries that lay ahead.

THE PATH BECAME INCREASINGLY treacherous as they continued on. Gnarled roots jutted out from the ground, threatening to trip the unsuspecting traveler, while thorny brambles snagged at their clothing, as if the forest itself was testing their resolve. The trio pressed on, undeterred by the obstacles in their way, their determination fueled by the promise of the secrets that lay ahead.

Finn took the lead, his keen eyes scanning the undergrowth for any signs of the elusive truffles they sought. Mystic, too, was on high alert, her nose twitching as she caught the scent of something hidden beneath the leaf litter. Suddenly, the dog let out a sharp bark, her tail wagging excitedly as she pawed at the ground.

Ethan and Finn rushed over, their hearts racing with anticipation. There, nestled among the roots of an ancient oak, was a cluster of forgotten truffle ground, untouched by human hands for who knows how long. The duo exchanged a look of pure joy as they carefully excavated the precious fungi, their hands trembling with excitement as they unearthed one valuable truffle after another.

As the light began to fade, casting long shadows across the forest floor, Ethan and Finn knew it was time to head back. But before they left, Finn pulled out his map, carefully marking the location of their newfound treasure. They knew that this secret was worth protecting, a hidden gem that could hold the key to a brighter future for their family.

With their packs heavy with the weight of their precious cargo, Ethan, Finn, and Mystic made their way back through the forest, their hearts filled with a sense of accomplishment and hope. They had faced the challenges of the wild and emerged victorious, armed with the knowledge that they had the skills and the determination to succeed in their quest.

ETHAN, FINN, AND MYSTIC made their way through the forest, their steps lighter with the success of their truffle hunt, they found themselves in a particularly secluded part of the woods. The air seemed to shimmer with an otherworldly quality, and as they walked, Finn and Mystic began to hear hushed whispers, as if the trees themselves were sharing secrets. The duo exchanged a glance, both feeling the mystical energy that permeated this hidden corner of the forest.

Suddenly, they froze in their tracks, their eyes widening at the sight before them. There, in a small clearing, stood a magnificent stag, its antlers stretching towards the sky like branches of an ancient tree. The animal's presence was imposing, its gaze seeming to pierce through Finn and Mystic, as if judging their intentions. The moment was infused with a sense of significance, as if they were standing before a guardian of the grove.

As quickly as it had appeared, the stag turned and departed, melting back into the shadows of the forest. Finn and Mystic stood in silence for a moment, processing the encounter. It was then that they noticed something at the base of a nearby tree - a cluster of truffles, nestled among the roots as if they had been placed there deliberately. It felt like an offering, a gift from the forest's guardian to those it deemed worthy.

Finn reached into his backpack and pulled out his journal, his hand moving almost of its own accord as he sketched the stag and the scene before them. He wanted to capture the magic of this moment, the whimsical elements of their adventure that seemed to defy explanation. Mystic watched on, her tail wagging contentedly as if she, too, understood the significance of what had just transpired.

Chapter 14

It was well after first light the next morning when Finn was pulled from sleep by his mother's call to come and eat breakfast. He stirred, the events of the past two days still fresh in his mind. The discovery of the ancient carvings, the mystical encounters in the forest, and the successful truffle hunt with his father and loyal dog, Mystic, had left an indelible mark on his young spirit.

As Finn made his way to the kitchen, he found his father, Ethan, preparing to leave for work. The aroma of freshly brewed coffee and the sizzle of eggs on the stove filled the air. Clara, Finn's mother, greeted him with a warm smile as she set a plate of toast on the table.

Finn slid into his chair, his eyes still heavy with sleep but his mind buzzing with excitement. As they began to eat, Finn regaled his mother with tales of their two-day adventure into the forest. He spoke of the ancient path they had discovered, the enchanting glade with the wise old oak, and the perilous journey that had led them to a hidden trove of valuable truffles.

Clara listened intently, her eyes widening with each detail. She marveled at the courage and determination her son and husband had shown, and at the mystical elements that seemed to guide their journey. Ethan chimed in occasionally, adding his own insights and observations, his pride in Finn's growth and skills evident in his voice.

Finn's thoughts turned to the truffles they had found. He knew their value, and an idea began to form in his mind. He announced his plan to ride into town on his bicycle and sell the truffles to Chef Jacques, the renowned local chef who had always appreciated the rare delicacies.

Ethan and Clara exchanged a glance, a mix of pride and concern in their eyes. They knew Finn was growing up, ready to take on more responsibility and forge his own path. With a nod of encouragement from his father and a gentle reminder from his mother to be safe, Finn excused himself from the table, eager to set his plan into motion.

He gathered the truffles, carefully wrapped them, and placed them in his backpack. With a final hug from his parents and a pat on Mystic's head, Finn set off on his bicycle, pedaling towards town and the promise of a new chapter in his adventures.

AS CHEF JACQUES TURNED the key in the lock of "Le Chêne Doré," he heard the sound of bicycle tires crunching on the gravel behind him. He turned to see young Finn Thornwood dismounting his bike, a backpack slung over his shoulder and a grin on his face.

"Bonjour, Finn!" Chef Jacques called out, his French accent thick with morning cheer. "What brings you here so early?"

Finn approached the chef, his excitement palpable. "Chef Jacques, you won't believe what I've got for you today."

Intrigued, the chef ushered Finn inside the restaurant. Once in the kitchen, Finn carefully opened his backpack and began to remove the truffles one by one, laying them out on the stainless steel counter.

Chef Jacques' eyes widened as he took in the sight before him. The truffles were a marvel to behold - some the size of golf balls, others as large as a fist. The aroma filled the kitchen, earthy and pungent, a scent that spoke of the forest's hidden treasures.

"Mon Dieu, Finn," Chef Jacques breathed, his voice hushed with reverence. "These are magnificent. Where did you find such a bounty?"

Finn beamed with pride as he recounted the tale of his and his father's adventure in the forest, the ancient carvings, and the mystical encounters that had led them to this trove of truffles.

Chef Jacques listened, enraptured, as he gently picked up each truffle, examining it with the keen eye of a connoisseur. He marveled at the variety - Bianchetto, Périgord, and the rare Mycelium Royale, each one a testament to the forest's secrets and the skill of the truffle hunter.

With great care, Chef Jacques began to weigh each truffle, jotting down the numbers on a notepad. The Bianchetto truffles, with their delicate, garlicky aroma, totaled a pound. The Périgord, dark and robust, weighed in at half a pound. And the single Mycelium Royale, the size of a small apple and pulsing with an almost otherworldly energy, tipped the scales at a quarter pound.

Chef Jacques' eyes sparkled with excitement once he saw the weight on his scales. He knew the value of this haul, not just in monetary terms, but in the culinary possibilities it presented. These truffles would elevate his dishes to new heights, and he could hardly wait to begin experimenting with them in his kitchen.

FINN THANKED CHEF JACQUES profusely, his gratitude evident in his beaming smile. "I can't tell you how much this means to me, Chef. Your support and willingness to buy these truffles have brought me one step closer to my dream."

Chef Jacques waved a hand dismissively, but his eyes twinkled with pride. "It is I who should be thanking you, mon ami. These truffles are a true treasure, and I look forward to creating culinary masterpieces with them."

With a final wave, Finn slung his backpack over his shoulder and headed back outside, where his trusty bicycle awaited. He mounted the bike and pedaled off, his heart light with the promise of adventure and the weight of the truffle money in his pocket.

His next stop was the Western Auto store, a haven for all things outdoors. As he entered, the scent of leather and camping gear enveloped him, and he felt a thrill of excitement.

Finn made his way to the camping section, his eyes roving over the array of tents, sleeping bags, and cookware. He knew he needed to stock up on supplies for his upcoming forays into the forest, and he wanted to be prepared for any eventuality.

A knowledgeable salesman approached Finn, sensing his enthusiasm. "Looking for anything in particular, son?"

Finn nodded eagerly. "I'm in need of some camping gear, and I'd love to get my hands on any books or guides you might have on camping and survival skills."

The salesman's face lit up, and he led Finn to a well-stocked section of books and manuals. "We've got a great selection here," he said, gesturing to the shelves. "Everything from basic camping guides to advanced wilderness survival techniques."

Finn's eyes scanned the titles, his mind already whirring with the knowledge he hoped to absorb. He selected a few promising volumes, including a comprehensive guide to edible plants and a manual on building shelters in the wilderness.

Next, Finn turned his attention to the fire-starting kits. He knew the importance of being able to start a fire in any condition, and he wanted to be prepared. After examining a few options, he settled on a compact kit that contained waterproof matches, a magnesium fire starter, and a small supply of tinder.

Finally, Finn made his way to the footwear section, where he tried on several pairs of lightweight hiking boots. He needed something sturdy yet comfortable, something that could withstand the rigors of trekking through the forest. After trying on a few options, he settled on a pair of boots that felt like an extension of his own feet.

With his purchases in hand, Finn headed to the checkout, his mind already planning his next adventure into the wilderness of Loblolly Springs.

BEFORE LEAVING TOWN, Finn stopped by his local Dairy Queen and ordered a burger and a shake. The familiar scent of sizzling meat and fries wafted through the air, and Finn felt his stomach rumble in anticipation.

As he waited for his order, he couldn't help but feel a sense of accomplishment. The weight of the truffle money in his pocket was a tangible reminder of his success, and he couldn't wait to put it towards his camping gear and education.

When his order was ready, Finn eagerly dug into the juicy burger, savoring the flavors that reminded him of simpler times. The cool, creamy shake was the perfect complement, and he sipped it contentedly, allowing the tension of the day to melt away.

Soon, with his belly full and his spirits high, Finn mounted his trusty bicycle and began the journey home. The familiar streets of Loblolly Springs passed by in a blur, and he couldn't help but feel a sense of gratitude for the town that had nurtured him and fostered his love of the great outdoors.

As he pedaled, his mind raced with thoughts of his future adventures in the forest. He couldn't wait to put his new gear to the test and delve deeper into the mysteries that awaited him among the trees.

Finn could barely contain his excitement as he burst through the front door, his feet barely touching the ground as he sprinted into the kitchen where his mom, Clara, was preparing dinner. Mystic trailed behind him, her tail wagging furiously as if to share in his enthusiasm.

"Mom! Mom!" Finn called out, his voice high-pitched with exhilaration.

Clara turned around, a warm smile spreading across her face at the sight of her son's uncontainable joy. "What is it, Finn? You look like you've just won the lottery."

"Even better," Finn said, panting slightly as he tried to catch his breath. "I sold the truffles to Chef Jacques today!"

Clara put down the wooden spoon she was holding, her eyes widening with interest. "Did you, now? And how did it go?"

"It went amazing, Mom. Chef Jacques was so impressed with what I found. He gave me $1,200 for the whole lot!" Finn's voice crescendoed with excitement as he relayed the news.

Clara's jaw dropped. "Twelve hundred dollars? That's incredible, Finn! I had no idea those truffles would be worth so much."

Finn nodded vigorously, his cheeks flushed with triumph. "Chef Jacques said the Mycelium Royale truffle was especially rare and valuable. He even said I have a real talent for finding them!"

Clara reached out, pulling Finn into a tight embrace. "I'm so proud of you, honey. This is a wonderful start for your college fund."

Finn hugged her back, feeling a warm sense of accomplishment wash over him. "Yeah, it feels great to know I'm helping out with something so important. And you know what else? It makes me even more excited to keep exploring the forest. There are so many more truffles out there waiting to be found!"

Clara pulled back, looking into Finn's eyes with a mix of pride and tenderness. "You're doing something very special, Finn. Not just for yourself, but for our family too. Keep following your passion, and who knows where it might lead you." With a final squeeze, Clara released Finn, who stood a little taller, a little more confident in himself and his abilities.

Finn was quite excited to be back home so that he could begin reading his guide to edible plants and manual on building shelters. He settled into his favorite chair, Mystic curled up at his feet, and opened the first book, his eyes devouring the pages with rapt attention.

He could almost feel the forest calling to him, beckoning him to put his newfound knowledge to the test. He knew that the challenges ahead would be formidable, but with his trusty gear and the wisdom contained within these pages, he felt ready to face whatever the wilderness might throw his way.

ETHAN SOON ARRIVED home from work, his boots leaving a trail of dirt on the hardwood floor as he entered the house. He shrugged off his jacket, inhaling deeply the aroma of Clara's cooking that wafted through the air.

"Honey, I'm home!" he called out, a warm smile spreading across his face as Clara emerged from the kitchen, wiping her hands on a dish towel.

"Perfect timing," she said, leaning in to give him a quick peck on the cheek. "Dinner's just about ready."

As if on cue, Finn appeared, his face flushed with excitement. "Dad! You'll never guess what happened today."

Ethan chuckled, ruffling Finn's hair affectionately. "Why don't you tell me over dinner? It smells delicious."

The family gathered around the table, where Clara had already set out steaming bowls of hearty stew and fresh-baked bread. As they dished out their portions, Finn could barely contain himself, bouncing in his seat with anticipation.

"So, you know those truffles we found in the forest?" he began, his eyes sparkling.

Ethan nodded, taking a bite of the savory stew. "Of course. Those were some impressive specimens."

"Well, I sold them to Chef Jacques today," Finn announced, his voice swelling with pride. "And you'll never believe how much he paid me."

Clara and Ethan exchanged a glance, their curiosity piqued.

"How much?" Ethan prompted, leaning back in his chair.

"Twelve hundred dollars!" Finn exclaimed, his hands gesturing wildly as if to emphasize the enormity of the sum. I used some of the money to buy some really cool stuff at the Western Auto Store."

He reached down, retrieving a canvas bag that had been resting at his feet. "Check it out. I got a fire starter kit, a guide to edible plants, and a manual on building shelters."

Ethan's eyes widened as Finn pulled out each item, laying them out on the table for inspection. "These are great, son. You're really gearing up for your next adventure, aren't you?"

Finn nodded, his eyes sparkling with determination. "You bet. With these tools and the money I made, I'm one step closer to being a real truffle hunter."

Clara reached across the table, giving Finn's hand a gentle squeeze. "We're so proud of you, sweetheart. Just promise us you'll be careful out there, okay?"

Finn met her gaze, his expression sincere. "I promise, Mom. With all this gear and Dad's guidance, I'll be as safe as can be."

The family continued their meal, the conversation flowed easily, with Finn regaling them with tales of his encounter with Chef Jacques and his plans for future forays into the forest. Ethan and Clara listened with rapt attention, their hearts swelling with pride and a touch of trepidation at the adventures that lay ahead for their son.

But for now, they were content to bask in the warmth of their family, united by their shared love of the great outdoors and the boundless possibilities that awaited them in the heart of Loblolly Springs.

FINN SETTLED INTO BED, exhaustion finally catching up to him after a long day. Mystic curled up at his feet, providing a sense of comfort and security. Finn allowed himself a moment of contentment, thinking about the truffles he'd sold and the gear he'd purchased for future adventures.

As sleep took hold, Finn's dreams quickly intensified. He found himself in an ancient forest, far older and more mystical than any part of Loblolly Springs he'd ever explored. The air was thick with tension and the soft glow of moonlight filtered through the dense canopy, casting eerie shadows.

In the dream, Finn stood at the edge of the Mycelium Haven, a once-hidden sanctuary now exposed. Beside him were figures from the past—ancient guardians dressed in robes, faces lined with wisdom and determination. Ahead of him loomed a shadowy adversary, indistinct yet palpable, a dark force threatening the existence of the haven and its precious truffles.

A fierce battle ensued. Finn, alongside the guardians, stood his ground, wielding knowledge and courage as their only weapons. The adversary advanced, its shape-shifting form drawing darkness around it. Finn shouted orders, his voice strong and commanding, as he led the charge to protect the haven.

Suddenly, the vision shifted. Finn found himself alone, standing atop a hill overlooking the Mycelium Haven. The once vibrant and lush sanctuary was now withering, shadows creeping over the land. An ominous voice echoed in his mind, "The battle is far from over, young guardian. Prepare yourself, for the true challenge lies ahead."

Startled awake, Finn sat up in bed, his breath rapid and his body drenched in a cold sweat. Mystic, sensing his distress, nudged his hand with her nose, offering silent reassurance. Finn's heart pounded as he replayed the vivid scenes in his mind. These weren't ordinary dreams—they felt like premonitions, warnings of the challenges to come.

He glanced at the Glimmerstone on his bedside table, its soft glow a constant reminder of the unknown power it held. Finn knew that his past adventures were only the beginning. The visions pointed to a conflict that would demand more than just his truffle-hunting skills. It would require courage, wisdom, and alliances he had yet to form.

Finn took a deep breath and lay back down, his mind racing with thoughts of the ancient conflict. He stroked Mystic's fur, drawing strength from her loyal presence.

Whispering into the stillness, Finn made a silent vow, "I won't let the shadows win. I promise, I'll protect the Mycelium Haven, no matter the cost."

Mystic's eyes gleamed with understanding, and Finn felt a renewed sense of purpose. The journey ahead was fraught with unknown dangers, but Finn was ready to face them head-on. With Mystic by his side, he was prepared to unlock the secrets of the ancient guardians and stand against the darkness that threatened their world.

Sleep had now claimed him once more, Finn's resolve strengthened. Tomorrow would bring new challenges, but he was no longer just the truffle hunter of Loblolly Springs. He was destined to be its guardian.

About the Author

Born in Little Rock, Arkansas, at the start of World War II, Wallace Berry grew up on a farm in the Arkansas countryside. His childhood, steeped in the rustic simplicity of farm life without modern conveniences, deeply rooted in him a love for the wilderness. The surrounding forests and hands-on experiences of rural living profoundly shaped his appreciation for nature and a life outdoors. As an adult, Wallace made the Texas Gulf Coast his home, carrying with him the values and passions developed during his formative years.

www.ingramcontent.com/pod-product-compliance
Lightning Source LLC
Chambersburg PA
CBHW050518260626
47157CB00004B/1371